I0787264

EVEN GROUND

WENDY SMITH

Edited by CREATING INK

Photography by GOLDEN CZERMAK / FURIOUSFOTOG

Cover Design by FURIOUSFOTOG

Model MICHAEL DEAN

All rights reserved. No part of this book may be reproduced or transmitted in any form, including electronic or mechanical, without written permission from the publisher, except in the case of brief quotations embodied in critical articles or reviews.

This is a work of fiction. Names, characters, businesses, places, events, and incidents are either the products of the author's imagination or used in a fictitious manner. Any resemblance to actual persons, living or dead, or actual events is purely coincidental. Wendy Smith is in no way affiliated with any brands, songs, musicians or artists mentioned in this book.

This book is written in New Zealand English.

© Wendy Smith 2021

❀ Created with Vellum

GLOSSARY

Wahine - Woman in Te Reo Māori
Boot - Trunk of car
Bonnet - Hood of car
Hongi - Traditional Māori greeting where people press noses together

1

REECE

"And that's a wrap. See you all at the party."

I drop my arms to my side, letting go of Sigourney and blowing out a long breath.

"Are you going to the wrap party?" She flutters her eyelashes at me. Ordinarily, I'd be taking up her unspoken offer. But, today, I've got other places to be.

"No. I'm heading back to LA."

"Today?"

I nod. "Josh's wedding."

Her eyelashes flutter again. "Need a date?"

"I'm the best man, and I'm giving the bride away. I'm not taking a date, but thanks."

After changing and saying my goodbyes, I head out to the car waiting to take me to the airport. I knew making it to the wedding after filming could be cutting it fine, but the role was only minor, and the movie only took a couple of weeks to film. In any case, finishing now gives me two days to prepare for the wedding, which is more than enough given I already have my suit, and Josh is being a control freak about everything.

Me: *I'm on my way back*

I flick a quick text to my best friend just so he knows what's going on. His head is full of wedding things, as most of the planning has been done by him.

Josh: *See you soon*

The car makes its way through the streets of Atlanta, heading toward the Hartsfield-Jackson Airport to where the jet I chartered waits. I usually fly commercial because I think private jets are a bit too over the top—even for me. But I wanted the ability to leave when I needed to, given the wedding is on the other side of the country.

My phone vibrates in my jacket pocket, and I pull it out to see who's calling.

Groaning, I roll my eyes. If I don't answer it, she'll just leave a voicemail and then call back again. And again.

"Jessie." I take a deep breath. There are only two things that Jessie Lane has ever called me for: booty calls, and to complain about Josh.

"What are you doing?" she asks.

"I'm on my way to the airport. Why?"

"Airport? Where are you going?"

I clench my fist. She wouldn't be calling if she didn't know what was going on. "I've been working in Georgia, and now I'm heading back to LA for the wedding." There's no point in beating around the bush.

"Do you need a chaperone?"

I bite down a smile. Even if I did, Jessie would be the last person I'd take to this particular wedding.

"Unfortunately no. I'm the best man, and I'm giving the bride away, so I'm not taking a date."

"I can't believe he didn't even invite me."

She lets out a sob, and my heart sinks. If Josh were marrying literally anyone else on the planet, he would have probably invited Jessie —she's been his friend for as long as she's been mine. But there's no way he's going to let her anywhere near Delaney. His soon-to-be-wife will chew her up and spit her out after the way Jessie treated her when they met.

Jessie turned up in Delaney's Diner when she and Josh shot a romantic comedy in New Zealand and was a full-on diva. She treated Delaney so badly that I don't think Josh will ever forgive her.

"I'm sorry, Jess. Maybe we can go for a drink one night and catch up?"

"Can you come and see me when you land in LA?"

I run my fingers through my hair. "Uh ... sure. I can't be there long, but I can stop by."

"Thank you." She sniffs.

I never thought it would come to this. Josh, Jessie, and Clarke were my instant friends when we all started the same acting class together. Josh and I were tight and soon became roommates. Jessie always had a crush on Josh, but it seemed harmless.

It's not like she's spent the years in between pining for him. It just becomes an issue when she realises he's out of reach. For good this time.

I've known people who have married and known ahead of time that it won't last. But that's not the case with Josh and Delaney. Those two are true soulmates.

"Gotta go, we're nearly there. See you when I reach LA."

"Okay." She sniffs again, but I disconnect the call. I feel bad even thinking about it, but I'm never sure with her whether she's faking it or not. But at the same time, I know I need to go and check up on her.

I'm not sure anyone else will.

APART FROM A LITTLE turbulence roughly halfway there, the flight is fairly uneventful.

It's simultaneously too long and not long enough as I think ahead about going to Josh's place versus knowing I need to check on Jessie.

I don't think she'd do anything stupid, but she'll be a mess as this wedding draws closer.

Why me?

Because she has no one else.

I've enjoyed a lavish lifestyle these past few years, but after I was raised in a house without much money, I'd like to think my feet are actually on the ground. Josh is the same.

But Jessie? She was the one in our group who let fame get to her. It's impacted her career in so many ways—I'm not even sure she realises there are people out there who will never work with her. And it's partly behind this fracture in her relationship with Josh, who went out of his way to try to help her out.

I still care about her, and I'm sure Josh does too. But right now, I'm the one friend she probably feels she can call on for sympathy.

My BMW i8's waiting for me at LAX in long-term parking, and I'm relieved to sink into the leather seats. It's good to be home again.

Jessie's place first, and then onto see Josh. I can do this.

Even though there's a part of me that wants to skip the visit to Jessie, I won't—she needs someone.

Her place isn't that far from Josh's home. She's in an apartment similar to mine. And I make my way there, enjoying the quiet of the car ride. It's been a hectic few days, and I'm glad to have a little downtime before the wedding madness.

Thankfully, there's a car park right outside her building, so I swing in there and jump out of the car.

Taking a ride in the elevator to the fourth floor, I do my best to brace for Jessie's inevitable tears. This isn't the first time I've comforted her, and no doubt it won't be the last.

She needs to move on.

The elevator comes to a stop, and I take the short walk to her apartment.

I take a deep breath and knock on the door.

"Who is it?"

"Jess, it's me. Reece."

She flings open the door. Her red-rimmed eyes tell me the whole story, and my heart sinks seeing her so miserable.

Before I know it, her arms are around my neck, and she's pulling me back into her apartment. Once the door's closed, we stand there for a minute while her hot tears soak the front of my shirt.

"Oh, Jess."

She raises her tear-streaked face to look at me. Jessie's gorgeous with her red hair and green eyes, and we've tangled in the sheets a handful of times on a casual basis. I went there because I always knew Josh wouldn't, but right now I almost wish I hadn't. I'm sure she thinks it gives her some power over me.

"Are you sure you can't take me? I want to see the wedding." Her lower lip trembles, but I shake my head.

"You know the answer to that." I lead her to the couch where we sit and wrap an arm around her shoulder. "I'll take a ton of photos, though."

She leans in, resting her head on me. "I just can't believe he's excluding me."

I raise my gaze to the ceiling. All Jessie had to do was pretend to like Delaney. She just had to make some effort. Instead, there's a sea of bitterness between them and Josh will always have Delaney's back.

"Maybe when this is all done, you could try and mend some bridges. Delaney's a good person, and she loves Josh. Reach out to her."

"I just want things the way they used to be." She lets out a long, dramatic sigh.

"Oh, honey, nothing's the way it used to be." I squeeze her shoulder. "We're all grown up now."

"You two get all the breaks. I'll never be as popular as you."

I plant a kiss in her hair. "You've had a ton of successes. That movie you did with Josh was a huge hit."

She rolls her eyes. "It didn't do anything for my career, though. People came to see it because of him."

"I'm sorry."

"You could always put me in your movie."

I close my eyes. "All the parts have been cast. And, again, I think what you need to do is to mend that bridge with Delaney, and maybe then it'll help repair your relationship with Josh."

She's silent for a moment. "Maybe."

"Think about it at least." I press a kiss to her temple. "I've got to get going."

"Can't you stay?"

"Not today, but I'll call you."

I stand, and she looks up at me. "Promise?"

"You know it."

Her smile's small, but it's there. Jessie can harbour so much sadness, and when she channels it, her performances are so much more powerful. But it sucks seeing her so sad, especially when I can't help her.

"I'll look out for wedding photos. I'm sure they'll have a wonderful day." She fiddles with the hem of her shirt. "Can you please tell Josh that I hope it all goes well and that they're happy."

I nod. "Of course I can. Give me a call if you need to talk."

Her eyes glaze over again. I wish she'd move on. We'll always be friends, but this is something she needs to deal with.

"I will."

Leaning over, I press another kiss to her forehead. "I'm sorry this didn't work out for you, Jess. I really am. I know this isn't much, me being here, but ..."

Her smile grows a little. "Thank you for always being my friend."

"You're welcome."

It's with a heavy heart that I make my way back to my car. But I get in and start it up, shifting the transmission into drive before moving into traffic.

My stomach grumbles, reminding me of one of the reasons why I'm going to Josh's home and not my own apartment.

I pull into Josh's driveway, switch off the ignition, and sit in the quiet for a moment. It sucks that I'm in the middle between Josh and Jessie, friends with both of them but unable to bring the two sides together.

We had so much fun when we were all in LA, auditioning, working out how to stay just a little longer in our attempts to become working actors. Josh was the one who got his break first, Jessie landed a part in a TV show, and then I got a movie role that helped launch my career. Clarke, the other part of our group of four, decided to go in a different direction—he's now in advertising.

And now our group is so fractured, I don't even know where to start.

I step out of the car and close the door, taking a deep breath as I get out.

Coming here is like coming home.

Spending so much time here is a recent development. I've always spent a lot of time with Josh when we've managed to be in the same place at the same time. But now he has his family, and he's more settled here, so I'm at his house more often than my apartment.

I can't deny Delaney is a big part of that. She welcomed me with open arms from the start, and I'm addicted to her cooking. Delaney and Josh are like the brother and sister I never had. And Delaney's bound to have food ready in the fridge for me—she usually does. I'm not sure she cooks it for me, but she never complains about me showing up to eat.

After walking up to the front door, I punch in my code and step into the entrance. Laughter floats down from upstairs. Josh used to rarely be here, and my visits were few and far between. But him bringing his family together has turned this house into a home in such a short amount of time.

Delaney and Amelia have turned both his and my world upside-down. Mine is just by extension, and I'm not sure I'll ever have what he does, but I cling to my visits here, and I push them as often as I can because I love being part of what he has.

And for the first time in my life, it's made me think of having a family of my own.

Delaney's voice echoes down the hallway, and I catch my breath when I reach the living room door.

Her back is to me, but she's a vision in cream, silk fabric, her dark hair tumbling down her back in big curls.

Josh is truly a lucky man.

2

———

PANIA

"If you don't stay still, I'll stab you." I look up at my best friend, Delaney, and meet her gaze.

"I can't hear you because of the pins you're not supposed to have in your mouth." She wiggles her hips, and I lose hold of the hem of her dress.

"Sue me." I grab the fabric again and slide in another pin.

"We don't have long. Josh could be home any minute."

I pull the pins out of my mouth and study her. The cream, silk fabric of Delaney's wedding dress hugs her curves. She's had me alter the neckline three times already to get the right amount of cleavage. She'll look incredible on her wedding day, but she's been a pain in the arse along the way.

"Well, if he does come home too early, I'll cut out his eyes. That'll stop him from looking."

She laughs. "I think that's a bit extreme."

"We're nearly done. I'm sure I won't have to do it." I grin. "You're going to knock his socks off."

"I hope so."

A low wolf whistle makes us both look around.

"Reece," Delaney exclaims.

I swallow hard. This is the moment I knew was coming but am still woefully unprepared for.

He hasn't even said a word, but Reece Evans's presence fills the room all the way from the doorway. What looks like a couple of days' worth of stubble covers his cheeks and chin, but it does nothing to hide those chiselled movie-star features, and his sparkling blue eyes are impossible to miss.

Before Delaney got back together with Josh and moved to LA, we spent many hours watching him on screen and drooling. Now he's one of her best friends. After me, of course.

I arrived in LA a week ago, and was horribly disappointed when Reece wasn't around. Delaney told me he was off filming for a movie. Patience and I don't really get along, and my anxiety over meeting him has only risen this past week.

And now he's here, larger than life.

Not looking at me.

"When did you get back?" Delaney asks him.

"My first port of call had to be my favourite girl. I've missed you." He crosses the room and holds his arms open. "You look fantastic."

She grins. "Thank you." She goes to him and kisses him on the cheek. "I'm glad you're back."

"It's not too late to leave him."

I raise an eyebrow, and he flicks a glance at me.

But Delaney just laughs. "That's enough of that."

"He's not around, then?"

She shakes her head. "No, but he'll be home soon. I need to get out of this dress."

Reece claps his hands together. "Now we're talking."

"Do you *ever* stop?" Delaney shifts her focus to me. "Are we good?"

I nod. "It's fine. I have enough to work on. We'll need another fitting before the big day, but we're almost done."

Reece catches my gaze. "You designed the dress? You must be Pania. I've heard a lot about you."

My heart seizes when he flashes his beautiful smile at me. I'm never lost for words, but this is the moment I've been looking forward to and dreading all at the same time.

"Help me unzip?" Delaney turns her back on him, and just like that the smile's gone, and I can't help but watch as he slides the zip halfway down her back. What I wouldn't give to be in her shoes right now. "Ta. I'll be back in a minute. Pania, I know you know this is Reece. Reece, take care of my best friend while I'm gone."

My eyes widen as she disappears out of the room. She just left me alone with a man she knows I have the major hots for. Then again, there was a time we both crushed on him even though Delaney's heart always belonged with Josh.

"You did an incredible job. She'll be the most beautiful bride." His blue eyes hit mine and it's so hard to look away.

"That's the plan." My cheeks burn just from being under his gaze.

I quickly look away and stick my pins into my pin cushion before throwing it into my sewing bag.

Reece extends his hand as I unfold my legs from under me and push myself to my feet. "I hope you don't have to cut my eyes out for seeing the dress."

"No." I laugh and take his hand in mine to steady myself. "You're fine. That only applies to Josh."

He smiles. "That's a relief."

Close up, Reece Evans is a work of art. Dimples grace his cheeks when he smiles, despite the stubble. And his eyes are so blue you could dive right in and never come up for air.

He's so cute it hurts.

"Are you all ready for the wedding?"

He nods. "Yes, Ma'am. I've got my tux, and Josh is uber organised. He's been ready for this for a long time."

"So has Delaney."

Reece looks down at our still-joined hands, and he gives them a small shake. "It's nice to finally meet you, Pania. Delaney's told me all about you."

I bite my bottom lip at the way he pronounces my name. It's not difficult to pronounce—the same as Tania but with a P, but his soft southern accent twists it a little. It's the kind of thing I'd usually try to correct, but he's making an effort.

"Don't believe a word of it."

"She only has nice things to say about you. I'm not sure what she'd say about me." He drops my hand.

"She's told me you're always hungry. But that's about it."

Reece chuckles. "That's accurate. But you can't blame me for liking her cooking. I hear you cook too."

I clasp my hands together. "We did our training together."

"And now you're a hot shot fashion designer."

Tilting my head, I shrug. "Learning to be."

"Well, I'm sure when people get a load of Delaney's wedding dress, you'll get a lot of offers." His dimples light up, and I suppress the urge to sigh. I'm not about to make a fool of myself over this guy. "You'll be here for a while, won't you? Seeing as we're all going to my place in Hawaii."

Shit. I never thought of that. Delaney and Josh's plan is to go to Hawaii for a week alone before Josh's parents, Reece, Amelia, and I join them. There'll be a week where I'm here with Reece. And the others too, of course, but *Reece.*

"Uh"—I shift on my feet then run my hand through my long golden-brown hair—"yeah. I'll be here until then."

His smile's so warm and genuine, it's confusing. "Good. I'm glad we'll be able to get to know each other better."

Wait. Is this is routine with women? Or does he mean it?

The number one thing I know about this guy is that he's never had a serious girlfriend. At least, not a public one. I can't read too much into this, but I know full well that tonight in that bed down the hall, it'll be Reece Evans who visits my dreams.

"Sounds great." My voice squeaks, but he doesn't seem to notice as he takes a look around.

"Where's Amelia? She's usually climbed me like a tree by now."

"She was in her room, playing. I'm sure she won't be far away."

As if on cue, there's a shriek from the doorway.

"Reece!"

He turns. "Hey, little lady."

Melly runs straight at him, leaping into his arms, and he laughs as he scoops her up onto his hip. Her dress is finished, and she refused to take it off once we got her into it.

"Mummy said I had to show you my dress."

"You're all dressed up too? You're so pretty." He plants a kiss on her cheek and hugs her before dropping her to the ground and turning back to me. "Do I get to see you all dressed up?"

"On the day of the wedding." My cheeks heat up again, and I take a deep breath to try and stop this stupid reaction.

He's just a man.

"Amelia." Josh's voice comes from the doorway.

Melly's eyes widen, and she claps her hands to her face. "Daddy can't see me in my dress."

"I'm pretty sure that just applies to your mom," Reece says. "Want me to sneak you out?"

She nods, her dark curls flying. I love this kid so much, and I'm so glad to see she's just slotted into this crazy world so well.

"Hide behind me."

She tucks herself in behind Reece's back, and I follow them as he steps sideways out of the room.

Josh stands just outside the door.

"I wasn't sure if it was okay to come in," he says to me.

"Delaney's upstairs getting changed, but I think someone else doesn't want you to see." I point to where Amelia is hiding.

He grins, and gives me a knowing nod.

"Has anyone seen Amelia?" he asks.

"Not me," Reece says. "I have no idea where she is."

"Guess I'm going to have to wait for that hug."

Melly giggles, then slams her hand over her mouth.

"What was that noise?" Josh looks around.

I shrug. "I think you're hearing things."

"You should get your hearing checked, old man." Reece turns his head and winks at me. I almost turn into a puddle on the living room floor.

"Old? You're six months older than I am." Josh laughs.

Reece looks back at Melly. "You ready to move?"

She nods, giggling again.

He reaches behind and clasps her hands in his before taking another step sideways, and then another. One step at a time, they make their way toward the hallway that leads to the bedrooms, Melly laughing the whole way.

Josh walks toward me, shaking his head. "How did today go?"

"It went well. Your bride looks beautiful."

He grins. "No offence, but she could wear a sack and she'd still be the most beautiful girl to me."

"Offence not taken, but that's because she's my BFF and I agree."

Josh never has to tell me how he feels about Delaney. It's so clear by that lovestruck look in his eyes. And I love that he wears his heart on his sleeve as far as Delaney and Amelia are concerned. He's everything Delaney ever deserved, and I know he'll love her forever.

"Are you settling in okay?" he asks. He's been working at his new production company during the day, and he and Reece are making a movie of their own. It's all so exciting, and I feel like I should be asking him the same question given that he's no longer tripping around the world to make films. At least, not for now.

I nod. "It's all a little overwhelming, but Delaney's happy and that's all that matters to me."

"I'm glad I have your approval." He flicks a glance toward the door. "I hope Reece was behaving."

"We just met."

Josh laughs. "Yeah, but he has a habit of being a bit much. Although, I think I know you well enough to assume you can handle him."

"Handle who?" Reece walks back in.

"I'm just warning Pania about you. Not that I think she needs warning. I'm sure Delaney's told her everything."

"From what I've heard, I'm sure Pania can handle me just fine." Reece flashes me that smile again, and my stomach flips. I'm not sure I can take two weeks of this.

"Oh, I've seen her in action. I'm pretty sure Pania can handle anything." Josh winks at me, and I look down at my feet. I know I can be pretty intimidating when I want to, but I'm not sure my nerves could stand up to my Hollywood crush. I lift my gaze again, and he's studying me closely with a small smile on his face. "She threw me out of their diner once. Too much testosterone, she said."

"To be fair, I thought you and Damon were about to out-man each other."

"I won the girl in the end."

Reece looks between us. "Sounds like there's a story there."

"Oh, just some guy who had a crush on Delaney back home. He never stood a chance against Josh." Josh's smile goes all the way to his eyes. He knows how protective I am of Delaney, and while he probably didn't appreciate it back then, he sure does now.

"Josh would have kicked his ass knowing how much in love he is," Reece says.

I shift my gaze to Reece. "That's exactly why I kicked them both out of the diner."

"Now that was a day." Delaney breezes into the room and walks straight to Josh. I roll my eyes and look away at their very affectionate greeting, only to find Reece doing the same. My cheeks burn as he copies my eye roll and grins at me.

"Are you here for dinner, Reece?" Delaney asks.

"I'm not travelling all this way and going home with an empty stomach." He lifts his shirt and rubs his washboard abs in a circular motion. I spend way too much time focusing on them, and blush yet again when he catches me. *Argh.*

"It's good to have you back." Josh breaks away from Delaney and grips Reece's shoulder. "We've got a lot to talk about."

"I hope you don't want too much out of me. I'm tired and I thought you had all this wedding stuff under control."

Josh laughs. "I do. We just have to go over what you're doing. I'm talking about the business."

Reece slinks out of Josh's grasp. "Can't that wait until after your honeymoon?"

Delaney looks between the two of them. "I'm going to go and sort out dinner. Want to get away from these two, Pania?"

"That might be a good idea. Let's have some real wine instead of listening to Reece whine."

She bursts out laughing. "Come on."

"I heard that," Reece calls out as we walk toward the kitchen.

"You were meant to," I call back.

My heart's racing, but I can't help my smart arse mouth sometimes.

3

REECE

I never thought I had a type.

But looking through my dating history, you would think I only ever hooked up with leggy blondes. It's probably mostly true, but not really a preference.

I'd seen photos of Pania on Delaney's social media, but she's even more stunning in person. Her long legs are about the only similarity to women I usually date, and she's showing them off in blue mid-thigh shorts. Her hazel eyes stopped me in my tracks the minute I saw them. Not that I would ever let her know that.

Pania's long hair looks like honey against her smooth brown skin.

And every time I make eye contact with her over the table, she blushes and drops her gaze.

There isn't much I know about Pania. Delaney's spoken about her at length, and I wrack my brain to remember everything she told me. But without the context of knowing her, it didn't mean much. I knew she was Māori and bilingual, that she's been Delaney's best friend virtually from birth, and that the two of them studied cooking together. Now she's studying fashion design although having seen that wedding dress, I think she's got a head start on the rest of the class.

Ordinarily, I'd make a move at this point, but given that she's Delaney's friend and we're having a family meal, it's probably not good behaviour.

"Your shoot's all done?" Josh asks.

I pitch my fork into my plate of tuna bake and meet his gaze. "Uh huh. Shot the last scene this morning."

"You're making a movie?" Pania asks.

"I've just finished one. It was only two weeks filming. My character comes in closer to the end of the movie, so it wasn't a long shoot."

"What's it about?"

I put my fork down. "Aren't you supposed to be a fan? Don't you know?"

Her eyebrows both arch, and I smile to myself.

"Reece. Stop it." Delaney laughs.

"I heard Pania can give as good as she gets. I just wanted to test her." I shrug.

Pania meets my gaze. "I'm sorry. I stopped caring about your career when Josh and Delaney got back together."

I grin. "And there it is."

"Reece is making a movie about kissing." Amelia covers her hand with her mouth and giggles.

I give her the side-eye. "Am I now?"

"That's what Mummy says all your movies are about."

Josh bursts out laughing, while Delaney is wide-eyed. "I don't remember saying that."

"So are Daddy's movies." Amelia giggles. "But he kisses Mummy now."

Delaney shoots Josh a pointed look. "I think maybe we need to explain a few things to our daughter."

He seems to try and evade her look. "That might be a good idea with us making our movie soon."

"I think so, seeing as you both have scenes with Gabby." She's still staring him down, and I try so hard to resist the urge to laugh. This isn't the first movie he's made since they got back together, but she's never wanted to be anywhere near the set while he's filming.

"*Hot* scenes with Gabby," I say.

He glares at me. "Don't make things worse. Your scene is more explicit than mine."

Pania looks between us, her hand poised over her meal with her laden fork hanging in mid-air, as if she's forgotten that she was taking a bite.

"Before we can make the film, Reece has to actually turn up to work."

"Ouch." I grimace.

"You made sure your schedule is clear from here on in, didn't you? No surprise absences?" Josh asks.

I nod. "It's all under control. Sara knows I'm not looking for anything else right now."

"Sara?" Pania asks.

Josh turns toward her. "Sara's our agent. She's also trying to sign Delaney after her viral cooking video."

Pania shifts her gaze to her best friend. "Someone's keeping secrets."

Delaney shrugs. "Those videos are just a bit of fun. One of us in show business is more than enough right now."

"I can't believe you didn't tell me. What. A. Bitch." Pania finishes the bite of her meal.

I stare at her. Josh and I joke around all the time with each other, but Pania's gruff tone takes me aback.

"Always. I thought you knew me better than that." Delaney laughs. "Might help if you answer your Skype calls more often."

Pania shakes her head. "What else haven't you been telling me?"

Delaney puts down her cutlery and taps her index fingers together. "Well, I am secretly already married to Ryan Reynolds. One flick of those hips as Deadpool, and—"

"Delaney." Josh growls.

She blows him a kiss. "You know you're really my favourite Canadian."

I look between the two of them. There's some private joke there that I've not asked Josh about, and the lovesick look in his eyes when she says it stops me from asking yet again.

"Are you two still going on about that?" Pania asks.

Delaney meets Josh's gaze across the table. "It's our thing."

"It's pathetic, that's what it is." Pania rolls her eyes.

I meet her gaze and shoot her a look that I hope conveys the question: what the fuck?

"I thought you would have known about it. Josh, here, made the mistake of thinking Delaney was Australian when they met. So she calls him her favourite Canadian," she explains. "I think they usually do it in private."

"No, I guess I missed that. But then I didn't meet Delaney the first time around. That makes sense." Delaney and Josh are still locked in some gaze competition, and I stab my fork into my food and scoop out a mouthful.

"To be fair, I made the wrong guess after she said *two* words," Josh says, swivelling his gaze to me.

"Big mistake to make, though, bro." Pania shakes her head. "I don't think Australians like being confused for New Zealanders either. You were probably screwed either way."

Josh's lips twitch. "Well ... I was screwed. Pretty spectacularly too. If you know what I mean."

Delaney throws a napkin across the table at him. "Joshua Carter."

"You sound like my mother." Josh screws up his face and takes a bite of his meal. "Did I tell you just how much I love your cooking, Delaney?"

"Oh it's *way* too late to kiss my arse now."

I'm used to their banter, but Pania's contribution adds a whole new dimension. And for the first time since I met Delaney, I'm feeling a little out of it.

Delaney smiles at me. "Would you like some more food, Reece? You're still in my good books."

"I'm fine right now, but thanks." I grin.

Josh's left eyebrow arches. "You can cut that out too."

"Cut what out?"

"The flirting."

I hold up my palms. "I literally just said thank you."

"With you, that's flirting." He smiles smugly at his fiancée, and she glances at Pania before they both dissolve into laughter.

I smile to myself and scoop more of my dinner into my mouth.

That's better.

I COULD HAVE GONE HOME last night, but after dinner, I was so tired, I crashed in my room. Before I left for Georgia, I'd started staying over here so much that Delaney allocated me a bedroom. And even though Pania staying here doesn't impact that, it still feels odd that there's another person staying in the house.

I'm acutely aware of it as I pull on my jeans and a fresh T-shirt from my bag. In the en suite, I take the time to wash my face, brush my teeth, and look presentable before making my way out of the bedroom and into the kitchen.

Josh, Delaney, Amelia, and Pania all look up as I enter the room.

I yawn. "That bed is so comfortable."

Delaney laughs. "You're just in time for breakfast. There's plenty of food."

I clap my hands together. "Immaculate timing as always."

There are a pile of pancakes in the centre of the table, and I take a seat, picking up a fork to help myself.

"Want a coffee?" Josh asks.

"I'll make one in a minute. After my stomach stops grumbling."

He stands. "I'm getting a refill anyway. Anyone else want one?"

Delaney shakes her head.

"No thanks," Pania says.

He heads behind the kitchen counter, and I fill my plate with pancakes before grabbing the syrup. "These look amazing, Delaney."

"Have as many as you like. I can always make more." She smiles. "Did you have any washing you want doing?"

I shake my head. "I had it all done before I came home."

"You do his washing?"

I shift my gaze to Pania. Her nose is scrunched up, her mouth hanging open.

"No." Delaney laughs. "But he's just got back from a trip, and you know what boys are like."

Pania rolls her eyes and goes back to eating.

My stomach grumbles, and I pick up my fork. This beats any hotel breakfast. Maybe I should just start paying rent.

It doesn't take long to eat my fill. Usually, I'm on an eating plan to keep in good condition for movies, especially with the love scene in our own production coming up, but I'll make an exception for this morning.

I lean back in my seat. "That was amazing. I missed your cooking so much when I was away."

"You're always welcome." She takes a sip of her coffee. "What are you two up to today?"

Josh stands. "We are getting out of here."

I look up. "Where are you going?"

"*We* are off to get new shoes."

I side-eye him. "I'm pretty sure that neither of us need new shoes. I've got—"

"Delaney's got her last dress fitting today, goofball. We're getting out of here."

I put down my coffee cup. "I've seen her dress. I helped her get out of it the other day."

Between Josh's glare and the death stare across the table from Pania, I'm surprised I don't end up a pile of ash on the floor.

I hold up my palms. "Okay. I get the message. Pania will kill me if I don't leave the house."

She leans back in her chair, a smug smile on her face. "Don't you forget it."

"I'm beginning to think you've got a death wish," Delaney says.

"I can't help it if she doesn't get my charm yet." I wink at Pania, and the satisfaction of seeing her blush and drop her gaze makes me warm inside.

"If that's what you're aiming for, you're missing your target." Josh pats my shoulder. "As Delaney would say, do better."

Delaney laughs, and I huff out a breath. "Fine. I'll come with you. But I want to see the finished product when we get back." I lock my gaze onto Pania, who's no longer blushing. "And if you need an opinion on what you're wearing ..."

This time, just one of her eyebrows arch. "If I want your opinion, I'll give it to you."

I push my chair out and stand. "Sounds fair. Let's go and get these shoes then, Joshua."

"Stop that."

I shoot a wink at Delaney. Josh hates being called Joshua. His mother usually only does it when she's annoyed with him, but it's enough to stop him wanting to be called that.

"See you ladies later. Don't have too much fun without me."

"Bye, Reece." Amelia waves from across the table.

"See you later, little lady." I blow her a kiss.

She giggles, and I also don't miss Pania's eyebrows rising yet again. She could tell a story just using them.

I raise my own eyebrows at the sight of Josh saying goodbye to Delaney. The wedding's the day after tomorrow, but they almost look like they're starting the honeymoon at the dining room table as he kisses her goodbye.

Pania's gaze is fixed on me, and she fights a smile as I pretend to put my index finger down my throat and point at Josh and Delaney.

She bites her bottom lip, and for the first time, I notice the freckle just above her top lip. She sucks it in, still not laughing, and it disappears before reappearing.

I draw in a breath at the mesmerising sight.

After picking up my dishes, I head into the kitchen and place them in the dishwasher. Josh follows, and then we're on our way out the door, leaving the ladies to themselves for the day.

He leads me down to the garage where his Mercedes waits.

"Do you really need new shoes?" I ask.

Unlocking the car, he pauses by his door. "I'm sure I could find a pair, but I think it's important for us to take some time out with everything that's going on."

I open the door and sit in the passenger side, sinking into the seat. Truth is, I'm glad to be out and about with him and not cooped up in the house with wedding talk that will inevitably happen today and tomorrow.

I'm excited for him, but I'll be glad when it's over and life can return somewhat to normal. Tomorrow, the house gets invaded by the wedding planner, and I'll probably hide somewhere until I'm actually needed.

Josh slides into the driver's seat, does up his seat belt, starts the car, and pulls out onto the road.

"What is up with you?" he asks.

"Nothing. Why?"

He glances at me, tightening his grip on the steering wheel. "I can deal with the way you flirt with Delaney because we're all friends, but you're not usually this annoying."

I shrug. "I don't mean to be. Maybe it's just a weird time right now, and I'm not sure how to deal with it." Sighing, I look out the window instead of at him. "My best friend is getting married, and it's the end of an era. Maybe that's it."

"It's not like I was ever a big womaniser. I left that up to you."

I look back at him. "Is that all you think of me?"

Josh frowns. "Of course not. You've always been so much more than what you think of yourself."

I don't say anything. It's hard to when I can only focus on what he just said.

"Reece, I love you like a brother. I'm not sure I've ever said that. And I can't imagine anyone else I'd want by my side for my wedding."

"I'm glad to hear it. I'd have to kill anyone else in my way." My voice croaks, even though I'm trying to be tough. I feel the same way about Josh. Before him, I didn't have siblings, and there was no one in my life that filled that space.

He chuckles, and I look out the window, not wanting to say anything else. I'm not a man afraid to cry, but there's a lot of emotion to come in the next couple of days.

"By the time we're finished, it'll be nearly noon. Want to go out somewhere afterward and grab a drink?"

I look back at him. "I think that's a great idea. It's been a while."

He nods. "It has been. With the wedding, and setting up this new business, it's been hard to find time for anything else."

"I'm not feeling neglected, if that's what you're concerned about."

Josh drives us to the Beverly Centre. "I'm not worried about that, but I think it's still important we hang out."

As we pull into the parking lot, I lean back in the seat. Josh stops to get a ticket.

"Now that we're here, do we really have to go shoe shopping?" It's not that I don't like shopping, but I'm still struggling to see the point.

"And when we go back home and Delaney asks to see what we bought?" He parks the car and turns off the engine.

"Just tell her the bride's not allowed to see the groom's shoes before the wedding." I give him a soft punch on the arm.

He shakes his head. "As if I'd get away with that."

"You might. Amelia played that trick on you."

"No." He laughs. "She actually thinks I'm not supposed to see her dress."

I roar with laughter. "That's the cutest thing I think I've ever heard."

"I don't think Delaney did it herself. I think it took the combined power of Delaney *and* Pania. But she freaks out if I go anywhere near her closet." He looks toward the building. "I've got to go into Tiffany's to pick up gifts for the girls. Don't you dare tell any of them."

I study him closely. "You left that to the last minute."

"I didn't want to try hiding anything in case Delaney found it. We got her engagement ring from the New York store, and she knows what the boxes look like."

I grin. "Understandable. If you need me to help hide anything ..."

"Thanks."

We get out of the car and head into the mall. The one good thing about being back in LA is that we can go shopping with minimal fuss. There'll be the odd person who wants an autograph or even a selfie, but it feels as if we blend in a bit better here.

"Where are we going for these shoes?" I ask.

"Fendi. That's where I got my last pair. And they're just across from Tiffany's."

Nodding in acknowledgement, I walk alongside him as we make our way to Level 7 where we turn into Fendi.

"I thought we could get patent leather to go with our tuxes," he says.

"Makes sense." I look around and blow out a long breath, thinking about the two pairs I have in my apartment closet. I guess another pair won't hurt.

"Is there anything I can help you with today?"

I turn at the sound of a woman's voice and can't help but smile. She's a brunette with brown eyes and full lips, those eyes widening as she looks between us.

"Stop it," Josh hisses.

"Stop what?"

"We're here to buy some shoes." He shoots me a pointed look. "We need two pairs of patent leather shoes to go with tuxedos for a wedding."

"We have a range over here. Come with me."

Trailing behind, Josh elbows me. "What are you doing?"

"I literally just smiled at her."

"No distractions. We have a wedding to get on with."

"You're the one getting married, not me." I shrug. "I'm not doing anything wrong."

"You know how much trouble that smile gets you in."

I laugh loudly, and the brunette looks back at us as she reaches the shelf.

Suitably chastised for smiling, I take a seat on one of the chairs while Josh has a look at the shoes.

He takes his time, trying on multiple pairs until he finds the ones he likes. They're nothing special, and I'm sure I've seen him wear similar pairs.

"I thought Delaney and Pania could do with some time without us for a bit. They've gone from seeing each other every day to living in different countries." He frowns. "It's the one thing I wish I could give Delaney, but it's not as if I can force Pania to move here."

The shop assistant returns, and he points at the shoes he wants. "These ones, and this size is perfect."

I put up my hand. "Can you make that two pairs? I'm the same size as him."

He watches me as she walks away. "What do you think of Pania?"

"We literally just met. What do you think I think of her?"

He shakes his head, rolling his eyes. "I just know what you're like with women, and you two will be spending some time together over the next couple of weeks. She's not the type you usually like."

I smooth my hands down my pants. "What is *that* supposed to mean?"

"She's tough, and smart. I know she has a soft side because she's fiercely protective of Delaney and Amelia. She loves the shit out of them."

I squint at him. "I'm not following."

"Don't even think about fucking and ditching her. Pania doesn't deserve it, and you'll ruin any friendship you're developing with my girl."

I tap my toe on the carpet, not even sure how to respond to that. It's fair. It's the kind of thing I might have done in the past. But even if I tell Josh I want to pull my life together, it's not like he'll believe me until I actually do it. And I've got no one to blame for that but me.

"I wouldn't do that to Delaney. Or Pania. I don't even know if she likes me."

His tone softens. "She's a big fan of yours. Just don't take advantage of that."

"You know, I should be angry that you even think I'm capable of that."

Josh's brows knit. "Probably. But I thought I'd say something because I don't want anything to upset Delaney." He sits on the bench beside me. "Until a few months ago, I didn't think I'd ever find her again. And, now, in two days, we're getting married. She's my whole life, Reece."

I smile, gripping his shoulder and squeezing. "I know. I'm pretty sure she feels the same way."

He nods. "I don't know how I went so long without her."

"Then don't you screw it up."

Josh laughs. "Let's get these damn shoes sorted and get out of here. Want to go somewhere for lunch?"

"If it includes a drink, yes."

"How long do we have to stay away for?" I ask before taking a sip of my beer.

Josh laughs. "Why are you itching to get back?"

I shrug. "I could do with a nap after being away for work."

Our waitress brings over a large platter of barbecue ribs and deposits it in the middle of the table.

I stare at it wide-eyed. "I could do with a nap after eating this."

"Enjoy," she says with a smile.

"Oh, I intend to. Thank you."

Josh tries his beer. "Damn that's good."

"A couple more days and you'll be an old married man."

Josh laughs. "Not so much of the old." He sucks on his bottom lip. "Can I crash at your place the night before the wedding? Delaney and I don't want to curse things."

"Of course you can. We can order pizza and have a boy's night."

His brows furrow. "No drinking though. I want a clear head for the wedding."

"Deal. I'm just looking forward to hanging out with you. It's been a while."

Josh nods slowly. "It has."

I chew my inner cheek. "I've got something to ask you, and I'm not sure you'll like it."

His smile disappears. "What is it?"

"It's about Jessie."

Josh looks away before taking in a deep breath and looking back at me. "What about her?"

"She's really upset about not being invited to the wedding. I wasn't going to say anything, but seeing as we're being open about everything …" I hold out my palms.

"You also know *why* she's not invited. She made a choice, and that was to treat Delaney like crap."

I chew on my top lip. "What if she apologised?"

Josh shakes his head. "It'd be up to Delaney to accept any apology. Not me."

"I wasn't there. You said she was nasty to Delaney. But what exactly did she do?"

He takes a long sip of his beer before answering. "When we were filming in New Zealand, she showed up at Delaney's diner and trashed her in public."

"Ouch." I screw up my face. Unfortunately, it's something I can picture Jessie doing, and being on Delaney's property, it would have been a shitstorm.

"Yeah. It wasn't pretty. Delaney was really upset. The only thing she ever did wrong was love me."

"It's you loving her back that Jessie struggles with."

Josh opens his mouth before closing it again and shaking his head. "It's not like I haven't been straight up with her. She's known for years I didn't want anything more than friendship. And I made that movie with her because she asked me. I'm glad I did because it lead me back to Delaney, but the fallout was our friendship."

I say nothing. There's nothing I can really say. There's no way forward for this until Jessie makes a move, which is what I suspected.

"But enough about her." Josh tilts his head. "What are you going to do while we're away? Mom and Dad are so happy to be looking after Amelia."

I take a sip of my drink. "I'm not sure. I thought I could give Pania a tour of LA. Maybe take her out somewhere quiet for dinner. It'll be nice to have some company, I'm so used to spending time with you and Delaney."

He chuckles. "She'll keep you on your toes. And I really appreciate it."

I lean back and smile.

While I don't know her well, I'm sure he's right about Pania keeping me on my toes.

The question is how I counter that.

4

PANIA

This evening is pure bliss.

Josh went to spend his last night as a single man in Reece's apartment. His parents arrived today, but they went to bed ages ago, and Melly is fast asleep.

Delaney and I are sprawled out on her bed, in our pyjamas, eating chocolate and watching some terrible movie on Netflix.

It's just like the good old days.

"You'll be Mrs Josh Carter tomorrow. How weird is that?"

Delaney laughs. "I know. It's so hard to believe there was a time I never thought this would happen. I hated him."

"I don't think you ever hated him. I don't think you're capable of hating anyone."

She pops a chocolate in her mouth and shrugs.

"I'm just glad you two sorted out your differences and got back together. I miss the shit out of you, but I know you and Melly are loved. And you're a rich bitch now, so I can eat all these chocolates and you can just buy some more."

Delaney coughs, her eyes bulging a little as she struggles not to choke as she laughs. "You did not say that."

"I did. And I'm really happy for you. No one deserves to land on their feet more than you, my brave *wahine*."

Tears pool in her eyes, but I'm not sure whether it's because of what I've said or because she's choking on her last chocolate.

"*I'm* so happy for me. And the money and the house is amazing, but Josh loves Melly and me so much. I still can't believe our little family's back together, and holy shit, I'm getting married tomorrow."

"Yes, you are."

Letting out a long, contented sigh, she lies flat on her back. "Do you remember when we were teenagers and we used to talk about this stuff?"

I laugh. "Yes, back before we discovered what a let-down men were."

"Not all of them." She nudges my arm and rolls over to face me. "Reece keeps looking at you." She pulls that smug look I know so well. "I think someone's interested."

I roll my eyes. "Oh, please. I'm a woman. That's enough for him."

Delaney shrugs. "I still think he's got his eye on you."

Snorting, I turn toward her. "Pretty sure he's got his eye on a lot of the ladies."

"They're not you, though. I'd be just fine with it if he fell in love with my bestie."

I swipe the air with my hand. "Oh, please. I'm not his type. There'll be more plastic at your wedding than a Tupperware party. That's his type."

"Stop it." She laughs. "Reece is a lot more sensitive than he seems."

"What makes you say that? He seems pretty annoying to me."

She's quiet for a moment as she reaches for the remote and then turns off the television. It makes sense when neither of us are watching it. And the topic at hand is far more interesting.

"When he's not being an outrageous flirt, he's a really sweet guy. He's not always the most dependable, but Josh can count on him when he really needs him. And he's so good with Melly. He mentions his parents sometimes, but I'm not sure if they're close. It's like he's adopted us."

I say nothing and pick up another chocolate.

"Or we've adopted him." She laughs.

I snort again. "Have you told Josh what a huge crush you had on him?"

She eyeballs me. "*We* had on him. Josh knows, but he also knows he's the only one for me. Besides, it's all a bit weird now with Reece being his best friend. And now that I've got to know him, there's no crush. Believe me on that."

I bite my bottom lip. "Is he that bad?"

Delaney rolls onto her back again. "No, he's just become like an old pair of slippers. Comfortable and easy."

"I hear easy is right."

She chuckles. "If you're jealous, he'll never be able to replace you as my bestie."

"I'm not jealous." I huff out a breath. "What other famous friends do you have that I'm going to meet tomorrow?"

Delaney shrugs. "No one really. Oh, except Gabby. Josh has a ton of people he knows coming, but I haven't met a lot of them yet."

"Gabby Reynolds?"

She nods. "You know I met her last time we were in Hawaii. She's going to be in Josh and Reece's movie, so we've hung out a few times." She links her fingers together. "If you think Josh and I are bad, wait until you meet her and Antonio. Those two practically eye fuck each other *all* the time. And he's hot."

"You seem surrounded by hot men these days." I yawn.

Delaney holds her arms in the air. "What can I say? I've become a hot man magnet."

"Can you rub some of that off on me?"

She laughs. "I'll be your wingman anytime, you know that."

"Can you do that when you're a married woman?"

Popping another chocolate in her mouth, she chews for a bit and swallows as she seems to ponder the answer. "There's probably another name for it. I'm sure we can make it work." She rolls her neck. "I think that's enough chocolate for the night. I'm going to brush my teeth unless you want to experience my morning breath."

I grimace. "No thanks."

"Remember when we used to camp in your mum's back yard? Did we ever last a whole night before caving and ending up in your room?"

I ponder her question for a moment before blowing out a long breath. "Not that I can remember. Dad hated it because that tent was such a pain in the arse to put up."

Delaney grins. "He'd get so angry and then your mum would come and sort it out."

"I don't miss those days. At least now we're sensible enough to sleep in real beds and not even try a tent."

She sighs. "I love my bed way too much for that these days."

"It is comfortable. Do you think Josh would mind if I moved in *and* slept here from now on?"

Leaning over to hug me, she laughs. "That'd be a no."

As she climbs off the bed and heads toward the en suite, I snuggle down into the pillows. "Are you sure? I don't snore."

"Neither does he," she calls out.

I shrug. "It was worth a try."

While she's gone, I look around the room. Delaney sent me photos when she first moved here, and since then she's really put her stamp on the decor. This room was so plain, and she hasn't done a lot, but the addition of new bedroom furniture and a beautiful blue floral duvet with her favourite hibiscus flower is so her. And then there are the family photos plastered all over one wall.

Anyone else, and I'd envy all that she has. But I know how much she's struggled at times because I was right there with her. I'm glad of everyone that I know, Delaney's the one who's fallen on her feet.

She walks back in. "Bathroom's free."

"Is that a hint you don't want *my* morning breath?" I tease.

"God no. Especially not on my wedding day." She grimaces, and then laughs.

I get out of bed and walk to the bathroom. My toothbrush waits for me beside the basin, and I stand in front of the mirror as I brush, my mind on tomorrow.

It was only months ago that our world was turned on its head by Josh's arrival in our small New Zealand town. All it took was for him and Delaney to work out the misunderstanding that drove them apart six years prior, and life changed for all of us.

After finishing up and cleaning my brush, I walk back into the bedroom. Delaney's tucked under the blankets, and I climb in beside her.

"We should get some sleep. The last thing I want are bags under my eyes tomorrow." She rolls onto her side, facing away from me, and reaches up to turn off the lamp. Soft light from the hallway illuminates the room enough for me to see what I'm doing as I wriggle down under the blankets and rest my head on Josh's pillow.

"Tomorrow will be amazing. You're marrying a good one."

"I am, aren't I?"

We lie in the dark for a few moments, and I roll toward her.

"Delaney," I whisper.

"What?"

"Do you remember when I told you that you were missing something after you came back from the states the first time? That you were never quite yourself after that?"

"Yes?" The bed shifts as she rolls toward me.

"It's back. And I'm so happy to see it. You're whole, my friend."

She sniffs. "You're not supposed to make me cry before I go to sleep."

I reach out and tuck her hair behind her ear. "Only happy tears now, bestie."

Delaney turns back over, and it's not long before she falls asleep given the gentle snores coming from the other side of the bed. I'm not so lucky as I stare at the ceiling.

It might be Delaney's big day tomorrow, but I think I'm more nervous than she is.

5

———

PANIA

I smooth my maroon dress down and take a look in the mirror.

Today is the most insane day of my life.

Delaney's backyard is filled with the who's who of Holly-wood, but only one man is on my mind.

Reece has been a bit of a dick, but I think Delaney's right in that there's more to him than what's on the surface. Although how far down I can scratch before he gets on my nerves is a whole other matter.

I reach for the diamond earrings Mum loaned me, and slide them into my ears. They were an anniversary gift from my dad. He died a few years ago, but he would have loved to have been here for Delaney's wedding day. As it is, Mum's terrified of flying—she'd never make it all the way here. Wearing the earrings makes me feel, a little, as if they're both with us today.

Taking a deep breath, I exit my room and head to Delaney's. She must have spent a fortune on getting hair and makeup done for us, my eyelids dusted in a silver shimmer, my lips glossy and pink. I delicately sweep my carefully pinned, honey curls off my shoulder and let them cascade down my back. I feel like a princess.

I hope it feels that way for her too.

Reece meets my gaze as I step in the doorway. Delaney asked him to give her away in the absence of anyone else, while Josh wanted him as best man. Somehow, he's performing both roles today. It's weird, but so is this whole world I find myself in.

"Aren't I lucky? Surrounded by beautiful women."

Delaney fiddles with her earrings. "So full of compliments today."

"Just because you're getting married doesn't mean that I can't try and win your heart."

I clamp my lips together as she shoves him. "Good luck with that."

Cocking an eyebrow, I meet his gaze. "We should get this show on the road before Josh thinks you've abandoned him."

"Look what I got, Pania."

I glance down to see Melly holding out her arm. Around her wrist is the most dainty bracelet I've ever seen.

"That's lovely."

"It's from my daddy." She beams. God, how I love this kid. She took her own chunk of my heart the day she was born, and I was so lucky to see every moment of her childhood until she moved to the US.

"Your daddy has very good taste. It's so pretty. Just like you, Miss Melly." I tap her on the nose, and she giggles. "Are you ready to get your mum and dad married?"

Melly nods, and picks up her basket of rose petals.

I raise my gaze to meet Reece's. There's a look in his eyes that I can't read, but he's not paying any attention to Delaney chatting beside him.

For just a moment, it's as if we're the only two people in the room.

"Pania, we gotta get Mummy and Daddy married."

I look down at Melly. Her lips are pursed, and her expression is so serious, I have to clamp my lips together to suppress a smile.

"Right you are. Let's go."

Taking Melly by the hand, I look at Delaney. "Ready?"

"As I'll ever be." She adjusts the sweetheart neckline of her dress then fiddles with her diamond necklace.

"Do I have lipstick on my teeth?" She bares her teeth and grins at me like the Cheshire Cat.

"No. It's a lip stain, silly. It won't budge."

Her smile is radiant as she inhales and puffs her chest. "Okay. Let's do this."

"We'll be right behind you," Reece says. "Lead the way."

I take Melly's hand, and we walk out of Delaney's room, along the hallway, and down the stairs before exiting the house through the kitchen and out of the back door.

Caterers bustle around us, and the wedding planner stands to one side, delegating through a headpiece while watching us with a big smile on her face.

We have a short walk around the pool fence, and I spy Josh standing with his back to us at the other end of the aisle, flanked by rows of chairs.

An instrumental version of Katy Perry's Firework begins to play. I clamp my lips together in amusement. It's a detail I didn't think to ask Delaney, but I know it's the song she first danced to with Josh a little over six years ago in some LA club.

It's almost enough to keep me distracted from the walk down the aisle, a little like being at the Oscars, the way the chairs are all laid out in rows.

Especially with Hollywood's elite sitting in them.

Melly skips, and I grab her hand and gently tug her back to me. "We're supposed to do this together, Miss Melly."

She giggles. "Can we throw the petals now?"

I nod. "Just a few like we practiced. Don't go too crazy."

She screws up her face, but plunges her hand into the basket and brings out two petals. "Like this?"

It takes everything in me not to laugh, but this little girl makes me so proud. "Just like that. Let's go."

Melly watches me as I scatter the petals as we walk. At one point, I look at Josh, and a lump forms in my throat at the pride on his face, his eyes fixed on his daughter.

And then his gaze shifts, and the lump grows bigger as tears well in his eyes. I don't need to look around to know Delaney's behind us. I can see it written all over his face.

I want that one day. I want someone to look at me in the way he's looking at his wife-to-be right now. His face is so open and full of pride. The way his mouth curls into a faint smile at the edges, but his eyes are so expressive and tell a story of his love for her.

Melly and I reach the altar, and she grabs my hand tight as her father winks at her. She beams up at me, and I lean over to plant a kiss on her cheek. "You did good, sweet pea. I'm so proud of you."

"Here's Mummy," she whispers.

I straighten up to see Delaney arrive, and my gaze meets Reece's for just a split second. My heart stops. All those jokes over the last few days, but I've never seen him so serious. He gives Delaney a kiss on the cheek and passes her hand over to Josh's. The two of them exchange a glance before Reece steps back, out of the way.

And then he looks at me.

The sound of blood rushing in my ears stops me from paying much attention to the ceremony until Melly tugs on my hand, forcing me to look down to see Josh squatting in front of her.

"I promised your mama that when we got married, I'd make a commitment to you too. And that is that I promise to always be a good father to you, Amelia. I'll listen, and make you your favourite hot chocolate with more whipped cream than your mother usually lets you have. I love you," he says.

"Love you too, Daddy." She wraps her arms around his neck, and he picks her up onto his hip, smothering her face in kisses as she giggles.

He places her down on the ground, and I hold out my hand which she takes again before snuggling into me.

After the ceremony, the guests head inside for the reception while our little group poses for photos.

"I hate having my photo taken," I mutter.

"You and me both." I look over to find Reece standing next to me.

"It's not that I think I look awful, I just hate the posing."

He laughs. "That's exactly it. I feel like a performing monkey."

I fold my arms, watching as Josh and Delaney snuggle up and kiss.

"How do you do it? You must have photographers in your face all the time. I've seen interviews and photo shoots in magazines."

He leans in. "Honestly? I just pretend I'm a kid again, and it's just a game. There are a lot of photos of me you haven't seen where I'm poking my tongue out."

I grin and shake my head. "They're the photos they should print. You might seem more human and less godlike."

"Is that what you think of me?" He places his palm on his chest.

"Maybe before I realised how annoying you are."

He opens his mouth, as if he's about to say something.

"And now the best man and bridesmaid," the photographer announces.

Reece holds out his hand. "Come on."

I swallow hard as I take his hand and we walk to the spot Delaney and Josh have just vacated.

"Stand nice and close together."

Sucking in a breath, I move closer to Reece.

"Are you ready?" he murmurs.

It takes everything in me not to laugh as it dawns on me what he's about to do.

"Say cheese." The photographer steadies his finger on the button.

Reece and I look at each other, screw up our noses, and poke out our tongues right as the flash goes.

All I can hear is Delaney's laughter

I DON'T THINK I've ever eaten so much in my life.

But the food is good, and the wine flows. And then there's that big cake right in front of our table, taunting me. It's chocolate—Delaney would never choose anything else, and it's beautifully decorated in white fondant with silver ferns around the sides to represent her and Melly's homeland.

Josh's father stands up and taps a spoon against his glass.

"On behalf of Josh and Delaney, I'd like to thank you all for coming. I believe Delaney's bridesmaid, Pania, and the best man, Reece, have a few words to say." He smiles down the table at me. "Pania?"

My knees knock together when I stand, which is the oddest feeling. I'm no fan of public speaking, but it doesn't usually intimidate me this much. Then again, I've never been in a room full of celebrities before.

This is my best friend's wedding.

I look down at Delaney, and she's smiling up at me with so much pride.

"Tēnā koutou, tēnā koutou, tēnā koutou katoa. Greetings, greetings, greetings to you all." I take a deep breath. "My name is Pania Wilson, and I'm Delaney's bridesmaid and her best friend. At least I was her best friend until this one wormed his way back in."

Josh grins at me as I meet his gaze.

"Delaney and I met when we were small, and she's been my bestie my whole life. I've never seen her so happy. Josh is the love of her life as she is his, and I could not be happier for the two of them."

"And me," Amelia calls out.

Laughter fills the air, and I nod toward her. "And you, too, my sweet girl. Love you." I look back at the sea of faces looking at me and hold up my glass. "To Delaney and Josh. You'd better take good care of my girl, Josh. She is one amazing *wahine*."

Delaney's eyes glisten with tears, and I blow her a kiss.

"To Delaney and Josh." A chorus of voices make my heart swell, and I sit back down next to my best friend.

She takes my hand in hers and squeezes it. "I love you."

"Love you too. You make sure he's always good to you. You deserve the best, Delaney."

Tears spill down her cheeks, and she wraps her arms around my shoulders and hugs me tight. "Thank you. For everything," she whispers. "All the years you were by my side and fought along with me to build the life we wanted. And now you're following your dream, too, and I'm so happy. I just wish you were closer."

"I'm only ever a phone call or Facetime away. And who knows? Maybe some designer will fall in love with your dress and offer me a job."

Delaney pulls back, searching my eyes. "Would you take it?"

"When I've finished my course, I won't say no. Maybe I'll be able to pay off the student loan if I can get a decent job."

Her smile lights up her whole face. "That works for me."

"Besides, I need to work Mum up to that. I might not live with her, but me moving will be a really big deal."

Delaney lets me go. "I know. I'm sorry your mum couldn't be here."

"I—"

Josh leans over. "Uh … are you two finished? Reece wants to make his speech."

"Fuck Reece." I poke my tongue out at him.

Delaney laughs. "We'll have plenty of time to talk when we all get to Hawaii." She claps and turns back to me. "I can't wait. Did you know—"

"Delaney." Josh nudges her arm, and she settles back into her seat. His grin tells me he's not really upset with her. He's so besotted, I don't think she can do wrong in his eyes.

"Sorry, Reece."

Reece just shakes his head. He catches my gaze and winks, which doesn't help my pounding heart.

"I'm not quite sure how to follow that up, and you lot know me; I'm never short of words." He pauses to laughter. "But from the bottom of my heart, I congratulate Josh and his beautiful bride, Delaney. And unlike Pania, I'm going to congratulate Amelia for getting her parents safely married."

He flicks a glance at me, and I roll my eyes in return with a smile.

"Yay!" Melly applauds, and the room dissolves into laughter.

"Anyway, Josh, I wish you and Delaney all the love in the world. You two were always meant to be, and I'm just so happy to be here for your big day. Love you guys." He raises his glass. "To Josh and Delaney."

"Josh and Delaney." We all raise our glasses and sip our drinks as Josh and Delaney snuggle up beside me. Their love is so heart-warming.

It really does make me wonder what I'm missing from my own life.

6

REECE

What a day.

I got to give the bride away, and stood as my best friend's best man. And then I even got Pania to play with me.

I hold out my hand to Amelia. "May I have this dance?"

Her eyes twinkle. "Mummy, can I?"

"Of course you can," Delaney says.

I bend and pick Amelia up, settling her on my hip. "I get to dance with the most beautiful girl here."

"Reece." She giggles, and I peck her on the cheek.

"It's true. You're the prettiest girl in the room."

I catch Pania's gaze. I'm still not sure what she thinks, but I've never been so anxious that someone likes me. Maybe it's because her best friend is family now, but maybe it's because she has these hazel eyes that don't miss a thing.

My best friend just married the love of his life, and she's his whole world. It's made me rethink my priorities, and losing myself in woman after woman in an attempt to avoid any kind of commitment is rapidly losing its appeal.

"Reece, come on." Amelia cups my face and drags it to look at her.

She presses her nose to mine, and I can't help but smile. If I ever have kids, I'd love them to be like this one. She's a queen, just like her mom.

With large steps, I sweep her onto the dance floor, and she lets out a whoop as we spin in circles and as I dip her.

I fall a little deeper in love. Amelia's my best friend's kid, and she's so much like him that I'm not surprised when she claps her hands to her cheeks and laughs.

"I think I'll take over here." Josh extends his arms, and Amelia abandons me for her father.

I raise the back of my hand to my forehead. "You're leaving me?"

Amelia leans her head against Josh's.

"I'm not going to see my girl for a week while you get to hang out with her. Of course I'm taking her for this dance." Josh's eyes shine with happiness. Everything's lining up for him now in a way that they've never lined up for me, and I can't resent him for it.

"You have fun with your dad. And we are going to do some fun things while he's away."

Amelia nods, and then Josh whisks her away to the other side of the dance floor where Delaney's waiting. I'm sure this will be the longest she and Amelia have been apart, so I get their need to be together right now.

I'll work with Josh's parents and Pania to keep Amelia distracted.

Pania.

I scan behind Delaney and Josh until I find her again. I'm not afraid to admit I like her—she has the same spunk as Delaney—and the next week will be fun being around her. I also love that freckle on her upper lip that I just want to ...

Stop it. You can't think of her that way.

Even if there was a chance of something happening between Pania and I, I'd only screw it up and hurt her. And that would only complicate my friendship with Delaney. I'm not sure she'd ever forgive me.

But we could be friends.

Apart from Jessie, I've never really had female friends. And

Jessie's near obsession with Josh made it easy to be her friend because she never wanted anything more from me. Except maybe for those handful of times we had sex—the times Josh doesn't know about.

I make my way to Pania, and she seems to take a deep breath as I approach. This wedding must be so weird for her, considering there's not many people she knows. The least I can do is take care of her if Josh and Delaney take off for their honeymoon soon.

Slipping my hands in my pockets, I draw closer to her, and she looks up at me and smiles.

"Hey."

"Hey, yourself." Her smile widens.

"What a night, huh?"

"The whole day's been a bit crazy." She lifts her hand to the back of her neck and stretches. "But it was a perfect wedding. Those two really are meant to be."

I slowly nod and reach for two champagne glasses as a waitress walks past with them. Pania accepts one when I offer it to her and takes a sip, closing her eyes. "Damn, that's good."

"It probably costs a ton of money. It should be good."

She laughs, opening her eyes and meeting my gaze. "I should make the most of it and drink a lot, then."

"You should." I take a sip too. "The best part is whatever's left over at the end of the night, stays here, so we can keep drinking it all week."

Pania grins. "Sounds great to me."

She holds up her glass, and I clink mine against hers. "To new-found friendships."

"To new-found friendships." Her hazel eyes sparkle.

"Pania, come and meet Gabby," Delaney calls out.

Pania looks at me, so I nod toward them. "Go. We have the next week to spend together."

She raises her glass again before walking over to Delaney. I try desperately not to let my eyes fall to her ass, which is typical for me. Is this day one of me trying to be a better man?

I grimace at the thought.

"Are you okay?" Josh asks from beside me.

"I'm fine. And could you not sneak up on me?"

His brows knit. "Seriously. Are you okay? Because that face you just pulled made you look constipated."

I chuckle. "Maybe I am."

Josh slaps me on the back. "Whatever it is, I hope you work it out of your system."

"I'm behaving. There's no chance of that."

His mouth falls open, and he nods slowly as if acknowledging my meaning. "You're doing a good job of it. Delaney tells me you only tried to talk her out of marrying me twice today."

"Guess I'm losing my touch."

I scan the crowd until I find Delaney. She's with Pania and Gabby, and they're all laughing. I smile at the sight. It must be hard to uproot your life and move half a world away, but Delaney's making friends and settling in just fine.

"Thank you for everything today. We really appreciate it."

Swivelling my gaze back to Josh, I hold up my fist for him to bump. He responds by bumping it, a grin on his face.

"You're welcome. I love you guys."

Delaney turns, sending him a dazzling smile that even makes *my* knees weak.

"We're going to sneak off," Josh murmurs.

I give him the thumbs up. "I've got this."

"Mum and Dad are already upstairs with Amelia. She's out cold." He chuckles.

"I'm not surprised. Today was a big day."

He blows out a breath. "Sure was. I'm going to miss her like crazy for the next week."

I punch him lightly on the arm. "Whatever. You have the luscious Delaney to keep you occupied. Speaking of ..."

Delaney and Pania walk toward us. Delaney's smile lights up as she locks gazes with her husband. It's a beautiful sight to see.

"We'll see you two next week. Have fun while we're gone." Delaney pulls me in for a hug and pecks me on the cheek.

"I'll show Pania around."

Her eyes shine with happiness. "Do that. Please. Convince her when she's finished her studies she needs to move here."

"I'll do my best."

Delaney lets me go and moves onto Pania. She throws her arms around Pania's neck and hugs her tight.

"You're cutting off my circulation." Pania laughs.

"Have fun while we're gone. And see you next week in beautiful Hawaii." Delaney lets her go and waves her hands in the air like she's doing a hula. "You're going to love it."

"I can't wait."

"In the meantime, I'll leave you in Reece's capable hands. But Josh's parents will be here, too, so I'm sure you'll be well looked after even if he neglects his duty."

I look between them. "What?"

Delaney and Pania burst out laughing, and Pania pats me on the shoulder. "Don't worry. I'm not expecting you to babysit me."

I pout. "But I'm looking forward to that part."

"You're insufferable," Delaney says, the affection obvious in her voice.

"I know, but you all still love me. Anyway, get going with that husband of yours. He's probably anxious to get laid."

"He's not the only one." Delaney blows me a kiss before turning away. "Mile high club, baby."

Pania covers her eyes with her palm and shakes her head. "Can't take you anywhere."

"Not even to my own wedding." Delaney grasps Josh's outstretched hand. "Bye."

Once they're gone from sight, I turn to Pania. "The crowd's thinned out a little. Want to hang out with me until they're all gone?"

She nods. "Sure."

I lead her to a table, and we sit while people dance.

Gabby slides her arms around my neck from behind and pecks

my cheek. "Antonio and I are going, and we've managed to persuade a few to leave with us. Are Josh and Delaney gone?"

"They've left for the hotel already. And, thanks, we're looking after the place until everyone leaves."

She laughs. "Thought you might be. We'll take the party elsewhere."

"Thanks, Gabby."

"You're welcome." She lets go of me and straightens up. "It was so nice to meet you, Pania. Maybe I can get you to make me a gown someday. Delaney looked gorgeous."

Pania's whole face lights up. "I'd love to."

"I'll be in touch."

She reaches for Antonio's hand, and they lead a group out the front door. Their absence cuts down the numbers quite a lot, and for that I am grateful. I'm wired, but I still really don't want to be up all night.

"Thank God for Gabby. Now to work out how to get rid of everyone else."

Pania places her hand on my arm. "It's not that bad. I think now there are only a few stragglers, it won't take them long."

"Maybe."

"Does it really matter? We have plenty to drink in the meantime."

That's a very, very good point.

It's late by the time everyone leaves, and after the final farewell, I turn to Pania. "Want to grab a bottle of that champagne and head up to the living room?"

She stretches. "That sounds good. I think I'm too wound up to sleep yet."

"What a day, huh?"

The smile that graces her face lights up the whole room. "It was wonderful, and everything Delaney ever deserved."

I look over my shoulder at the room. At least we don't have to clean up; there are cleaners coming in to take care of that in the morning.

Pania's already on her way up the stairs, and I grab a bottle before following her. I can't help but watch the way she moves. Her maroon dress hugs her curves, and there's a split up the side, exposing her left calf. She has amazing legs.

And I'm not supposed to think this way about her.

I drop my gaze and pay attention to my own footsteps. It's the longest trek ever up the stairs and into the living room. Josh's parents have long since gone to bed, and the living room is lit with gentle lamplight.

Pania drops into one of the recliners and puts her feet up, kicking off her shoes. "That's so much better."

"Want a foot rub?"

She cocks an eyebrow at me, then closes her eyes.

"I'll grab some champagne glasses."

"Good boy," she says.

I can't help the smile on my face as I walk into the kitchen. I must be some kind of glutton for punishment, but I really like this woman.

"Somewhere in here ..." I mutter to myself. Opening cupboards, I finally find the one with glasses inside, and to the left are a set of champagne flutes.

Carrying them to the kitchen counter, I pour champagne into the two flutes and return to the living room.

Pania's stretched out with her eyes still closed.

"Are you awake?" I ask.

Her eyes slowly open, and I catch my breath.

"I'm not about to turn down free booze."

I grin and hand her a glass. She takes it, her hand brushing mine. This is ridiculous.

Don't fuck and ditch her.

I tap my glass against hers. "Cheers." *And thanks Josh for thinking so little of me.*

"Cheers," she says.

Loosening my tie, I walk to the couch and sit before taking a long sip of my drink. It goes down easily, and my only regret is that I left the rest of the bottle in the kitchen.

I place my drink on the coffee table then tug off my jacket, pulling my phone out of the pocket before dropping the jacket on the arm of the couch.

Scrolling through my Instagram, I pick up my glass and take another sip of champagne, smiling to myself at the photos already posted to social media. Josh and Delaney discussed asking their guests not to post, but with the stories already out there speculating on their reunion, they decided not to worry about it.

My social media feed is so full of love.

During the afternoon, I'd taken my own photos and sent some to Josh. It's an honour to see he's used one to post his own special message about his wedding today.

The photo is a closeup of Delaney, her eyes shut, Josh kissing her cheek. It's the look of total bliss on her face, the curve of her smile, his nose pressed against her skin.

The caption reads: *Today, I married my best friend and the love of my life. Turns out they're the same person.*

And then I make the mistake of scrolling down.

"Some of these comments." I frown.

"What's going on?" Pania asks.

I look over at her. "I sent Josh a candid photo I took of him and Delaney and he posted it on Instagram. Most people are great, but you know there are always some …"

She rolls her shoulders like she's prepping for a fight. "The ones I want to punch in the face?"

"Uh huh. There's a lot of jealousy out there."

Pania stands and moves over to the couch, dropping onto it. "I've seen all kinds of comments about her. What are they saying?"

I sigh. "The usual. He can do better. She's a gold-digger. So much bullshit."

"It makes me so mad."

I grin. "I'm going to comment."

Her eyes widen. "You are not."

"I've had just enough to drink, and I'm not going to let anyone bash Josh's girl."

I press the icon to comment and type out. *No fair. I want a Delaney too. Can we clone her?*

Pania's gentle perfume breaks through my senses, and I turn my head to see her watching over my shoulder.

Her lips twitch. "I like that."

"I don't know if it'll teach anyone to be better, but it makes me feel good."

Hope you've got a prenup.

I blow out a breath and shake my head.

"Delaney's worked hard her whole life, and people say dumb stuff like she's a gold-digger and they hope Josh has a prenup. If those two ever broke up, Delaney wouldn't take a cent." Pania frowns.

Really? You could do so much better than her.

My blood boils reading these comments. And the way Pania makes little growling noises in her throat behind me, tells me she feels the same way.

I hit reply. *Are you serious? I'm fucking bitter I couldn't steal her from him. She could do so much better than Josh Carter.*

Pania giggles, and I grin.

"Want to join in?" I ask.

She shakes her head. "I don't use Instagram. Never got it. Delaney ran all the social media for the diner."

I turn back to the screen.

Leave him and marry me, Delaney.

Pania roars with laughter. "That'll set Josh off."

"Nah, he'll be fine. It'll annoy the mean girls, though. Losing him is bad enough, but if they think we've both fallen for the charms of the lovely Delaney ..."

"You're wicked."

I drop my phone on the table and lean back on the couch. "Only some of the time."

Our gazes lock, and Pania's smile slowly disappears the longer we look at each other. She bites her top lip, and I let out a long breath as that freckle disappears and then turns back up again.

"I should really get some sleep," she says.

I rub my cheek. "Me too."

"Don't forget to drink some water. You'll feel like shit in the morning if you don't." She stretches her legs out before standing.

"Good thinking. I'll do that." I push myself to my feet. "Goodnight, Pania. Tonight's been fun."

She flicks her hair back behind her ear. "It has been. I'm looking forward to Hawaii."

I nod, slowly. "Me too. It'll be great for us all to spend some time together."

"Goodnight." She raises her hand and gives me a little wave before turning and walking away.

Tonight's been the most fun I've had in a long time. It's been good to relax with a woman that I find attractive but also enjoyed just hanging out with.

Pania shares my sense of humour, and her loyalty to Delaney is unquestionable. I admire that because that's how I've always felt about Josh.

I pick up my phone and throw it in my jacket pocket before making my way to the kitchen. Helping myself to a glass of cold water from the fridge door, I gulp it down before refilling and drinking that too.

It's nice someone cared enough to remind me. I've had way too many events where I've woken up the next morning feeling like crap.

Walking up the hallway, I pause at Pania's door. If she were anyone else, I'd be tapping to be let in followed by charming my way into her bed.

But there's no way I'm pulling my usual shit now.

Instead, I walk a little farther to my room.

Throwing my phone on the mattress, I strip off my clothes and climb into bed, naked.

Sure enough, Delaney's changed the sheets, and they smell of that lightly scented laundry powder she uses. It feels even more like this is home.

Maybe it's time to sort out one of my own.

PANIA.

There's a rat living in my head.

At least that's how my brain feels, as if it's being nibbled on from the inside. And that's *after* I consumed about half a litre of water before bed.

I grab my phone from the bedside table to check the time, and wince: 11:12 a.m.

Delaney and Josh will be winging their way to Hawaii about now. I close my eyes and pretend just for a moment that I'm lying on a beach, the sun bathing me in its warmth, a soft breeze tickling my skin. The weather's nice in LA, but Hawaii will be magical.

But that's next week.

For now, I need to haul my arse out of bed and see how Josh's parents are doing.

The sooner I'm up and about, the sooner I'll feel better. I know there are painkillers in the kitchen somewhere, and once I get some into me, along with a decent meal, it'll make all the difference.

I roll out of bed to get dressed, tugging on a pair of shorts and a tank top before heading toward the bathroom to pee and splash water on my face.

The best part about staying here is the en suite. I don't have to leave the room until I get hungry. But almost on cue, my stomach grumbles.

Once I'm done, I head out of the bedroom and straight toward the kitchen. A faint smell of toast floats in the air, and again my stomach reminds me it wants food.

I pat it. "Patience, padawan. You'll be fed soon enough."

"Pania." Cal, Josh's dad, smiles as I walk into the kitchen. "I was just about to leave you and Reece a note."

I scratch the back of my head and yawn before clamping my hand across my mouth.

He laughs. "Don't worry. Ros and I figured you two would be sleeping most of the day. Good night?"

I nod. "It was fantastic. Lots of wine."

"I was impressed this morning at how quickly this place was cleaned up." He pauses. "We're heading out with Amelia to the zoo now. Did you want to come with us?"

I shake my head. "Thank you, but I'm not feeling that great after last night. I think I'm going to grab something to eat and head back to bed for a while."

He chuckles. "That's fair. You have a good day."

"You too. I'll cook dinner tonight."

Cal nods and turns toward the door. In the doorway, Melly waves at me. "We're going to the zoo."

"I know, sweet pea. Have fun."

She blows me a kiss before heading out with her grandfather. Now left in silence, I close my eyes and let out a long breath.

"Is that hurricane Amelia gone for the day?" Reece's voice comes seemingly out of nowhere, and I open my eyes to him standing right in front of me. It's the most casual he's been dressed—jeans and a tight T-shirt—and I swallow hard at the sight of his rippling muscles through the material.

"They just headed out. Want some breakfast?"

His lips twitch. "I won't say no."

"Good. I'll probably cook way too much for me anyway. I need a lot to conquer this hangover."

He bows his head slightly. "Did you follow your own advice and drink some water before bed?"

I laugh, giving his shoulder a push. "I sure did. Probably would have felt a lot worse if I hadn't. My brain feels as if something's gnawing at it."

"Mine too. I'm sure there's a carpenter working in my head, hammering in nails."

"Let's get something to eat and take some pills to end our suffering." I walk around the kitchen bench and look back at him, his smile disappearing from his face, his feet shuffling. "Are you okay?"

Reece looks up. "I'm fine. Want me to make coffee?"

I shake my head. "Just take a seat. I'll do it."

He all but collapses on a stool on the other side of the bench. "I'm so glad you said that."

"Drama queen." I bite down a smile. "Eggs and bacon?"

His mouth hanging open, Reece seems to be drooling. He makes a sound I can only describe as one of those noises a zombie makes in the movies.

"Are you okay?" I ask again, tilting my head.

"Hungry." He growls.

"You're such a clown. Fried eggs or scrambled?"

"However you want them."

I head to the fridge and grab everything I need before placing it on the bench. By the sink, there's a fresh loaf of bread, and I pick it up to take a deep breath. There's nothing better.

"Fried eggs on toast with bacon. The grease will suck up all the alcohol."

He chuckles. "I'm pretty sure that's not true."

"Of course it is. Want a coffee first?"

"I'm not sure there's enough coffee in the world to get me through today."

Retrieving a pan from a hook on the wall, I then place it on the cooktop and turn it on. A big, shiny coffee machine sits on the other side of the kitchen on a bench. Delaney's made the coffee since I've been here, and I think she's in a love affair with the machine. I shake my head; she's got everything set out just like she did in the diner.

"You look like you know what you're doing," he says.

I roll the hair tie that usually resides on my wrist off and scoop my hair into a ponytail. "I was a barista in a former life. I'm so impressed at Delaney's coffee machine."

"Josh used to have a much smaller one, but you know what he's like."

"I know what Delaney's like with shiny appliances. How do you take your coffee?"

"Any way you want to make it."

I laugh and then get to work, heating the pan and adding the eggs to it, and then the bacon. In between checking it's not burning, I make the coffee and pass Reece a cup before popping some slices of bread in the toaster.

"You make it all look so effortless," he says. "I would have burned something by now."

"Try making breakfast with a diner full of customers. This is easy."

He takes a sip of coffee. "Damn, this is so good."

"Here we go." I slide a plate of food in front of him, and then pick up my plate and coffee, walking around the bench and dropping onto a stool next to him.

"This smells amazing. My stomach is churning, but I know it'll be better once I eat this."

"Oh, I nearly forgot. Do you want any painkillers? I saw some in a drawer somewhere."

He shakes his head. "No, I'm just going to eat this, drink my coffee, probably have some more water, and then head back to bed."

Pushing myself off the stool, I walk back around the bench and start opening drawers, punching the air when I find a packet of Tylenol.

I read the back of the packet and hold it up. "Is this okay for a hangover?"

Reece looks up and nods before returning to his food.

Grabbing a couple of tablets, I go back to my seat, swallow them with my coffee, and get stuck into my food.

Reece's knife scrapes his plate, and at a glance, it's already nearly empty.

"Do you want some more?" I ask. "There are plenty of eggs and a ton of bacon in the fridge."

Reece turns to look at me, and for the first time, I see his eyes are still a little bloodshot. I think he's right that he needs more sleep. I probably do too.

"No, thanks for the offer. This is really good."

"Do you cook for yourself? Josh sucks at cooking."

He chuckles. "I rate myself as slightly better. I can cook a steak, but not much more."

I shrug. "That's easily better than Josh."

Reece scrapes up the last of his food and swallows it down before draining his coffee. "Thank you so much for that. It was great."

He gets up and walks around the bench, rinsing off his plate and cup in the sink. "I don't mean to be rude, but I'm not sure I'll be good company today."

Pushing myself back from the bench, I slip off the stool to stand. "I could do with a nap myself after that. How about we go and do something tomorrow?"

He makes his way back around past me toward the door. "That sounds like a great idea. I'll take you on a tour."

I smile. "I'd love that. I'm not sure what time Josh's parents will be back with Melly, so I'll cook dinner tonight, too, if you want to make it to the dining room."

Reece's eyes light up. "After that breakfast? You bet."

"See you later, then."

My heart flutters like he's my teenage crush.

Reece turns back toward the door. "Wouldn't miss it for the world."

I OPEN my eyes as my bedroom door creaks, just in time to see a little face peering around it.

"Pania?"

My head's still heavy, but it's better than it was earlier.

"Hey, sweet girl. Come and tell me all about the zoo."

Melly flies across the room and leaps onto the bed.

"Ooof." I grunt as her knee smacks my leg, then wrinkle my nose when a large piece of fluff tickles it.

"Look what Grandpa bought me."

The sound of knuckles rapping wood snaps my attention to the door.

"Yes?" I say to whoever is knocking.

"Pania?" Ros pokes her head inside the room. " I hope Amelia didn't disturb you."

"No, she's fine. It's time I got out of bed anyway. What's the time?"

"A little after five. I was about to start cooking dinner."

I sit up. "Don't. Go and put your feet up. I'll do it."

"Are you sure?" She smiles, and it makes me miss my mum more than anything.

"Absolutely. You've been on your feet all day, I'm sure. I've just been lazing in bed." I grab Melly for a hug. "I'll be out in a minute. Melly's just showing me what she got today."

"She's had a lovely time. But I'm sure she'll sleep soundly tonight," Ros says.

"I bet."

She closes the door, and I turn to look at the toy Melly's waving around.

It's a ring-tailed lemur with a long fluffy tail.

"Grandpa found King Julian." A small v forms between her eyes, her tone so solemn, and it's hard not to laugh.

"He did. Should we watch Madagascar before I go home? We can sing the song."

Her eyes light up. "Could we?"

"I'm sure it's streaming on something. It's a date, Miss Melly."

She flings herself at me, wrapping her arms around my neck. "I love you."

I plant a big kiss in her hair. "I love you too. Do you want to help me cook dinner?"

Melly nods.

"Should we put *you* in the oven for dinner?"

She blinks rapidly. "No. Don't be silly, Pania."

"Okay. Maybe not today." I hug her tight. "Let's go and see what's in the kitchen to cook."

She skips ahead of me all the way to the large freezer in the kitchen.

I swing open the stainless steel doors and scan the shelves. It's packed with all kinds of things, but organised into sections which I'm grateful for.

"What do you feel like eating?"

Melly squeezes in front of me to take look. "I like it when you make meatballs."

I ruffle her hair. "That's easy. If I can find some mince, let's do that. I'm sure there'll be some spaghetti in the cupboard."

Her hand darts in and pulls out a pack. "Mummy makes them for me sometimes."

I close the doors and take the meat from her. "Good girl. I'll pop this in some water to defrost and we'll go watch a cartoon for a while."

Running some lukewarm water in the sink, I place the meat pack in it and find some dried spaghetti in the pantry before taking Melly's hand. She leads me into the living room where Cal and Ros are.

"Everything under control?" Ros asks.

"It sure is. I told Melly we could watch a cartoon while the meat defrosts. It won't take long. And then she's going to help me make dinner."

Ros beams. "Just like your mom, Amelia."

Melly clasps her hands together and twirls. No wonder her mother thinks she'll follow in her father's footsteps.

I pick up the TV remote and switch it on. Almost predictably, *Nickelodeon* comes up on the screen.

"SpongeBob!" Melly yells.

Cal chuckles. "Your father used to love SpongeBob when he was your age, Amelia."

Her head nearly spins off her shoulders. "Really?"

He nods. "He sure did."

I flop onto the couch, and Melly jumps up beside me. I hold out my arm and she snuggles into my side.

"Will you help me roll the meatballs once the mince is defrosted?" I ask.

She looks up at me. "I like that job."

"It's all yours."

Two SpongeBob SquarePants episodes later, I head back into the kitchen with my assistant chef.

The mince is defrosted enough, and I turn to Melly. "We need to give our hands a good wash."

Melly smiles up at me. "Mummy lets me help sometimes. I always have to scrub my hands."

"So you already know how to do it. Good girl."

I leave her by the sink while I retrieve a dining room chair for her to stand on.

"Get up there." I pat the seat.

She clambers up onto the chair, and I turn on the tap then squirt some liquid soap on her hands. I'm not really sure who does the better job as she takes extra care to clean under her finger nails. She's been taught well.

I scrape the chair along the floor with her still on top of it, careful to hold her steady. I know I probably shouldn't have, but she shrieks with laughter and holds onto my shoulders as I move her.

"Here we go." I dump the mince into the bowl.

It only takes a few minutes to find some other ingredients to throw in, and because I know she likes it, I top it all off by grating some cheese into the mix.

"Go on then. Mix it up."

She leans against me as she digs her hands into the mixing bowl. "I like doing this."

"Maybe you'll be a cook like your mum one day."

She shakes her head. "Mummy says I'll be an actor like Daddy."

I bite my inner cheek to stop from laughing. "Either way, you'll be wonderful at what you do."

After it's mixed, I put a large plate next to her. "Now you have to roll them, like this." I take out a chunk of the mix and roll it into a ball. "Can you do that for me while I cook the spaghetti and make the sauce?"

She gets busy, and I find a saucepan and prepare some water to boil.

"Finished," she calls out.

I turn around.

The meatballs are a range of sizes from small to large, but Melly's so pleased with herself that I don't have the heart to make any changes to them.

"Thank you so much for your help. Would you like to help me make the sauce while these cook?"

Melly sighs. "I think I've done enough work today."

"Fair enough. Why don't you go and wash your hands?"

She jumps down off the chair.

"This looks interesting," Reece says as he enters the kitchen.

"Pania and me are cooking misketti and meatballs," Melly announces.

"Is that right?"

I meet his amused gaze. "That's right. I just have to cook the meatballs and make the sauce, but the misketti's cooked."

"I've never had that before. I've eaten spaghetti, but I assume this is an Amelia meal."

I look at Melly. "That's right. She helped roll the meatballs, didn't you, sweet pea?"

Melly beams and holds out her dirty hands. "Now I have to wash it all off."

She runs off, leaving me with Reece.

"You look rested," I say.

"I just took the longest shower. Don't be surprised if there's no hot water left." He shrugs.

"Dinner will be ready soon if you're hungry."

He steps around the bench and looks over my shoulder, and all I can smell is sandalwood and soap. *Damn he smells good.*

"Need any help?" he asks.

"No. Melly made the meatballs, and now I just have to cook them and make the sauce. Won't take long." I turn my head. "Why don't you go and watch cartoons in the living room?"

He laughs but says nothing else as he turns and walks away.

For a moment, I'm lost, standing in the kitchen because what I was about to do has completely slipped my mind.

I close my eyes and take a deep breath. Reece's scent lingers, which doesn't help my addled brain.

Bubbling water snaps me back.

"The spaghetti." I fist my hands and punch the air, congratulating myself for remembering.

If only Reece wasn't so distracting.

"THAT WAS GREAT, PANIA." Cal leans back in his chair and pats his stomach. "You could give Delaney a run for her money with that meal."

I grin. "Well, we did do our cooking training together. I'm only sorry you didn't get to eat at our diner. You would have loved it."

"I wish I'd been able to," Reece says. "Sounds like the two of you had a great little business going."

"We did until Josh turned up." I let out a dramatic sigh. "But I wouldn't change things for the world. Delaney and I are both doing what we love now."

"Delaney said you're learning fashion design?" Ros asks.

I nod. "It's always been a hobby, but I took a chance on it when Delaney decided to sell the diner."

"I hope it works out for you. That wedding dress was something really special." Her smile's so kind, and again it makes me think of Mum. "We'll sort out the dishes, Pania. You sit back and relax." Ros stands and walks around the table, patting me on the shoulder as she passes.

I look over at Melly. The poor kid's so tired, her eyes are closing on her before she sits up with a jolt.

"Hey, sweet pea. How about I help you get ready for bed?"

She gives me a tired smile. "Okay. Can you read Hairy Maclary?"

"Sure thing. You still reading that old book?"

Melly laughs. "Daddy reads it to me. It's my favourite."

"I think I still know it off by heart."

I turn to look at Cal and Ros. "I'll pop Melly to bed."

Ros smiles. "Sounds like she wants you to."

I shift my gaze back to Melly. "Come on, you."

After she's in her pyjamas and her teeth are brushed, I tuck her under her bed covers and start telling the story.

It's been months since I've done this, but I remember every word as Hairy Maclary goes for a walk with his other dog friends until ...

"They saw ..." I draw in a breath.

Melly holds her hands up like claws and deepens her voice. "Scarface Claw ..."

"The toughest Tom in town," we say together.

She collapses in giggles.

"Before I finish this story, Miss Melly, I think we need to snuggle you down to sleep. You don't usually last all the way to Scarface Claw."

"I like you reading to me."

She nestles down under the covers, and I pull the duvet up to her chin and bend to kiss her nose. "I like reading to you."

Melly purses her lips. "Daddy has to read the book. He doesn't remember the story like you."

I laugh. "Give him time. I've read that story so many times, I think it's burned into my brain forever."

"I miss Mummy and Daddy."

I reach over and stroke her cheek. "You'll see them soon. They'll be missing you too."

"Can you read Hairy Maclary every night?"

I nod. "Of course I can, *taku iti kahurangi*."

"What does that mean?" Melly asks.

"It means my little treasure. That's what you are to me." I tilt my head.

She lets out a big yawn. "I'm tired."

"Then close your eyes and go to sleep. I'll stay right here if you want me to."

I sit with her for a while. It's not often that she does last the whole story, but I guess it's the novelty of having someone else here to tell it. That, and she's missing her parents. I'm glad she has the comfort of her own bed and surroundings at least, and that I'm here to keep her company.

A couple of times, she stirs, her eyes opening a little, as if she's checking I'm still here, but she eventually drifts off to sleep. Thankfully, for Delaney, once Melly got past the sleepless nights, she loved sleeping. It's definitely made this easier.

I drop a kiss to her cheek before tiptoeing toward the door, turning my head just in time to realise Reece is standing in the doorway.

"That is one amazing kid," Reece says as I walk out into the hall.

I look back at Melly. My heart will break when I go home and leave her and her mother. Melly's been a part of my life since before she was born. I was the one who held Delaney up when she cried over Josh, and then her mother as she was thrown out of the house. I was Delaney's person when she gave birth, and the first person other than Delaney to hold that little girl in my arms.

"She's fantastic. I love the shit out of her."

Reece says nothing, so I look at him. His gaze is still fixed on that little girl in the bed. He sucks in a breath and turns to me.

"I always wanted kids." His eyes search mine. "What about you?"

"One day." I drop my gaze. "I thought I'd probably live the rest of my life working in our little diner, and settling down with a sheep farmer or something. But now ..." I pick at my finger nails. "I want to finish my course, start my own business, and live a little before I have kids."

Reece nods toward Melly. "She changed my life. I know I haven't known Delaney and Amelia for long, but that little girl in there is such a big part of Josh, and he's the brother I never had. I've been rethinking my future since I met those two."

He says it with such awe in his tone that I feel fortunate to be a part of this moment. Melly's birth had a big impact on my life—more than I've ever admitted to anyone. She's family.

"How about I make us a coffee and maybe we can talk some more?" I swallow hard. It's only been a few days, and while I have this almost constant reminder in the back of my head that Reece used to just be some movie star on the big screen to me, I like the idea that we could be friends.

Reece turns and smiles. "I'd like that."

Delaney's told me there's more to him, but he keeps it to himself. I don't know Reece well enough to judge that for myself, but these past few moments have told me there's something more.

Media coverage isn't any indication of what people are like. They're not always kind to Delaney, and yet I know she's the warmest, most caring person I know. Even if she is a little cynical at times.

"Come on, then."

By the time we get back to the kitchen, the table's clear and the dishwasher's running. There's no sign of Ros and Cal, but they're probably tired after the past couple of days.

The smell of coffee fills the kitchen as I grind it, and I take a deep breath.

And just like this morning, I make two cups and give one to Reece before we sit at the dining table, across from one another.

I pull out my ponytail with one hand and shake my hair loose.

His piercing blue gaze makes my cheeks burn.

"This coffee's really good." He holds up his mug.

"I know."

"I should get you to make my coffee all of the time." He shoots one of those winks at me, and I bury my nose in my cup.

"You couldn't afford me." I place my empty cup back on the table. I'm not about to let him get the better of me, no matter how cute he is.

"Probably not." He puts his drink down and rises from his seat, rounding the table until he's next to me. "So, what are we going to do for the next week until we join them?" he asks as he sits back down.

I shrug. "No idea."

"Want to hang out?"

I open my mouth to speak, but then pause as I take in the sly smile on his face. His reputation precedes him, and I should get up and walk away, but there's something behind that smile, and I want to know what it is.

"Is 'hang out' a euphemism for having sex?"

His eyes widen. "Well ... I ...."

My own smile must be pretty smug. "Have I rendered Reece Evans speechless? The one thing I know for sure you have in common with Delaney is the ability to talk a lot."

He just stares at me. His lips twitch, and it takes a moment, but soon enough his laughter fills the room, and he cocks his head. "You really are something, Pania Wilson."

I raise an eyebrow.

He leans forward a little. "Josh told me you scared him. I can see why."

"Josh is a pussy."

Reece chuckles. "I'm going to enjoy this week. I can tell."

"Maybe you will. If you like getting your arse handed to you by a woman."

"Oh you can handle my ass any time."

I study him for a moment. I'm usually pretty good at reading people, at least I think so, but Reece is hard to get a handle on. This Reece is a lot of fun, but what lies underneath?

Ugh. I'm sure I'm not the only woman to think this. Leopards don't change their spots.

"Well, nice as this conversation is, I'm going to bed to get some sleep. It's been a long day." I spring to my feet.

Reece grabs hold of one of my hands. "You've never been to LA before, have you?"

I shake my head. "First time."

His hand is warm and soft, and he runs his thumb over my knuckles. "I'll show you all my favourite places."

"I'd like that."

My heart races as he raises my hand to his lips and kisses it. It's corny but cute, and I draw in a deep breath.

"See you in the morning," he says.

I lift my chin in response. "See you in the morning."

And for the second time today he leaves the room while my heart pounds.

I'm not quite sure how to describe our budding relationship. I think we're definitely friends.

Is there any possibility for something more?

8

REECE

Before meeting Pania, I wasn't looking forward to playing babysitter for Delaney's friend. Now, all I can think about is how little time we have together.

She wanted a tour; I'm giving her a tour today.

Her eyes shine when she lays eyes on my car. I know the feeling, it's how I feel whenever I look at it too.

"This is yours?" she asks.

"I just bought it. Josh is the only passenger I've had. You're in exclusive territory here."

She claps, and it makes me think of Amelia.

I open the passenger door and she steps in. Rounding the car, I slip into the driver's side. Pania runs her fingers through her long hair, scoops it into a ponytail, and twists it into a knot, securing it to the top of her head with a hair tie.

"Is there anything you want to see in particular?" I ask.

"I want to see some movie stars." Her eyes take on a dreamy look.

"Ahem."

She screws up her nose. "Not you. You don't count."

"Thanks." I laugh.

"You know what I mean."

"Didn't you meet a ton of them at Josh and Delaney's wedding?"

"I did, but there are plenty more."

"You're crazy."

She shrugs. "Maybe, but I feel as if I need to make the most of being here before I go home."

Home.

The thought of her leaving stabs me right in the chest. Even if this doesn't take a romantic turn, I like her being around. Since Josh and I went into business together, and Delaney and Amelia moved here, I've never felt so settled.

Sure, I spend a lot of time at their place, but I'm beginning to think it's a sign that I need to do something about my life.

"I thought today we could just go for a big drive, and maybe somewhere quiet for lunch."

Her smile warms my heart. "I'd like that."

"I just think it'd be better if we didn't go out too publicly. The last thing we need is the media to get the wrong idea about—"

"Are you embarrassed to be seen with me?" Her brows furrow.

"No. Of course not. It's just ... I'm sure you know what Delaney has dealt with, and I don't want that to happen to you, especially when we're not actually dating."

She straightens herself up to her full height and looks me straight in the eye. "I can handle it."

"I'm sure you can, sweetheart, but I don't want you to have to."

"They say some pretty mean things about you. How do you cope?"

I lean back in my seat. "I know what's true and what isn't."

She's silent for a moment, dropping her gaze. "I don't read magazines anymore. Not since Delaney got together with Josh. Or those trashy gossip websites. It's so unfair."

"It is what it is. It only gets worse if you try and stop it."

"Delaney says she tries to ignore it." Her eyes are back on mine again, those hazel orbs penetrating my brain. Her lips twitch, and the small freckle above her mouth moves. The overwhelming urge to kiss it makes my chest ache.

I'll only hurt her.

"She's a strong woman. I admire that in her." I cock my head. "I think that's one thing you two have in common."

Pania crosses her arms. "Well, then maybe you should trust me when I say I don't care what anyone says if they see us together."

"Did you ever think that maybe I do because I don't exactly have a stellar reputation when it comes to women?"

She unfolds her arms and places a hand on my bicep. "No, I didn't think about that. It's nice that you want to protect me. I'm sorry."

"I'm not as bad as people make me out to be either."

Pania leans in until her face is inches from mine. "Are you pouting?"

"No."

"You *so* are."

"Can we go now?"

She leans back, tugs on the seat belt and clips it into place. "I don't know. You're the one who's driving."

I laugh and then let out a big sigh. "Is this our first fight?"

"If that was fighting, it's not just Josh who's the pussy."

I slide on my seat belt and start the car.

This could be a long but enjoyable day.

～

"Where are we going?" she asks about two minutes into the trip.

"Do you know where you are now?" I ask.

"Sherman Oaks." She covers her face with her hands. "That's all I know."

I nudge her arm. "That's okay. We're going toward Burbank because I know you'll want to see the Hollywood sign. Got your camera?"

"I've got my phone."

"That'll do. It also means we'll go past Universal Studios, and a few other landmarks. If you see anywhere you want to visit, we can always go later in the week."

She lowers her hands. "Thank you for this."

"You're welcome. I'm not hating spending time with you as much as I thought I would."

Pania snorts then covers her nose. "I'm glad. You're not as annoying as you were when we first met."

I slap the steering well. "That's good to hear."

"Maybe Delaney's right and there's more to you after all."

"She said that?" I glance at Pania, and there's no smile to indicate she's making fun of me.

"Yes, she did. And I trust her, usually, but I wasn't sure about you."

I point to my chest with my index finger. "Me?"

"Yes you. She's usually pretty cautious with people, but she took to you. I can see why."

My heart warms at her words. In all fairness, I don't know much about Delaney's past beyond that she and Josh dated several years ago before a misunderstanding broke them up. He was obsessed for a while at finding her, but over time it seemed to ease until he went to work on a movie in New Zealand and found her.

We became instant friends, but there's a lot I don't know about her. She knows nothing of me—there are things in my past that Josh doesn't even know about.

But her faith in me is rewarded by Pania adopting the same sentiment.

"Thank you. That means a lot."

Her satisfied smile makes me smile, and she raises her chin, pointing toward something at the side of the road. "There are so many shops here. Delaney must love it."

I deliberately drove along Ventura Boulevard so she could see something other than the concrete of the freeway. We have plenty of time.

"I'm not sure she goes out much still other than taking Amelia to school and back. It's all a bit intimidating."

Pania looks ahead. "I can see why. And you're driving on the wrong side of the road."

I look at the road, then the steering wheel, then back at the road.

She snickers. "Did you just double check what side you were driving on?"

"Maybe."

"I'll behave now. Promise. Don't need you having an accident."

I huff out a breath. "You'd better behave. I'll tell on you to Cal and Ros if you don't."

A gentle breeze fills the car as Pania puts down her window a little. "I'm always good."

"I'm not commenting."

She laughs, reaching for the hand hold above the door. I make a few turns until we're on the freeway. It's clear she has no idea where we are as she looks around, but I make my way to the end of Ledge-wood Drive.

"This is my favourite spot to look at it. It's maybe a three minute walk from here."

Pania grimaces. "I'm not hiking. Don't you have some movie star pass to just drive up there?"

I laugh. "Not that I know of. It's not far. Let's go."

Pulling over to the side of the road, I open my door and step out of the car. She joins me at the front of the car, and I lock it before we walk up the road.

She grumbles the whole time. "I thought we were just going for a drive."

"Do you want to get photos?"

Her lips curl. "My mum would love it."

"Do it for her, then."

She comes to a halt and gasps. "It really was a three minute walk."

"Told you."

It's the weirdest thing. I guess when I moved to LA it was a novelty to see things like the Hollywood sign, but it's just a part of my daily life now. Seeing Pania smiling and taking photos makes me look at it again through fresh eyes.

Maybe that's symbolic of the choices I make in my life going forward.

It's not always easy to leave the past behind, but it might be time to do just that.

It's a little after four when I approach Josh's house and slowly pull into the driveway, maybe too slowly, because I've enjoyed the day so much. I'm not sure I want it to end.

"Thank you for today." Pania looks at me from under the longest eyelashes I've ever seen. How did I not notice those before?

"You're welcome. I enjoyed it. Next time, we might even get out of the car a bit more."

Pania laughs. "To be honest, I'm still tired from the wedding. Staying inside the car for most of it was fine with me."

I suck in my bottom lip as I draw the car to a halt and switch off the ignition. "Josh has this pizza place he recommended. I thought we might try it for dinner. He feels comfortable enough to take Delaney and Amelia there, so it should be okay."

"Sounds great. I'm pretty hungry considering how long I haven't moved today."

I laugh. "We moved. Just not on our feet."

"Good point." She takes a deep breath. "We should probably head in and let Ros know before she starts cooking dinner."

Opening my door, I stretch my leg out. "I might have a shower and get changed too."

"Why? You don't smell bad." Her eyes meet mine, and her cheeks flush. "How do I smell?"

Pania's tilt of her head makes me lose focus. "You smell pretty good to me. That's impressive given we've been trapped in a car together for hours."

She opens her door and steps out, and I'm not quite sure how today went. We talked a lot, laughed, and I smile at the thought of how enthused she was in a city that drains me sometimes.

"Are you coming with me?" she asks.

Hell yeah.

"On my way."

I follow Pania inside and up the stairs.

The sound of cartoons comes from the living room, and I laugh softly to myself. Amelia has her grandparents twisted around her little finger, just as she does everyone else.

"Hello, you two," Cal says. "Did you have a good day?"

"It was amazing." Pania drops onto the couch beside Amelia. "It doesn't feel like we did much, but it was a long day."

"Did you want dinner, you two?" Ros asks.

I shoot a glance at Pania. "Actually, we were going to try a pizza place Josh recommended."

She smiles. "He's mentioned it. I understand Amelia's a big fan. Maybe you could take her."

"Can we get pizza?" Amelia climbs onto Pania's lap.

"Melly, did you want to go to—" Pania turns toward me "—What's the name of the pizza place?"

"Lorenzo's." Amelia claps, and I chuckle. It figures she knows all about it.

"Yes, Miss Melly. Lorenzo's."

Amelia's forms an O with her mouth. "I know Maria from there. We have playdates."

Pania looks at me with one eyebrow raised, and I hold up my hands, palms up.

"I'll grab her spare car seat," Cal says.

Pania turns to me. "Did you ever think your car would have a child's seat in the back?"

I shove my hands in my pockets. "There's a first time for everything."

Cal chuckles. "Come on, Reece. I'll help you install it."

He ends up doing all the work because I have no idea, and then Pania and Amelia wait while I have a quick shower.

When I walk back into the living room, Pania stands and walks toward me. Her back's to everyone else, so no one sees her as she takes a subtle sniff at my chest.

"Oooh, that is better."

Playfully ignoring her, I look over at Amelia. "Wanna go get some pizza?"

She leaps off the couch. "Yes."

"Come on, sweet pea," Pania says, holding out her hand. She looks up at Ros. "We won't be too late."

"See you soon." Ros blows a kiss to Amelia who pretends to catch it before grabbing Pania's hand.

I lead them to the car, and Pania helps Amelia into her seat. She buckles her in before climbing into the passenger seat beside me, and I sigh with relief because it all looks like a tangle of belt and buckle to me.

"Let's get going.." I look up directions for Lorenzo's, press the GPS to start, and turn on the ignition. "Ready to go fast, Amelia?" I ask.

Amelia claps, and I grin.

"Don't you dare." Pania elbows me.

"I know. I was just kidding."

She waves her arms in the air. "How Delaney puts up with you, I'll never know.

"True love. That's what it is."

Pania snorts. "You keep telling yourself that."

Amelia sings all the way to Lorenzo's, and when we pull into the parking lot, she strains to lean forward. "I hope Maria's there."

"Is that your friend?" I ask.

"Lorenzo is her Poppa."

I exchange a glance with Pania and we both nod, slowly. That makes sense.

We barely step in the door when Amelia's recognised.

"Amelia." A young man with a name badge approaches us. He holds out his fist and Amelia fistbumps him. I clamp my lips together in amusement, and notice Pania doing the same. He smiles at us. "Would you like Josh and Delaney's usual table?"

"They have a usual table?" Pania asks. She leans forward a little, looking at his badge. "That sounds great, Jason."

Amelia grabs her hand. "It's this way."

She leads us to a quiet corner of the restaurant and slides into a booth. I slip in beside her and look around.

There are burgundy leather booths around the outside of the room and circular tables in the middle with table cloths that match the colour of the booths. Soft lighting makes the room look cosy and welcoming.

"Josh said Delaney loves the garlic rolls." I look over the menu at Pania.

"Is that right, Melly?" Pania asks.

Amelia nods. "Daddy eats *all* the pizza and Mummy likes the bread."

"And what do you like?" I smile at her.

"I like all of it." Her eyes are so wide, and she holds out her arms like she's describing the one that got away.

I chuckle. "What type of pizza should I get?"

"Pepperoni." She nods, her ponytail flying.

"Amelia." A deep voice behind us brings a beaming smile to Amelia's face. "It's so good to see you."

I look up to see a white-bearded, older man beside me. "I'm Lorenzo. Welcome."

"Reece Evans." I hold out my hand and he shakes it. "Josh and Delaney are on their honeymoon, so Pania and I are helping take care of the munchkin."

He cocks his head. "Ah yes. I read about the wedding. Such a beautiful couple. Please give them my best wishes."

I nod. "I will."

"Is Maria here?" Amelia cranes her neck and scans the room, but Lorenzo shakes his head.

"Not tonight, my sweet, I'm sorry to say. Maybe next time."

Amelia juts out her bottom lip.

"How about we order this pizza and I'll talk to your mum about another playdate," Pania says.

"Maria loves the playdates with Amelia. I'm sure she would love more." Lorenzo looks between us. "What would you like to order?"

"Pepperoni pizza sounds good according to Amelia, and she said Delaney likes the bread?" I look to him for a hint.

His wide smile tells me he knows exactly what I'm talking about. "The garlic rolls. I'll bring some of those too. Anything else?"

"I'd love an orange juice." I look toward Pania and Amelia. "What do you two want to drink?"

"The same as you," Amelia says.

Pania smiles at Lorenzo. "Three orange juices, please."

"I'll get them brought to your table. Your food won't be too long." With another smile, he turns and walks toward the back of the restaurant.

"You can be the daddy." Amelia hands me a napkin, and then passes one to Pania. "And you can be the mummy."

Pania clamps her lips together and meets my gaze.

"Does that mean I get to eat most of the pizza? Like your dad?" I ask.

Amelia frowns. "No. You can get your own pizza."

Pania laughs. "You've been told."

"I ordered one pizza. I guess we'll have to share." I meet Pania's gaze. "Unless Amelia eats all the pizza and we'll just have to go without."

The giggle that comes from Amelia melts my heart. "I can't eat a whole pizza. Mummy says the slices are as big as my head."

Our drinks are delivered to the table, and then it's not much longer before Lorenzo arrives with a huge pizza and a plate piled with bread rolls.

"This looks amazing." I meet his gaze.

"Enjoy."

"The slices really are as big as your head, Melly." Pania laughs. She lifts a slice of pizza up and places it on Amelia's plate. "Careful, that's hot."

Amelia blows all over her pizza, and I exchange an amused glance with Pania.

Pania picks up a bread roll. They're cute, the dough tied into a knot, and she takes in a deep breath before biting into it.

Her moan catches me by surprise, making my cock jump to attention, and I can't stop watching her as she closes her eyes and chews.

After a moment, she slowly opens her eyes and her gaze hits mine. Her lips curl into a smile. "You should try one. They're so good. All doughy in the centre."

"Reece. You need to eat the pizza. Daddy likes the pizza." Amelia pokes my arm with her index finger.

"Okay. You're so bossy." I reach for a slice.

She giggles, and then takes a big bite of her own piece. "Yummy."

"Let me try this."

I take a bite, and the spicy pepperoni and cheese hit my taste-buds, and I let out a moan before I know it.

Pania's eyebrows rise and a bemused expression hits her hazel eyes.

"Damn, that's good. No wonder Delaney and Josh love this place."

"You have to try these rolls. They're amazing."

She holds one up to my face and my lower lip grazes her thumb as I take a bite. Pania blinks a bunch of times and drops the rest of the roll onto my plate.

I swallow the food, but can't stop watching her drop her head and turn back to the food.

"Finished." Amelia pronounces. Pania picks up her napkin and wipes the sauce from around Amelia's mouth. "Can I have some bread?"

"Of course you can." Pania places a roll on her plate, and Amelia picks it up, taking a big bite.

Over the next half hour, we finish off the pizza—or rather I do because Pania is enamoured with the garlic rolls and Amelia admits defeat after her head-sized slice and a single roll.

Leaning back in my seat, I pat my stomach. "I'm going to have to do double time at the gym after all this good food this week."

Pania drains the rest of her drink and puts the glass down. "Aren't you starting your new movie soon?"

"Not long after we get back from Hawaii."

"I can't wait to see it."

I knit my fingers together. "It's exciting. I never thought Josh and I would be making our own movies, but here we are."

Amelia yawns, and Pania reaches across the table for her hand. "Are you tired, sweet pea?"

She nods.

"Let's get you out of here."

"I'll go and pay the bill."

Pania gets up and rounds the table, taking Amelia's hand in hers. "Want to go home?"

Amelia wriggles off the chair and leans against Pania. "Will you read me Hairy Maclary when we get there?"

"Of course I will."

For a moment, I just watch as Amelia wraps her arms around Pania's waist and snuggles in against her.

We make our way to the entrance where I pay the bill, and then move out into the warm night.

"Did you have fun, Amelia?" I ask.

"I'm full of pizza."

Pania and I laugh; it's the best answer there is.

Once she's buckled into her seat, I drive my way back to Josh's place, contentment settling over me. My plan had been to take Pania out, but I'm not upset with the way things transpired.

We pull up to the house, and Pania turns to look at the back seat.

"Melly's asleep."

I chuckle. "I'm not surprised. I'll carry her inside."

Pania's eyes smile. "Are you still being the daddy?"

I look back at Amelia. Her head's flopped against her seat, and her mouth's wide open as she sleeps.

"Just until we get inside. Josh is such a lucky man. He gets to do this all the time."

"She's always made me feel clucky too."

I shift my gaze back to Pania. "Always?"

"From the moment she was born. I held that little baby in my arms and fell in love. That feeling's never gone away."

"It's all new to me."

Her entire face lights up. "It's not like anything else. Must be a whole other level when it's your own child."

I gulp. For a long time, I'd pushed settling down and having children to the back of my head. It's not like there's any rush when I'm still in my mid-twenties, but Amelia has made me second guess myself.

Pania places her hand on my arm. "I'll unbuckle her belt."

Cool night air floods the car as she opens her door, and I take a deep breath.

The longer I spend with this family, the more I see what I'm missing out on.

9

———————

PANIA

Flying from New Zealand to the US is draining, but it's nothing compared to flying from LA to Honolulu with a five-year-old as company.

"Are we there yet?"

I look over at Melly, lying in her comfy bed, just as I am, on this flight that never seems to end.

"Are you serious?" I screw my nose up at her.

"I want to see Mummy."

Her big brown eyes turn even bigger if that's at all possible, and she does the best hang-dog expression of any kid I've ever met.

"Me too, sweet pea. We'll see her soon. You know she'll be counting down the seconds until she has you in her arms."

Melly's lips lift slightly from the pout she's had going on all day. A week probably feels like a lifetime to a kid who's never really been apart from her mother. But we've all managed to keep her busy and distracted, and now she'll be reunited with Delaney, who I know is desperately missing her too.

A week in Reece's company has eased us into a friendship. There's a part of me that wants to jump his bones whenever I see him, and I occasionally get side-tracked by his shameless flirting, but my feet are firmly on the ground as far as anything more goes.

"It's not much farther, and they'll be waiting for us at the airport."

"Pania—"

"If you ask me if we're there yet," I say, interrupting Reece who's sitting in the next seat down from me. "I'll get up and throttle you."

He chuckles. "No, I just thought you might like to go for a drive when we get there. I can show you around."

For most of the week, we went sightseeing in LA. Reece took me to so many famous places, and I have a ton of photos for Mum. I might have even sneaked in a few of him when he wasn't looking.

"I'd like that."

"I don't think we'll do too much this week. Just enjoy the sun and get in some swimming."

"I can swim," Amelia says. She forms an O with her mouth like she does when she's excited about something. "We can go to the beach."

"We can, and there's a pool," Reece says.

He and Amelia talk about swimming while I close my eyes. At least this trip is more comfortable. I might have to insist on a bed on the way home.

Grimacing at the thought of the length of my flight home, I open my eyes again. Reece is standing over Amelia, pressing some buttons on the in-flight display. "There you go. Now you can see how close we are to your parents."

Melly sits up and claps as Reece returns to his seat.

"Now she might stop asking you how much longer there is."

It seems to take forever to get off the plane, but before too long, we're heading out to meet Josh and Delaney.

Delaney's right at the front of a small crowd, waiting. She opens her arms, and Melly tugs her hand out of mine before running at her mother.

It brings tears to my eyes to see them reunited as Delaney lifts Melly up and buries her face in her neck.

"Pania." Josh pecks me on the cheek. "How was your flight?"

"Long, but comfortable. Little Miss has been anxious to see Delaney. And you."

He chuckles. "It's okay. I'm not offended if she's been asking for her mom and not me. I'll still get to tuck her into bed tonight."

"She's had a lot of fun this week. The zoo, the movies, Lorenzo's."

"You went to Lorenzo's?"

I nod. "I can see why you love it there. The food was amazing."

He grins. "It is. And you and Reece have been spending some time together, I hear."

My cheeks give me away. I feel it. I know it. And Josh confirms it as he casts his gaze over my face and presses his lips together.

"Enough said." He looks over my shoulder. "Reece. Good to see you, man."

Reece walks past to shake hands with Josh, pulling him into a hug. I draw a deep breath as the now familiar scent of sandalwood washes over me.

"Good to see you too. How's the honeymoon going?"

"Great. We've had a wonderful time, but we missed all of you. I'm glad you're all here."

"I bet you're not," I say. "Pretty sure there's only one of us you really missed."

Josh laughs.

"Daddy." Melly reaches for him, and he takes her from Delaney to hug her tight while Delaney greets Cal and Ros.

"Let's get the luggage and get out of here. The limo's right outside."

He drops Melly back down to the ground, and she takes Delaney's hand while we walk over to the luggage claim.

And after we've grabbed our bags, Josh takes hold of the handles of my luggage trolley.

"What are you doing?" I raise an eyebrow.

"Being a gentleman. Reece can't do it, he's got his own crap to push."

I laugh and take a step back.

"You could have pushed my trolley." Reece calls as we walk away.

"She's better looking." Josh winks at me, and I laugh.

Reece doesn't respond, and as we make our way out the airport door, he pulls up alongside me.

"He's right. You are. I should have pushed both our trolleys."

I'm left open-mouthed as he moves past me and he and Josh start loading the suitcases into the boot of the car.

After climbing into the open door of the limo, I sit next to Delaney and she gives me a quick hug.

"I'm so glad you're here," she says, pulling back.

"Me too."

"Did you have a good week? Reece didn't do anything dumb, did he?"

I take a moment to think, but all that comes to mind is the laughter and teasing, and the way he smells after the shower, and ...

Delaney's brows knit. "Was it that bad?"

Laughing, I lean against her. "No. I was just trying to think of anything dumb he did, but it was all pretty good."

She smiles. "I'm glad."

"I've got a ton of photos to take home with me. And now I'm looking forward to putting my feet up for a while."

Delaney squeezes my arm. "There'll be plenty of opportunity for that. Wait until you see the house. I think you're just going to fall in love."

"That good, huh?"

Cal and Ros join us, followed by Josh and Reece climbing into the limo. After buckling in and helping myself to a glass of sparkling water from the limo's bar fridge, I'm transfixed by the palm trees, crystal clear blue ocean and mountainous views we're passing by, until a security guard waves us through a gate.

I gape at the lush green spacious grounds and gasp as the house comes into view. Josh and Delaney's home is amazing, but it's love at first sight when it comes to Reece's mansion.

It's a beautiful two-storey blue and white house with a veranda running around the outside.

Reece nudges my arm. "You like it?"

"It's beautiful."

I swear he puffs out his chest as he smiles at me.

"It's my getaway for when it all gets too much." His eyes shine with pride. "It was the first big thing I bought. I love it here."

The limo parks parallel to the house, and the door opens. I step out into the warm breeze, the scent of frangipani hanging in the air, and take a deep breath.

"Aloha. You must be Pania. Delaney's told me all about you."

I shift my gaze to the direction of the voice and smile at an older woman walking toward me.

"Pania, this is Leilani. She's the boss around here." Delaney grins.

Leilani reaches for my arm, and instinctively, I step toward her as we hongi, placing our foreheads and noses together. There are some traditions that span pacific countries, and that's one of them.

"It's so good to meet you. I know you took good care of my friend last time she was here." I smile as we move apart.

She places a fragrant lei around my neck. "She's good at getting into trouble, I'll give her that."

Delaney slams her hands onto her hips and looks between us. "You're not supposed to gang up on me."

We both laugh, and Delaney finally caves and grins.

"This is such a beautiful house," I say, shading my eyes from the sun as I look up.

Leilani holds out her hand. "Come inside. I'll show you your room, and there's plenty of food ready for you all. I know airplane food is awful."

I laugh. "It wasn't too bad, but there's never enough."

She pats me on the back. "I understand."

I follow her inside, and it's as beautiful as the outside—similar to Delaney and Josh's home with large rooms and a sweeping staircase.

We head upstairs and down a hallway until we reach one of the rooms where she comes to a stop and opens the door.

Leilani doesn't say anything, just gestures I step inside, which I do, shocked and in awe of a pale blue room with a four-poster bed, and a balcony that I head straight for. The doors are open, and I step out to see a view of the backyard with a large pool and grounds that seem to go for miles.

Turning, I smile at Leilani. "It's gorgeous."

"Anything you need, just pick up the phone and dial zero for the kitchen. When you're ready, come downstairs and turn right to get to the dining room."

"Thank you so much."

She hesitates, as if she's unsure to say something, and I frown.

"I'm not supposed to tell you this ..." There's a cheeky glint in her eye as if she's about to let me in on a big secret. "Reece wanted you in this room. It's the best guest room because it has the best bed and the best view from the balcony. He's never given me any advice on where to house his guests before."

I bite my bottom lip "Thank you for telling me."

She smiles. "See you downstairs."

After she's gone, I walk back out to the balcony and look around. LA was so busy and noisy, even from the car, but this? This I could live with forever.

And I haven't even ventured beyond the gate.

10

PANIA

I don't want to open my eyes.

It's our first morning here, and the warm breeze floats through the open window carrying the fragrant scent of flowers through the air. I could lie like this all day.

The bed dips beside me, and I shake my head to wake myself up.

"Good morning." Delaney sounds way too chirpy, and I let out a moan.

"What are you doing in my bed?" I rub my eyes.

"Waking you up. We have places to be." Delaney leans her head on my shoulder. "I'm borrowing one of Reece's cars and we'll go for a drive. We can't get *that* lost on an island."

I push myself up to sit. "Just don't let Josh drive. We'll get lost if he does."

Delaney bursts out laughing. "You're not wrong." She wriggles. "Your bed is so comfortable. This is such a nice room. Maybe I should sleep in here with you."

"You're supposed to be on your honeymoon." I raise my hands above my head, clasping them together and stretch. "With the gorgeous Josh."

"I live with him. And I only have you here for a week before you go home." She rolls off the side of the bed to her feet. "Leilani's made breakfast. That woman can bake."

My mouth waters at the thought of food. I crawled into bed early last night, tired from our flight and full of the seafood feast Leilani had put together.

Swinging my legs out the side of the bed, I sit there for a moment as Delaney makes her way around the bed.

"You, me, and Melly. It'll be like the old days." Her smile's so wide, I don't have the heart to tell her I just want to stay in bed.

"The old days a few months ago."

Delaney grabs one of my hands and swings my arm. "Yes. I don't know when we'll get to do this again."

"That's fair." I pull my hand away and scrub my face with my palms. "Give me a few minutes to get dressed and I'll head downstairs for breakfast."

"See you soon."

She floats out the door, and even though I'm tired, I can't help but smile at her enthusiasm. Delaney's right. I don't know when I'll get to spend time with her again—we have to make the most of every moment.

I pull on a pair of shorts and a shirt. I'm looking forward to taking a tour. Going to LA for the wedding was my first international journey, and I'm eager to see the sights of Hawaii before it's time to head home.

As I make my way downstairs, I pass Leilani coming up. Her welcoming smile just makes me feel even more at home.

I moan when I reach the doorway of the dining room. The scent of fresh bread wafts through the air, and my stomach grumbles in response.

Reece stares at me.

"That food smells amazing."

He grins. "Leilani makes the best croissants. They're why I don't stay here for any length of time because I'd have to spend twice as much time in the gym."

"It's so yummy, Pania," Melly mumbles, her mouth full of food.

I take a seat next to her. Delaney smiles from across the table. "Eat up."

"I hear you're going out with Delaney today," Reece says.

Plucking a croissant from the centre of the table and placing it on my plate, I tilt my head to look at him. "That's right."

"Save some time for me this afternoon. I want to take you somewhere."

"Ooooh." Delaney waggles her eyebrows.

"I told Pania about some of the sights around here and just want to show her." He winks at me, and even though my stomach grumbles again as if reminding me that the food is right there, I ignore it for a moment to squint at him.

He didn't say anything of the sort, but I'm not about to announce that with the way Delaney's gaze sits expectant on me.

"I want to see everything." I beam a smile before breaking open and buttering my croissant. Spreading jam on it, I then take a big bite and moan again. "Damn. That is good."

"Told you Leilani was an amazing baker. Maybe I can convince her to come home with me." Delaney flutters her eyelashes toward Reece who snorts.

"No way. You're not stealing her."

"I'm not sure you could handle sharing your kitchen anyway." Josh nudges Delaney's arm and she leans her head on his shoulder.

"Probably not."

"Where are you going today?" Reece asks.

"We're checking out the markets." Delaney reaches for another croissant. "Have credit card, will shop."

"Sounds dangerous."

"It is. You haven't seen her credit card bills." Josh winks at his wife who slaps his arm.

"Be gentle with her. She's shopping for two." I wrinkle my nose at Josh.

He stills, glancing between Delaney and me.

"I'm talking about me." I shake my head and start eating again.

Reece chuckles, and Josh seems to fight a smile.

I don't want this time together to ever end.

After breakfast, we walk outside where a shiny new-looking Toyota RAV4 sits.

"This is Reece's?" I ask.

Delaney pulls open the back door, and Melly climbs up into a booster seat. "Yeah. He's got a few cars in that garage. Not sure how often he gets to use them."

I open the passenger seat and climb in, sinking into the soft leather seats. "I like hanging out with you rich people."

She laughs, closing Melly's door and opening her own. "Stop it."

"You know what my car is like. This is luxury."

Buckling her seat belt, she then adjusts the rear view mirror and slides the key into the ignition. "Let's go spend Josh's money."

We take in the soft breeze as we drive along a long road with houses few and far between, and a lot of foliage. That soon changes to a more urban setting, and Delaney parks the car not far from a sea of brightly coloured stalls.

I climb out of the car and take a deep breath.

We've just eaten ourselves silly, but the smell of fried chicken and donuts floats through the air and makes my mouth water.

"Last time I was here, I walked from Reece's house to get to the markets and ended up with heat stroke," Delaney says, opening Melly's door.

"Oh, that was coming here?"

She nods. "I was so low. Josh and I had argued and then I ended up in hospital and all I wanted was to come home."

"But you didn't."

She walks around the car and grips my arm. "No. And I'm glad I didn't because I loved my time here. Last week, we didn't get out a lot to go shopping, so this week I plan on making up for it."

Leaning my head against hers, I laugh. "Josh won't know what hit him."

"That's the plan."

∼

By the time we get back to the house, I'm just about dead on my feet, but happy.

I've got bags and bags of gifts to take home—Delaney spent a small fortune, and I got to spend the day with two of the people I love most in the world. It'll be hard going back to a world where they're not with me.

"Ready?" Reece asks.

I whine, "I'm tired now."

His lips curl into a smile. "I promise it'll be worth it."

"Is there any walking?"

Reece cocks his head. "Maybe about thirty seconds worth."

Delaney walks up behind me and grabs my shopping bags. "Go. I'll get all this unloaded, and you go for a drive with this one."

"We have to get going otherwise we'll miss it," Reece says.

"Miss what?"

"You'll see."

I hold my arms up. "Okay, let's go."

Delaney hands Reece the car keys, and I get back in the passenger seat while he loads a basket into the back.

My mouth waters at the familiar scent of freshly baked food.

Reece climbs into the driver's seat and clicks his seatbelt on. "Leilani packed a picnic for us."

I lean back. "She's so good to you."

He starts the engine, and we move off down the driveway. "I'm very lucky to have found her. She worked for the couple who owned the house before me, then stayed on when I begged her. I never have to worry about anything. She just takes care of it."

"And you."

He flicks a bemused glance at me. "And me. I don't get to stay here as often as I'd like, but I try and make the most of it when I do. Leilani fusses over me about as much as Delaney does."

I snicker. "You're such a big baby."

"I like the attention. What man doesn't?" He grins and takes a turn that leads us up hill.

"Where are we going?"

"My favourite place. Where I go to think."

We drive the opposite way to the route I took with Delaney, eventually following a road that winds up a hill. There are no houses up here—trees and greenery line both sides of the road, which seems to get narrower until we pass through some gates that lead to a car park.

"Where are we?"

He smiles. "Tantalus lookout. There's a great view of Honolulu from here." After pulling the car into an empty park, he turns off the engine. "There's a short walk, and we can sit on the grass and eat while we watch the sunset."

My heart.

I swish my open palm toward him. "Lead the way."

Reece grabs the basket of food, and I follow him along a concrete path. He's right, it is only a short walk, and there's a large grassed area where other people are already sitting.

I catch my breath at the view. The city lies below us, and in the distance the blue-green ocean beckons. I think we might just have to visit the beach tomorrow.

"What do you think?"

"It's beautiful." There's so much to look at—the suburban houses that surround the city, to the taller buildings in the centre.

"We moved around a lot when I was a kid, but the first time I came here it felt right."

He's gazing out over the view, but my eyes are firmly on him. We've shared a lot of laughs, and a few confusing moments, but this is the most serious I've ever seen Reece.

"I'm glad I came on this trip."

Reece focuses his blue-eyes on me.

"Thank you for bringing me up here."

He drops the basket to the ground and digs his hands into his pockets. "You're the first person I've brought here. But I figured that we've spent the week together, and I've heard a lot about your life, so maybe it's time for me to share."

I nudge his arm. "Let's have something to eat because the smell of that food teased me the whole way here. Want to sit down?"

"There's even a picnic blanket in the basket."

I grin. "Even better."

He opens the basket and pulls out a red checked blanket. Spreading it out where we stand, he then moves the basket onto it while I slip off my shoes.

Leilani's packed cold meat and salads with freshly baked bread. A small package with two sweet muffins sits in the basket too—a little dessert for afterward.

There might be a handful of other people here, but quiet falls over us all as sunset approaches. And when we've finished eating, Reece clears the basket away to one side and moves closer to me.

He says nothing. But we end up sitting so close, I can smell his aftershave. I press my eyes shut and take a big breath. It's still a bit surreal to be here with this big movie star, but the more time we spend together, the less that plays on my mind.

This must be how Delaney feels being around Josh all the time. For a while, I didn't get how he was just Josh to her, even if they met before he became famous.

Now, I know.

Orange hues slowly fill the sky, and the white fluffy clouds become dark against them as the sun sets.

I've seen so many sunsets in my life, but this is breathtaking.

"This is why I love it up here." Reece nudges my arm.

"It's beautiful."

He opens his mouth, as if to say something, but his mobile rings, and instead he wrinkles his nose.

Reece pulls his phone out of his pocket and frowns at the screen. "Sorry. I have to take this. If I don't she'll just keep calling back."

She?

I don't even know who she is, but I smile and nod, and he turns away to take the call. And of course I try really hard not to listen in, but he's right there, and ...

"Hey."

My throat tightens at his soft tone. For a moment, he says nothing, but whoever's on the other end is reading him the riot act. He has his back to me, but his free hand tightens into a fist before he straightens it out.

"I'll be back in LA next week, and we'll go out for dinner." He rubs his forehead with his palm.

Jealousy ripples through me. We've spent the past week together, and he never mentioned seeing anyone. Not that he owes me any insight into his personal life.

"Geez, Jessie, when did you get so needy?"

Oh. I narrow my gaze.

Reece glances back at me. "I've got to go. I'll call you later. Yes. I promise." He grunts. "I know I promised to call you last week, but I was busy. I'll make it up to you. Bye."

I bite my bottom lip. Hard.

"Sorry." He slides his phone back into his pocket.

"Problem?" I ask.

He drops his head. "Just something that can wait until I go back to LA."

"Jessie Lane something?" I cross my arms. It shouldn't irritate me —I'm not sure I have the right to be pissy about him talking to her. But I am, and I've never been one to hold back.

Reece screws up his face, and I know I've guessed right. His eyes dart from side to side. "You heard that, huh?"

"My bitchiness radar's on high alert."

He raises his palms. "I'm not sure what I'm supposed to do. We've been friends a long time."

"Jessie called Delaney a whore."

He recoils.

"In her own diner. Full of people, including Melly."

Reece's jaw sets. "Josh told me she'd treated Delaney like trash, but I didn't know exactly what she'd said."

I drop my hands to my sides. "Delaney told Josh it was okay to invite her to the wedding, because she knows they've been friends a long time, and she's a forgiving person. I'm not."

"Point taken," he mumbles. A V forms between his eyebrows. "She's not a bad person, Pania. She's just always had a thing for Josh."

"Yeah, I figured."

"Things are ... complicated with her."

It shouldn't. It really shouldn't, but that word, *"complicated"*, has a loaded meaning. And it slams me right in the chest.

"You and Jessie?" I say, my voice cracking.

Reece breaks eye contact.

Woah.

"We're not together. We hooked up a few times in the past." His gaze hits mine again.

"I'm not going to judge you. Hell, we don't really know each other. I'm just surprised."

He leans forward. "I hope this doesn't come between us."

I swallow hard. It shouldn't, but I'm loyal to Delaney, and while I knew about the friendship between Jessie, Josh, and Reece, this is an unexpected piece of news.

I'm not even sure how to process it.

"I don't really know what to think. But it's none of my business." I look around. The sky has grown darker, the bright colours fading. The other people sitting at the lookout are packing up, so I suggest we do the same. "We should get going."

He nods.

It's a silent ride home. I'm not sure if it's petty to feel disappointed in him, but he has a past with a lot of women in it, and it shouldn't be surprising Jessie's one of them.

Delaney greets us as we walk in the door, her hand in Melly's.

"I'm just putting this one to bed, then you can tell me all about your mysterious trip," she says.

I glance at Reece as I answer her. "I think I'm just going to have an early night. We'll catch up tomorrow."

Swallowing hard, I meet Reece's gaze. "Thank you."

Delaney's eyes dart from Reece to me and back again. "Fair enough. It's been a long day." She looks down at Melly. "Say goodnight to Pania and Reece."

I bend so Melly can give me a hug. She wraps her arms around my neck, and I close my eyes, holding her tight.

"Goodnight, Pania," she whispers.

"Night, sweet pea." I press a kiss to her ear, then let her go.

And then I climb the stairs without looking behind me, tiredness taking over.

I've got some thinking to do.

11

REECE

Things change after that night.

Pania hasn't told Delaney or Josh about Jessie, or one of them would have said something. Instead, she's avoiding me, spending all her time with Delaney. And when we do come into contact, I'm left unsure whether we're flirting or sparring. It's unfamiliar territory. And Josh's words still ring in the back of my mind. I can't just have a fling with her. Not that I really know if she'd want that anyway.

On our last night, after dinner, I'm left alone. Ros and Cal have gone to bed early every night this week—the effect the islands have when you bounce out of bed at some ridiculous hour.

Delaney took Amelia upstairs for a bath a while ago, and Josh followed them sometime later. But at some point in the evening, I lost track of Pania.

This is my last chance to tell her I'm feeling ... something.

I find her out the back of the house, dangling her feet in the swimming pool and looking up at the stars.

"Sorry to disturb you," I say as I step up beside her.

She tilts her head back and looks up at me. "I heard you coming. You're not exactly quiet."

"Thank you for not telling the others about Jessie. It's just awkward. And in the past."

Pania smacks her lips together. "It's not my story to tell. Whatever it is."

"Well, thanks." I slide my hands into my pockets and rock back on my heels. "What are you doing?"

She takes a deep breath. "I love it out here. I know I'm far away from New Zealand, but this feels like home. And it's not just your house, which is amazing, but it's the people and the culture. Thank you for letting me stay."

I drop to the ground beside her, and dangle my feet in the water too. Leaning back on my palms, I look up at the night sky. "You're welcome. I'm glad to see you've enjoyed your time here."

Her gaze meets mine. In the soft light, I can see the flecks of green that surround her hazel eyes. It's so hard to remember my promise to Josh when I find her so damn attractive.

"I loved it. You're so lucky to have this place to escape to when you need it. It's so relaxing, but at the same time, the city's not too far away."

"You're welcome to come here any time."

She smiles and drops her gaze. "I'm looking forward to going home, but I'll miss this. I'll miss all of you."

Her lips twitch, and my eyes go straight to them. What would it be like to kiss her? My heart thuds. I move my hand a little closer.

"And then I think about how our lives have changed, and how I have to get on with the new challenges of my life without the people who mean the most to me." She raises her head again. "I'm so glad I came here, though. I got to be by my best friend's side as she married the love of her life."

I sit up and rub my neck. "It's kind of weird to think about how much all our lives have changed these past few months."

Pania shrugs. "Yes, but it's all good. Those two inside make love look so easy, but I don't think it happens that way all the time."

I swallow hard. It feels as if, sometimes, she sees right through me, even though she seems to be talking about her own experiences.

"Have you ever been in love?" I blurt out.

Pania scrunches her nose. "I've thought so a couple of times. But I don't think I'm the easiest person to love. A lot of men don't like a woman who speaks their mind."

I cock my head. "I think it's great. It's what I respect about you and Delaney. I can see how the two of you made such a great team for so long."

She laughs. "We've had some good times. Some really shit ones, too, but the good outnumbers the bad by a lot."

"I'm going to miss you when you leave." I take a deep breath. "I just wanted to say how much these past two weeks have meant to me. You're really one of a kind, Pania Wilson."

She blushes, looking down at her feet.

I reach for her chin and tilt her face up until her gaze hits mine.

Her hazel eyes widen. "I bet you say that to all the girls," she whispers, her chest rising as she holds her breath.

I shake my head and lick my lips as my eyes lock onto hers. "I'm not sure I've ever said it to anyone before. But then, I've never met anyone like you."

"Reece."

Her eyelids flutter before they close, so I let go of her chin and run my knuckle along her jaw.

Her breath hitches.

"Pania," I whisper.

My mouth meets hers, and I kiss her gently, the rushing noise in my ears calming as she kisses me back, her soft lips caressing mine. She opens up, and I slide my tongue in, tasting the sweet wine we've been drinking this evening.

I kiss her with everything that I am and everything I hope to be. She's the first person I've met that'd make it all worthwhile.

It feels as if we bicker like an old married couple, the gentle sniping that doesn't hurt but leaves you wanting more, and I've only known her two weeks.

She stares at me when the kiss ends, and for the first time I think she's left with nothing to say.

"I've been wanting to do that for a while."

"I've been wanting to do that since before I met you." Her lips quirk in amusement.

"Maybe I just want to kiss you some more."

She grins and drops her gaze. It's coy and cute, and it makes my heart sing.

"That'd be nice, but I'm not sure it's a good idea."

My eyes narrow. "Why not?"

Pania stretches her legs out and sighs. "I live on the other side of the world, and I leave tomorrow. I'm not looking for a quick hook-up. I don't know if you want anything more than that."

I suck on my bottom lip. "Truth is, I don't know what I want."

"What do you mean?"

I turn toward her. "I've spent years avoiding commitment and seeking the hook-up, but those two inside are making me reconsider all of it. What if there's more out there for me?"

Her lips twitch, and she tilts her head. "I'm sure there is if you give it a chance." She touches my arm. "I've enjoyed getting to know you. I'm not star struck anymore."

"You mean you were at the start? I couldn't tell."

Her cheeks flush with colour and she laughs. "For about the first thirty seconds. And then you opened your mouth and it was all over."

I chuckle. "I'm usually good with words. Or so I'm told."

She shoots me a wry smile. "When the first words are flirting with my bestie, they're not so impressive."

Oh.

"I hope I've made up for that."

"You're not too bad." She leans back "Especially at kissing."

"I've been told I'm pretty good at that."

She drops her gaze, and I suck in a breath. *What a dumb thing to say when I don't want to spar with her right now.* "I didn't m—"

"What are you two doing, hiding out here?" Delaney places her glass on the nearby table and flops into a chair.

"Just talking. Amelia asleep?" I ask.

She nods. "Josh will be down in a minute. He's just having a shower."

Pania pulls her feet out of the pool and walks over to the table, taking a seat next to Delaney. After a moment, I follow suit.

Delaney grips Pania's arm and shakes her. "I'm going to miss you."

Pania frowns. "I'll miss you too."

"I'm going to talk to Josh about a trip home. He never got to meet your mum or see where I grew up. That, and I really want to spend some time in our house there and cook in that beautiful kitchen."

I laugh. "You and your kitchens."

Pania meets my gaze again. "She's got it bad for shiny cooktops. It's really the way to her heart."

We all laugh as Josh appears at the back door, beer in hand, his skin looking decidedly red after our day in the sun.

"You need to learn how to use sunscreen," I say.

"He does." Delaney nods. "I've been extra careful after my last visit. The last thing I need is sunstroke again."

Josh sits at the table. "It's not that bad."

"It'll be me picking you up from the hospital if you're not careful." Delaney purses her lips, and he leans over and kisses her.

"I'll be more careful tomorrow. Promise."

I look across the table at Pania. She meets my gaze, and gives me a small smile.

At least I'll get one more chance to talk to her before she leaves tomorrow.

I wish I came here more.

My schedule has been crazy for years, so I employed people to run the estate and just visited when I could. But every time I come here, I wish I'd stayed longer.

Maybe that's one of the changes I can make to my life.

Things will slow down for the next few months anyway. Josh and I aren't racing to get this movie of ours finished. We're taking our time and learning new parts of the industry as we go. It's been a huge undertaking, but one that will hopefully pay off for us big time.

I yawn as I make my way downstairs for breakfast. Pania leaves in a few hours, so once I've eaten, I'll have to find a way to take her aside, and we'll talk. About what yet, I don't know, but I'd like to continue our interrupted conversation from last night.

Sitting alone at the dining room table when I enter the room is Josh. He takes a sip of coffee while poring over the newspaper.

"Morning."

He looks up. "Hey."

"Where is everyone?"

His eyes narrow toward the clock on the wall. "Delaney should be back any minute. She and Amelia took Pania to the airport."

Shit.

"What? I thought her flight was later in the day."

"It's not for a little while yet, but she had to get there early with it being an international flight."

I sit down hard on the chair in front of me.

"Are you okay?" Josh tilts his head. "You've got a soft spot for her."

"It's nothing."

He straightens up. "Yeah, looks like nothing."

"I like her. We're friends. There's no law against that."

Josh chuckles and holds his hands up in surrender. "No, there's not, but—"

"I remember your warning."

He frowns. "It wasn't a warning."

"Whatever it was. Doesn't matter. Are you ready to leave tomorrow?"

He nods, not saying anything more.

"I need coffee," I grumble.

That last chance is gone.

12

PANIA

I think I'm in shock.

I'm not sure I can really remember anything from the morning, apart from climbing out of bed, grabbing my things and leaving. And then I was on the plane and flying home, all the while my body hummed with the memory of Reece.

Reece Evans.

I didn't see him before I left. And it's probably just as well. I didn't get much sleep after we kissed, and I'm not sure what I would have said to him this morning.

It was hard enough leaving Delaney and Melly behind.

When Delaney got back with Josh, I made her promise to find me a Hollywood boyfriend. I was only half serious. She's moved into a world I still struggle to wrap my head around, and she does it with all of the class Delaney has.

I press the buttons on the inflight entertainment, flicking through the screens in some vain attempt to distract myself.

Reece and I kissed.

Chuckling as one of Reece's movie posters catches my eye, I pause and take a deep breath. It's an older movie, and I've seen it before. He's one of those gorgeous men everyone seems to fall in love with when he's acting. It's impossible not to. And then he's equally impressive in real life.

But he scares me.

I know he's a player, and no one's ever managed to tie him down. I have no intention of even trying. I'm not even sure it'd be more than just sex for him.

Pressing play, I tug on my headphones and settle back into my seat. If I remember this movie correctly, there's a really hot sex scene halfway through, and if I never see those abs up close again in real life, at least I can watch them move on screen.

And those hips.

The only problem's going to be that every time I see that damn smile of his—it might just break my heart.

AFTER SLEEPING for a chunk of the flight, I wake reluctantly in time to land in Auckland. The familiar sight of home makes me ache. As we fly over Manukau, I try in vain to look for my little flat, but there's no way I can see it among all the houses. And when the wheels touch the tarmac, I close my eyes and breathe a sigh of relief for being home.

Thankfully, it doesn't take too long to clear customs and get my bags, and despite sitting on my arse for hours, my feet feel like lead by the time I get out of the plane and into the airport.

"Pania."

I look up to see my cousin Wiremu waiting for me. Eternally in a pair of trackpants and a singlet—at most a T-shirt, he's taken the time to dress up for once, and is wearing a collared shirt.

That has to be my mother's influence.

I pull my luggage trolley to a stop when I reach him and fling my arms around his neck.

"Are you okay?" He plants a kiss in my hair.

"Just really tired and glad to be home."

He chuckles. "Your chariot awaits. She's running like a dream."

I'm not looking forward to a drive to Whakatane, but I made a promise to my mother before I left that I'd see her first before coming back to Auckland. She worries about me flying too.

Wiremu has been doing some maintenance work on my car while I've been gone. At least he knows how to do an oil change and all those other little things I've never wrapped my head around.

I let him go, and his eyes roam my face.

"You look like shit."

"Hey!" I slap his arm. "What the fuck? You're not supposed to say stuff like that to me."

He shrugs. "It's true. I thought you would have slept on the plane. Instead, you look like you haven't slept in a week."

That's exactly how I feel.

"I just need to get home and get some rest."

He grins.

I love my cousin. Apart from Delaney, he's the best friend I've ever had. I don't have siblings, but I have Wiremu and Delaney. That he's driven all the way from Whakatane to pick me up means a lot to me.

I'm not so sure I love his attitude, though.

"Yeah, you tell yourself that, cuz. I think you look like shit anyway." He nudges my arm, and that grin makes me smile. It's infectious, and for the millionth time, I wonder about just who we can set him up with. He needs someone to pull him into line.

Just like Reece does.

Reece.

Wiremu grabs my trolley and leads me out of the airport and into the car park. I'm relieved when we reach my good old Honda Accord. She might have a couple of hundred thousand kilometres on the clock, and be a bit worse for wear, but she's never let me down.

"I'll put all this in the boot. You get in the car," Wiremu says, pressing the key fob and unlocking it.

I'm happy to plonk myself in the passenger seat.

After the luggage is stowed, Wiremu laughs as he opens the driver's door.

"I thought you would want to take the wheel."

"I'm not keen on crashing."

He slides into the driver's seat. "Let's get you home."

It doesn't take long for the gentle hum of the car to send me back to sleep.

"WE'RE HERE."

I jerk as Wiremu elbows me in the ribs, and shake my head to wake myself up. Home has never looked so good.

Mum opens the door and steps out onto the landing, a broad smile on her face.

"What do you want to do with the bags?" Wiremu asks.

"I'll grab what I need. Thank you for everything."

He smiles. "You'd do the same for me."

Climbing out of the car, I walk around to the boot and open it, grabbing my bag full of gifts. Thanks to Leilani, I don't have any dirty washing, so all my clothes can stay here until I take them home with me.

Mum's already inside when I reach the back door, so I kick off my shoes and step into the kitchen.

"I'm in here, my love," she calls from the living room.

I drop onto the couch beside her, and she wraps her arms around my neck.

"I'm so glad you're home safe."

Leaning my head against hers, I resist the urge to close my eyes again. "I'm happy to be home."

She drops her arms.

"How's Delaney?"

I smile. "She's doing so well. I think she was born for that life, Mum. She's like a princess living in her castle with the handsome prince who worships the ground she walks on."

"I'm so glad she fell on her feet. What about you?"

"What about me?"

"Did you meet anyone?"

This is what Mum does. Ever since Delaney and Josh got back together, my mother seems to think it'll lead to a happy ending for me. Probably because Delaney and I have done so much together over the years.

"Mum, I—"

"You did meet someone." She beams.

"Kind of."

"And ...?"

I shake my head. "Nothing will come of it, Mum. I like him, but I'm not sure he likes me enough."

"Then he's just not good enough for you." She sticks her nose in the air and sniffs.

"I love you, Mum."

"Love you too. How long are you home for?"

I shrug. "A couple of days, and then I'll head up north again. Do you want to see the photos of the wedding?"

Mum stares as me as if I've just said something stupid. "Of course I do. How's my *moko*?"

"Melly is"—I pause—"well ... she'll follow in her father's footsteps if she keeps up the dramatics. But she's happy."

"One day I'll get brave enough to fly over for myself." She slides her arm around my shoulders and squeezes me against her again.

"I'm sure they'll come and see you when they visit."

I hand her my phone and she flicks through the photos and sighs. "She made a beautiful bride. And that dress is so special." Her mouth falls open. "So many movie stars. Is that Reece Evans?"

Sucking on my bottom lip, I nod. "You know Reece is Josh's bestie."

"I know, but he's so handsome." Mum gets this faraway look in her eyes. "Like the old time movie stars."

"He's also a terrible flirt."

She turns her head, her eyes wide. "Did he flirt with you?"

"Yes, Mum. But he flirts with everyone. You should hear him with Delaney."

She waves her hand as if dismissing what I've just said. "But he flirted with you. Such a lucky girl."

"Mum." I laugh.

"He looks like a good man."

I swallow hard. She's right, but Reece buries it under so many layers of bullshit.

"He is. He's just a little lost at times."

Her eyes search mine. "I think there's a bit more than flirting, then."

I drop my gaze. "We spent some time together before we went to Hawaii. Reece isn't a bad person, but he's not the man for me."

Her slow nod tells me she doesn't really believe what I'm saying. Mum could always see right through me.

"You like him."

"Everyone likes him."

She takes my hand in hers, and I look up into her dark eyes. "No, my love. *You* like him."

I shrug. "I do. But I'm back here and he'll already be off on another conquest."

Her eyebrows rise. "Another ..."

"I didn't sleep with him. I might have let him kiss me."

Her lips twitch. "Sometimes, you have to kiss some frogs to find your prince. I did plenty of kissing when I was your age."

I laugh. "And Dad?"

"Your dad was a prince among men. I miss him." She pats me on the knee. "Did you want a coffee?"

"I'll make it. You sit here and look through the rest of the photos. There are some gorgeous ones of Melly in there."

She flicks through a couple more. "Amelia will be a little heart-breaker."

"That she will, Mum. That she will." I smile and push myself to my feet. Hours in a plane and then in a car have left my joints stiff, and I wince as I stand.

"Are you okay?"

"Too much sitting on my bum." I chuckle. "I might have to go for a walk to get all the kinks out. You keep looking at the photos. Reece took me all over LA and I took pictures everywhere I went."

I walk toward the door.

"And, Mum, if we can ever get you to fly, you'd love Hawaii. It's magical."

She presses her hand to her chest. "I'd love to go."

"Maybe one day."

Pulling open the back door, I step out into the sunshine and rub my neck. How is it possible to still be so tired when I've had so much sleep? How can I feel so happy to be home, but still feel like some part of me isn't?

I'm not sure I can take another journey for a while to see Delaney.

Not until I work out how I feel.

13

PANIA

The two days at my childhood home go much faster than I hoped they would.

It's been wonderful to be at home with Mum, poring over wedding photos and sharing my stories of my time away. But real life beckons now, and I've got my studies to get on with. The first term was pretty basic—I've been making my own clothing since I was a teenager, but not everyone is that knowledgeable about the whole process, and this term we should get into more detail.

Wiremu runs his hand over the bonnet of my beaten old Honda Accord before handing me the keys.

"She's running like a dream again, but you're gonna have to look at replacing her sometime soon."

"Thanks, cuz. I owe you one."

"I used most of the money you gave me. I'll keep the rest as a tip."

I laugh. "You do that."

"Have a safe trip. And good luck with your training course. Maybe you can make me something to wear."

Opening the boot of the car, I stop for a moment to look at him before dropping my bag in. "I'm sure I can sort something out."

He opens his arms, and I hug him tight. "You take care of yourself. If you need anything, call me."

"I will. Take good care of Mum."

We let go of each other. "She takes care of me, more like it."

"Pania." Mum comes out of the door. "Are you leaving now?"

"No time like the present."

She cups my face in her hands. "I'm so proud of you. Shine like the star you are."

"I love you, Mum."

"I love you, too, my favourite *tamāhine*."

I laugh. "I'm your only daughter."

"Still my favourite."

She places a kiss on my cheek and hugs me tight. "Be safe on the road."

"I will."

It's always hard to leave Mum, but at least I can see her a bit more often now I'm living in the North Island. When I lived down south, I didn't get to see her very much.

The thought of the three hour drive back doesn't exactly fill me with joy, but the sooner I leave, the sooner I'll get there.

I'm nowhere near as tired as I was when I got here, but my thoughts still linger on Reece. At some point I'm bound to see him again. Will things be the same between us, or will it be awkward.

As nice as that kiss was, I'm still undecided about whether it was a good idea or not.

ALL THE WAY HOME, the sunshine and a soft breeze keep me company. I've never been so happy to turn into my driveway and pull into the carport next to my flat. I unlock the front door and unload my bags into the living room.

My bed beckons to me like a giant white marshmallow, and I drop onto the duvet, face first, and let out a long groan.

This tiny apartment isn't much, but it's home for the next three years.

It's hard to reconcile the past couple of weeks with that, but for the moment, I have to settle into student life.

After I flick off a quick text to Mum and Delaney to let them both know I'm home, I lie on my back on the bed and close my eyes.

My stomach gurgles, reminding me I'm going to have to fill it at some point. I didn't get anything to eat on the way home, but there's meat in the freezer, and I have a few potatoes. Tomorrow, after class, I'll go shopping.

Delaney: *Skype?*

I grab my laptop from beside the bed and plug the charger in. It takes a moment to come to life—it's not the newest thing around, but when it's loaded I text her back.

Me: *Call me.*

The call comes up, and I click accept.

Delaney's face appears, filling up most of the screen.

"Woah! That's way too much you. Back up a bit." I laugh.

"Sorry. Just getting used to this new setup. Josh replaced my laptop *again* after Melly dropped a drink on it. All that money and the damn thing still wasn't waterproof."

I laugh. "I hope you had your data backed up."

"It's all in the cloud. You'd be so proud of me."

"I'm so proud of you. What's up?"

She leans back a little and smiles. "I just wanted to check in and see how you were doing. How was your trip home? How's your mum?"

"Mum's great. The trip was long. I just got back to Auckland today, and I'll be cooking up something to eat before falling asleep in front of the TV."

"Sounds perfect. I miss you." Her brows knit, and I can't help but tear up a little. For years, we were in each other's pockets apart from the year she spent in the US when we were eighteen. Being there for the wedding and spending time together afterward doesn't make up for no longer having my best friend on tap.

"I miss you too. What have you been up to?"

She stifles a yawn. "Melly went back to school today. It was such a mission to get out of bed on time, but we made it. Reece is thinking about buying a house, which is just bizarre, but Josh thinks it's because he's watching us settle down and maybe he'll do the same thing."

My heart stops. "Really?"

"He's lived out of a suitcase forever, and he has an apartment even though he spends most of his time living at our place. It'll be good for him." She blows out a breath. "Though, he's staying with us full-time while they film their movie."

My eyebrows rise. "Are you okay with that?"

"I'm used to him, but I didn't think we'd have a flatmate at this stage in our lives." She facepalms. "I think Josh just wants to make sure he stays on the job. He missed some days of work at the start, and then he was away for those two weeks filming."

"Fair enough. He seems to be serious about their movie. He talked about it a little when I was there, and he was pretty proud."

Her lips curl. "They both are. It's so cool. They started filming today, and Antonio and I are going shopping tomorrow. I wish you could've spent another week here."

I chuckle. "I would have loved to, but I'm also glad to be home. This term should be more of a challenge."

She flaps one hand as if waving that away. "Screw that. Just come back. You can start a business. I could be your manager. Except you don't have to pay me. Seeing you do well is payment enough."

I roll my eyes. "I don't know ..."

"You're so talented. You always have been. I know you want to finish your studies, but whenever you're ready, my home is always open, and you know I'll help you in any way I can."

"You don't have to do that."

Delaney cocks her head. "You studied cooking with me when it wasn't really your first love. You set up the diner with me in the middle of nowhere because we're family. Supporting you to live your dream is the least I can do."

I shake my head. "I love you."

Her face lights up. "Love you too."

"Where is Josh? Isn't it late over there?"

Delaney screws up her nose. "Yeah, but I knew he'd be working late tonight. He had a night scene to shoot."

"Stink."

"It's so boring. Reece is there, too, so I don't even have him around to keep me entertained."

"So you called me?"

She shrugs. "I was planning to regardless. The house feels weird without you." She glances off screen. "I even spent some time looking up stories about the wedding. Probably not the smartest thing to do."

"What are you talking about?"

"Josh has some ... I'm not even sure what to call them. He has some rather obsessive fans who make stuff up."

I narrow my gaze. It's bad enough they say shit about her online. "Like what?"

"Oh, there are all kinds of random stories about his life that they've made up. They're like amateur detectives looking for clues that we're not really together."

I close my eyes, shaking my head. "What? Why are you reading this stuff?"

"I can't help it. Josh tells me not to look, but it's so funny. They get so agitated that he's not telling the truth, and they hate on me, but the only people I care about know it's all shit."

I chew my bottom lip. "I've seen the public stuff. You mean there's worse?"

"I'll send you some links. To be honest, part of the reason I bother is that there are posts about Melly, and it's her safety I worry about the most. It also helps pass the time."

I laugh. "You have the world at your feet. Are you really *that* bored?"

There's a pause, and Delaney sighs. "Sometimes. The diner kept me busy all the time, and I love my life, but there are days I haven't worked out how to fill yet. But I'm happier than I have been in a long time. I just miss you."

"Miss you too."

"One day I'll convince you to move over here with me."

I laugh. "Maybe."

"Anyway, I should go. Josh just walked in the door, and we're due some mummy and daddy time."

I screw up my nose. "Ew. I don't want to know."

"That's why I told you. I'm leaving you with that image." She chuckles. "Oh, by the way, Reece asked for your number."

I swallow hard. "Why?"

"Someone asked him about my wedding dress. He wants to put you in touch. I didn't think you'd mind, but now I'm thinking that I shouldn't have done it."

I close my eyes. I'm not sure I want this—we shared a kiss that's not likely to mean anything to him, and I'm not interested in getting hurt. But then again, he wants to contact me …

I can't read anything into it.

"That's fine. I mean, it's all good if I can pick up some work."

"I thought it would be. And it's way better to go through him than someone randomly contacting you. Let me know if it turns into anything."

Clamping my lips together, I shift my gaze to the ceiling. "Sure will."

"Talk to you soon."

Once the call disconnects, I stare at the blank screen for a moment. It's so tempting just to throw it all in and go back. Delaney would let me stay while I found my feet, and if there are people asking about my designs …

My phone buzzes, and I shake my head to get me out of my stupor.

Reece: *Hey. It's Reece. Delaney gave me your number.*

I raise an eyebrow. Looks like that didn't take too long.

Me: *She told me. I was just on Skype with her.*

After dropping my phone on the table, I head to the cooktop. I fill a pan with water and place it on the element, flicking on the gas.

My life would be so different if I moved to stay with Delaney—even for a little while. But I always looked up to the way she lived her life when she started her own business. She went for what she wanted, and while she had to make sacrifices, she never gave up.

I want to follow my dream and not take shortcuts. That means three years of study and building my own little empire. Delaney had her diner, and I'll have my own fashion business one day.

After wandering back to the table, I pick up my phone.

Reece: *I never got to say goodbye. You cheated.*

A smile tugs at my lips despite me not wanting it to.

Me: *We both know it's for the best.*

Reece: *Probably, but I'm going to pester you from time to time.*

Me: *Until I change my number.*

I laugh and put my phone back down. This isn't getting my dinner cooked. But it's a pleasant distraction.

Reece: *You wouldn't do that to me.*

Me: *Probably not. I have to cook my dinner now. Talk to you later.*

It's not easy to ignore the phone while I peel the potatoes and put some sausages in the oven. Even when it buzzes again after I've left it there.

But my stomach no longer gurgles, instead grumbling. And when everything's cooking away, I return to the table and pick up the phone.

Reece: *Just wanted to make sure you were okay. If you're responding I know you're alive. Talk soon.*

I smile and save his number into my phone. God knows if I'll hear from him again, but it can't hurt to have his contact details—just in case of an emergency.

I'm not sure what kind of emergency I'd have to contact him for, but that's what I tell myself as I put the phone back down.

Makes perfect sense to me.

14

PANIA

The past three weeks have been a fairy tale, but as my alarm blares in the morning, I come down to earth with a bang.

I rub my face with my palms, trying to wake myself up. Maybe a cool shower will help.

Yawning as I climb out of bed, I then make my way to the bathroom and turn on the shower before adjusting the heat a little.

Ten minutes later, I'm refreshed and wide awake.

I scrape some butter and Marmite onto toast and wolf it down before making my way out to the car. If I don't get to my favourite parking spot early enough, it'll be gone. It's bad enough that I then have to catch a bus into the city, but city carparking is ridiculous, and I like the freedom of having my car nearby.

It would be a great idea if it weren't for the fact that so many other people do the same thing, and the quiet little side street I found last term fills pretty quickly, so I can't afford to run late.

An hour later, I walk into the building and take my seat in my class. Back when I started taking an interest in fashion, Judith Brookes was at the top of her game. She had stores throughout the country, and while not quite cracking the international scene, there were some stores in Australia.

Very exclusive, very expensive, and everything my teenage-heart desired.

When I had an inkling that Delaney would want to go to Josh in LA, I looked at my options, and my heart leapt when I saw Judith was teaching fashion design. A few years ago, her business tanked and most of her stores closed, but she still has one in Auckland.

Now looking up, I see her glaring right at me. She reminds me of Edna Mode in *The Incredibles*, only blonde and with a ton of red lipstick.

"Miss Wilson. It's so good of you to join us today."

The venom is dripping in Judith's tone. I knew she'd be pissy with me missing a couple of days class, but most of my time away was Easter followed by the holidays. So overall, I haven't really missed much.

"I'm glad to be back."

"Congratulations."

I swear she spits the word out as if it's an insult. She's well known for her frosty demeanour, but she's going real ice queen on me now.

"I'm not sure—"

She smiles, but it's so fake I'm half expecting her face to crack. "Your name is in all the magazines this week." Holding one up with Delaney and Josh on the cover, she flicks through some pages.

The penny drops. It's something I knew would happen, but I was so invested on seeing my best friend marrying the love of her life, I'd pushed it to the back of my mind. Of course Delaney told people who made her dress. I'm so grateful to her, but right now I'm thinking I could have done without it.

"Thank you."

"It's a shame they couldn't mention that you're doing this class with me." Her grip tightens on the magazine.

"I didn't really have any control on what they reported. I made a dress for my bestie."

"It's not what I would have dressed her in."

"She loved it, and so did Josh."

Her eyes widen at the mention of Josh's name. I should use it more often.

She smacks her lips together. "I suppose that's what's important."

I let out a sigh of relief when she drops her focus on me and turns to someone else.

"Welcome back." Sam, the woman who sits beside me on class nudges my arm. "I saw the dress. It's beautiful."

"Thank you."

"And ignore Judith. She's just jealous. She'd kill for the publicity you got."

My cheeks burn. I know Delaney's life is a far cry from mine—from the life she used to have—but this whole Hollywood thing is like a different world. Coming home from that hasn't been easy. I miss my friend, but I'm not sure I miss the craziness.

"So, who else did you meet over there? I saw the wedding photos. Reece Evans was the best man, wasn't he? He's so gorgeous."

I swallow hard. "He's a good guy," I croak.

"I read he's about to start making a movie with Josh Carter. *Coming Home*? I would have killed to be Gabby Reynolds getting to kiss both of them. What's he like in real life?"

My nostrils pick up the scent of sandalwood out of nowhere, as if Reece is right there. I drop my gaze and shrug. "He's a guy."

She giggles. "Yeah, but what a guy. Those pictures of him on holiday in Hawaii ..." I look up, and as our gazes connect, her eyes widen. "Oh. You were there, weren't you?"

I nod slowly. "I was."

"You're so lucky. I'd kill to get that close to him. I mean, Josh Carter is gorgeous too. It must be crazy hanging out with them."

"To be honest, I was really hanging out with Delaney."

Her expression blanks for a moment. "Delaney? Josh's wife."

"The one in the beautiful dress."

Her wistful smile makes me clamp my lips together. I've seen enough reaction on social media to the wedding. It's a mix of people who are supportive, and then there's the crowd who hate Delaney with a passion just for being the one to snag Josh.

But they don't know those two—they were made for each other.

I'm not sure which category Sam fits into.

"Anyway, I'm really glad you're here. I'm sure you have a ton of stories about the wedding."

I do. And I'm not sharing them with you.

My phone buzzes in my jacket pocket, and I pluck it out.

Reece: *Just checking in. I wanted to make sure you got home okay.*

I bite my bottom lip and smile.

Me: *I'm back at school today. Thanks for checking up on me.*

"Pania?"

Dazed, I meet Sam's gaze. "Sorry?"

"Stories about the wedding?"

"Oh." I shrug. "It was beautiful, and there were so many famous people, but I mainly stuck around Delaney and her daughter. I don't really have any stories."

Sam screws up her nose. "Stink. Never mind. Want to go for lunch together? If you've got any close-ups of that dress, I'd love to see them. My sister's getting married in a few months, and she's got a similar figure to Delaney. And she's got a big thing for Josh Carter."

I'm not sure this is really a good idea. But my best friend is half a world away, and after my run in with Judith, maybe lunch with a friendly face would be a good idea.

"Sure. Sounds good. I have a ton of photos of the dress."

JUDITH SAYS nothing more all morning, but she's not an easy person to read.

I'm still relieved when it gets to lunchtime, and Sam and I make our way across the road to the seats on the berm opposite the building. It's not the ideal lunch spot, but it gets us outside for a while.

I eat my leftovers from last night while Sam polishes off her sandwiches, and then I pull out my phone to show her the photos.

I flick through the pictures of the dress. I took photos well before the wedding, so there aren't any personal moments in them. And I know to stop when I hit photos of my own dress.

"Wow. Looks amazing. They just look so much in love. It's so sweet."

I lock my phone and put it down. "They really are."

She smiles wistfully. "That's awesome. It's so weird when you see celebrities and there are stories about them, and you never know what to believe."

I rub my forehead. "Probably none of them."

Sam laughs. "I'll keep that in mind."

My phone buzzes. I pick it up and swipe to open.

Reece: *Hope your day goes well. I'm on the set of our new movie and bored.*

My lips twitch.

Me: *Bored enough to text me.*

Reece: *You answer. Josh and Delaney might have finished their honeymoon, but they're still tucked away together. So boring.*

Me: *Nice to know I'm third on your list to contact, then.*

Sam nudges my arm. "We should get back."

I look up and blink a few times. "What's the time?"

"Nearly one. I don't want to get the evil death stare."

Laughing, I drop my phone in my bag and stand. "Fair point. Though I'm told I'm pretty good at those too."

She shivers. "Judith scares me."

"She's just a person. Don't let her intimidate you. We're paying to study here."

Her eyes widen. "I hadn't thought of it that way."

"We're all adults. If she wants to be petty, then whatever. I'm here to learn."

Sam laughs. "I like you, Pania."

"I'm glad to find a friend in class after this morning. I'm sure she'll forget about it."

She pushes herself off the bench. "I'm not so sure she will, but I guess we can hope."

There's still a few minutes left after we get back to class, and I pull my phone back out of my bag.

Reece: *You're not third on my list. You're right at the top.*

Heat floods my body. But I know him and his reputation. He says that now, but he's bound to pop up in a magazine with a beautiful woman on his arm.

Me: *Glad to hear it.* I pause, sucking on my bottom lip. *It's really nice of you to text me. I know you're busy.*

His reply takes my breath away.

Reece: *I'll always have time for you.*

15

———————

REECE

It's been three months since I last saw Pania, but we've kept in touch. I know I probably shouldn't, but nearly every day we've exchanged text messages or used Skype. We joke with each other, and there are times when we both open up about things happening in our day-to-day life.

Mine's not really that exciting right now, even though there are a lot of men out there who would kill to be me today.

"Is it weird getting naked on screen?" Pania asks. She takes a sip of the tea she brewed while chatting to me on Skype.

"Someone has to see all the work I've put into myself." I grin. "It's not my favorite thing to do, but it's okay. Gabby's pretty relaxed about it, which helps."

Pania screws up her nose. "I don't know if I want to see this when the movie comes out. It's weird knowing both of you."

"No excuses. You have to see this. It's going to be amazing."

I jump when someone taps on my trailer door. "I've got to go. Talk to you later?"

She claps. "Have fun."

"That's so not appropriate."

She grins as I terminate the call. I hadn't planned to call her, but when I'm tense, her down-to-earth manner calms me. It's impossible to be egotistical around her, and for the first time in a long time, I'm able to relax and just be myself.

I make my way out of my trailer and toward the set.

Gabby Reynolds is easily one of the most beautiful women in Hollywood, and she's standing in front of me in a bathrobe, ready and waiting for our big sex scene in the movie.

These scenes always make me nervous, but I've spent hours working out to get my physique as toned as possible. Especially when it comes to women like Gabby who are just spectacular.

She smiles. "Ready?"

"No. Never. But I guess we get this done?"

She laughs. "These aren't my favourite scenes either, but I love the way it works in with the story. And I guess I'm lucky enough to have one scene with you and another with Josh. I'm going to get so many bitchy comments on my social media because of it."

I raise my eyebrows. "You don't mind that?"

"I think it's hilarious. I know how lucky I am to work with amazing actors such as yourselves. And I'm really honoured that you two thought of me when it came to casting this role. I guess I met the Delaney seal of approval."

At that I roar with laughter. "I think she really just loved the idea of shopping with Antonio while we worked."

"That'd be right." She rolls her eyes. "Our credit card bill since we started this movie is sucking up the money you've paid me to be here."

I swallow hard. At the mention of his name, her whole face lights up. I want that. I've spent so long avoiding commitment, but I want someone who I'll make shine like that. Not because of anything else but her loving me.

And all I can think about is kissing Pania.

Now is not the time to think about that.

We've practiced this scene fully-clothed all week with the help of the intimacy choreographer we hired. She's a genius. Gabby and I are ready to do this and are completely comfortable with each other and the scene.

I've done these scenes before, and I don't know if it's because it's our movie, but I'm particularly proud of this. Josh's character is on deployment, and I'm his best friend who crosses a line with his wife. There's been so much lead up to this, and this is the only time our characters have sex, so getting it right is really important to all of us.

Once we're on set, I slip off my robe and climb into the bed. I'm in my boxers, and Gabby's wearing a pair of leggings, but there's also additional padding to make us both comfortable. There's enough skin revealed to make it sexy, and even though we both hope there are no slip ups, any clothing revealed will be removed in post-production.

Gabby's the one with the most on show. She's topless, and there's a point where I touch her breasts. But it's not as explicit as some scenes I've shot, and Gabby's not shy, which is a huge advantage. Although, if she had been, we would have made the changes to make her comfortable. This was her suggestion.

She straddles my hips and looks down at me. I keep eye contact because the last thing we both need is for our performance to cross into real life.

"Ready?" she asks.

"As I'll ever be."

We start when the director tells us to. Gabby leans over to kiss me, and once that's done, she pushes back up and starts moving against me.

I close my eyes.

We follow the directions, but instead of blanking like I usually do, all I can picture is Pania.

I'm not sure if it's because Gabby's grinding against me, but that can't be helping. I'm not even sure what Pania looks like naked. I do not want my mind to wander, but ...

Gabby leans over to kiss me. Again, it's all scripted, but my eyes are closed ,and all I smell is the vanilla scent that Pania seems to always smell of.

What would she be like in bed? Pania astride me, my cock deep inside her, her ample breasts swinging as she ...

My eyes fly open.

Gabby's gaze is fixed on mine, and she never falters.

"James," she whispers. "We can't do this again."

I swallow hard. "We should never have done this in the first place."

Those moments give me enough time to recover my thoughts, and she laughs as I flip her onto her back. I drop down the bed a little so my hips are rutting against her instead of my groin.

Her eyes search mine. There are so many layers between us, surely she can't feel my erection. *Please don't let her know.*

Shit.

I'm going to have to apologise just in case.

"Cut," the director yells.

I've never been so glad to hear one word in all my life. One of the assistants brings me my robe and I take it, wrapping it around my body as I climb out of bed. Gabby takes her robe and follows suit, smiling as she stands beside me.

"Great work, you two." The director, Daniel Harmer, smiles as he approaches us. "That was just fantastic. All in one take, too."

Gabby laughs. "I think we just wanted to get it over with."

He fixes his gaze on me. "Whatever you were thinking about when your eyes were closed, it was perfect."

I'm simultaneously proud and embarrassed.

"Just thinking about how good I wanted the scene to be."

Liar.

"Well, it was great. That's it for the day, folks."

"Thanks, Daniel."

Gabby wraps her robe, tighter, around herself as we watch him walk away.

I wait until he's nearly out of sight before saying, "Gabby, I am so, so sorry."

She turns and smiles, but her brows are knitted together as she dips her head, closer to me. "It's fine."

"No, it's not." I look around to see if anyone can hear us. "I'm not that guy. I don't do that." I walk away before she can say anything else.

I'm so disappointed in my own behaviour. Nothing like this has ever happened to me. Sure, I've dated a lot of women, but I've never let my work life and my personal life intersect like that.

Ignoring anyone else, I head into my trailer and close the door.

My heart races. I've never been this rattled.

I need to pull myself together.

I need to apologise to Gabby again.

What the hell am I doing?

Pania has me all tied up in knots and I barely know the woman. Maybe it's because she's so down to earth and would never let my ego get away from me. Lord knows I've let that happen often enough.

I sit down and rub my face with my hands.

Being in here is stifling.

There's no more filming today, so I get up and grab a cold can of Coke from the fridge. Taking a sip, I open the trailer door.

Sitting on the doorstep, my shoulders slump as I cool down and relax.

"Reece? Are you okay?"

Gabby's still in her bathrobe, but now she's wearing a shirt underneath it. I feel self-conscious sitting in my boxers and robe, but I don't move.

She sits on the step beside me.

I drain the can, crushing it and throwing it at a nearby bin. "No."

"You heard Daniel. That scene was great. We don't have another one like it."

"Thank God." I slam my head back on my trailer door. "I'm really, really sorry. I don't know what came over me."

She swipes at the air. "Don't worry about it. It's not the first time that's happened, and it won't be the last. There was so much padding between us, the only reason I knew was the look on your face."

"It's just so unprofessional. I've never had that happen before. It wasn't you. I swear."

Gabby laughs. "Well, that's good for a girl's ego."

"That's not what I meant." I rub my forehead with my palm.

"I'm teasing. I'm guessing whoever you were picturing was what caused it."

I frown. "How did you—"

"We rehearsed that scene. Your eyes were open in rehearsal. Once you closed them …" She cocks her head. "I know it wasn't me, but you were thinking of someone."

I look away. Gabby is close with Delaney too. I'm not sure I know her well enough to spill my secrets to her.

I turn back toward her. "Can I ask you something?"

"Anything." The corners of her mouth curve up a little in a curious smile.

"How did you know Antonio was the one?"

Her whole face lights up, her blue eyes twinkling. "He was just right. I don't know how to describe it."

"How did you work it out?"

She places her hand over mine. "We just worked. We talked, we laughed, we were just the perfect fit together." Her cheeks grow pink. "That was before the sex."

I laugh. "I don't want to know."

Gabby smiles again. "The point is that while we were definitely attracted from the first day, it didn't take long for both of us to just know. I can be myself with him, and we can sit and not talk and it's just as comfortable when we do." She cocks her head. "Why do you ask? Is there someone special?"

"I've just been thinking a lot since Josh's wedding …"

She blinks rapidly. "Don't tell me it's Delaney. He'd kill you."

I shake my head. That's the last thing I need her to think. "Oh, I love her, but not like that. It's one of her friends."

She slowly nods. "The one I met at the wedding? I'm sorry, I can't remember her name. Tania?"

"Pania."

"That's the one." She seems to study my expression. "I didn't meet her for long, but she seemed nice."

"She's fiery, and smart, and not like any woman I've ever been with." I gape. "Not that I mean the women I've been with aren't smart. Or fiery."

Gabby chuckles. "I understand."

"When I'm with her, I can't think straight. That's so not me with women."

"So I hear."

I raise my eyebrows. "What's that supposed to mean?"

She leans back on the step. "It means you have quite the reputation when it comes to women."

Running my fingers through my hair, I sigh. "I'm sure I do."

"I'm not judging you. I had my fair share of men before I found Antonio. You've got to try before you buy." Her lips quirk up, and I laugh. "I don't know you that well, Reece, but you seem like a decent guy to me."

"I try. You know? I'm not sure if I succeed all of the time, but I try."

"That's all anyone can ever do." She shrugs.

I look down at my feet. "Can you not mention any of this to Josh? I don't want it getting back to Delaney because she'll make way more out of it than it is right now. At least, until I work things out in my head."

Gabby nods. "Of course. If there's anything else I can help with, just let me know. Talk to Antonio if you need to."

"Thanks, Gabby." I pause. "And I'm sorry about … you know."

"Don't worry about it. At least you had the decency to apologise."

I stare at her. "You mean other actors don't?"

"I'm never sure whether it's rudeness or they're embarrassed. Either way, you did good. And that scene will be smoking." Gabby leans over and kisses me on the cheek. "I've got to run, but don't be too hard on yourself. And take your time working out how you feel. If she feels the same way, she'll wait."

She grips my shoulder as she pushes herself to her feet, and walks away in the direction of her own trailer, leaving me with my thoughts.

I need to prove to myself that I'm good enough for Pania. She deserves better than the man I've been in the past.

He's just not good enough for her, but I can be.

16

PANIA

Sam's mumbling is driving me nuts. The last thing I need is more of Judith's negative attention, so I put my head down and do my best to ignore whatever Sam's talking about beside me.

"Reece Evans and Gabby Reynolds, huh? Funny. I thought she was madly in love with that other guy and probably getting married."

Wait. What?

I turn to her. "What are you talking about?"

"Check this out." She shoves a magazine under my nose.

Of course there are photos.

The two of them, sitting in their bathrobes on the steps of some trailer, hand in hand. And there's even a photo of her kissing his cheek.

Delaney deals with this kind of stuff all the time, and I have no idea how she does it. I know for myself how connected Gabby and Antonio are—I've seen it with my own eyes.

It was only a few months ago that I saw it, but I guess a lot can change in a short time.

I hate this doubt.

I hate that this hurts even though Reece and I are just friends.

We're just friends. It doesn't matter how much he flirts, or how he tries Skyping me at three in the morning when he screws the time up. I'm not the type for him to be interested in, not compared to someone like Gabby Reynolds.

The woman's a goddess.

I hate the way this makes me feel. I've never been a woman who compared myself to other women. I always thought my close friendship with Delaney was one of the reasons that just didn't happen. We spent our whole lives building each other up and supporting one another.

Sometimes I'm hard on myself, but I'm not competing with anyone. Except now I'm suddenly doubting myself.

Where I have romantic thoughts about Reece, what would he ever see in me when Gabby's right there?

"Pania. Are you okay?" Sam nudges my arm.

I blink a bunch of times to snap myself out of my thoughts. "I'm fine. I'd be really surprised if this is true. She and Antonio were all over each other at Delaney's wedding."

"Ladies, how are those designs coming along?"

Judith's voice penetrates my brain. I look up to see her walking toward us. We're designing gowns for our end of term projects. Everything counts from the design to choosing the right fabrics. It's been easy to be inspired—I just think of what would look good on the red carpet for Delaney.

"Sam's just showing me a dress. I've been telling her she's more than talented to make something similar."

She smiles. "I agree. I'm also interested to see what you come up with, given the fuss over the wedding dress you created. The fabric has arrived for your projects. So, go and take a look, and choose wisely. Good luck."

It's the first time I've seen Judith smile in a while. I'm never sure whether to trust it when she does. Although, I guess this is the project where some of our work goes on display in her retail store and she can show off her student's progress.

As much as I don't like her, I want one of those spots.

Sam grabs my arm. "Come on, let's get in now."

It's all a bit crazy. Everyone has such different ideas, but Judith has given us some general guidelines and there's a generous selection.

I gasp at the first things I lay eyes on. It's a soft, royal blue crepe fabric, and there's also a roll of a similar colour tulle with tiny pearls embedded in it. It's the sort of thing I could make an evening gown for Delaney in, but in her absence, I'll make one that fits me.

Smiling to myself, I grab the rolls and make my way back to my desk.

"You've made your decision already?" Judith asks.

I smile. "They're all so beautiful, but it was an easy choice. I'm already planning what I want to do."

Her smile is uneasy. It's going to take a lot to get past her defences, but all I can do is keep on working and hope that my work speaks for itself.

By the end of the day, I have my design done and have started working on my pattern. It's been a productive day, and I feel confident for the first time in a while.

Before I can go home, though, I still have to go to my part-time job. My student allowance covers my rent—just—but I work a few hours most evenings doing office cleaning to pay for all my incidental costs.

Things are tight, but manageable.

When Delaney sold the diner, she made sure I got a share of the proceeds, even though it was the inheritance from her grandmother which enabled her to buy it in the first place. That's my nest egg in case things go bad. I haven't had to touch it yet, but there have been times when I've come close.

It might as well be an eight-hour shift, I'm so tired. I love my study, but keeping under Judith's radar while still learning what I can is exhausting.

By the time I've vacuumed and wiped down the kitchen, it's nearly eight and time to go home. I miss my old life. The diner wasn't easy work either, but once we had things up and running, it just happened. It wasn't stressful, and Delaney and I had fun.

This isn't fun.

I knew it would be hard, and I'm loving the learning that I'm doing. And one day, I'll turn it into something more. I just have to be patient.

After my drive home, I throw myself on my bed and scream into the duvet. Another couple of days, and the term will end. I'll have two weeks to take a break, though I don't think I'll go anywhere, as travelling costs money I don't have.

My phone vibrates, and I open one eye to look at the incoming message.

Reece: *Are you home? Want to talk?*

No matter how tired I am, there's no way I'm passing this up. It gives me a chance to ask him about the photos. I'm sure I can just slide that into the conversation.

I roll onto my back.

Me: *Sure.*

My phone lights up, and I'm glad he's voice calling and not using video. I must look like shit.

"Hey." I close my eyes, cradling my phone to my ear.

"Hey." The deep rumble of his voice comes down the line. I'll never get over that initial rush when we talk. Even after the past few months of us talking, there are times when I still can't quite believe my life and that I'm talking to *the* Reece Evans.

Not that I'd ever tell him that. His ego's big enough as it is.

"What are you up to?" I ask.

"We have a break from filming for a few days, and I've had a few drinks. I was just lying here and thinking I hadn't talked to you in a while."

I can't help but smile. "We spoke about three days ago."

"Did we? It feels like a lot longer."

My mouth's suddenly dry, and I lick my lips. "Wait. Is this your flirty shit? Don't you try this on me."

Reece laughs. "I love it when you tell me off."

"I'll have to tell you off more often."

The duvet is soft, and lying here with my eyes closed, it's easy to drop off as he talks. I love the sound of Reece's voice, the way that soft southern drawl relaxes me, and I let out a contented sigh.

"You okay?" he asks.

I force my eyes open. "Just a little tired. Why?"

"I seem to be talking while you say nothing. Which I'm fine with, but it's not like you."

I don't want to ask, but I've also never backed down from anything in my life.

"One of the women in my class had a magazine with photos of you in it. You and Gabby Reynolds. I just thought it was weird you hadn't said anything."

He's silent for a moment. "I didn't have anything to say. What was in the photos?"

"You and her sitting on a step holding hands. She kissed you."

He's quiet again, and my chest tightens as irritation builds.

"Are you jealous?"

Yes.

"No. I just thought that with us being friends, you might tell me if something was going on. I'm not sure any girlfriend would be keen on you calling me so often."

He laughs. "You are *so* salty."

"No, I just thought that we were friends. I'm sure I'd tell you if I was dating someone."

This time, the laughter stops.

The silence is unexpected.

"Are you?"

"Am I what?" Now I'm confused.

"Are you dating anyone?" His tone is weird as his voice sounds shaky. What's with that?

"No. But how did you just turn this around on *me*?"

He blows out a long breath. "There's nothing between Gabby and

I. She's still head over heels with Antonio. She did sit with me one day a couple of weeks ago when I had an issue and gave me some advice. That's the only time I can think of when we sat together like that."

My heart thuds. "Okay."

"Believe me?"

I swallow down a sigh. "I've seen Gabby with Antonio. My first thought was that I didn't think they'd split."

"Those two are for life. Just like Josh and Delaney." His tone softens, as if he's reassuring me.

"That's what I thought."

"How's class?"

I let out a growl and then laugh. "You know. Same old. I'm learning a lot, but the tutor isn't the person I thought she was."

He says nothing at first. I never told him about the way Judith reacted when I came home—I told no one. I thought it would just cause drama when all I want to do is forget about it and get on with proving myself.

"What do you mean?" he asks.

"Nothing. I just think you should never meet your heroes."

He chuckles. "You met me, and I didn't let you down."

I facepalm. "You clown."

My phone buzzes.

Delaney: *Skype*?

I roll over. The laptop's on the bed beside me, and I open the screen.

It only takes a moment before Skype tells me there's an incoming call.

"Delaney's calling. I've gotta go."

He laughs. "Want me to tell her you're busy."

"No." I laugh. "It's still weird you're in her house."

"I'm quite enjoying it. I'll let you go and talk to Delaney. Catch up some other time?"

I nod. "Sounds great."

"Goodnight, Pania."

"Goodnight."

With our call disconnected, I grab a hair tie and pull my hair into a ponytail. I need a moment to gather my thoughts. As far as I know, Delaney doesn't know Reece and I have kept in touch. I don't want to keep anything from her, but at the same time I don't want her thinking it's a bigger deal than it actually is.

Especially when I don't really understand it.

I prop myself up on one arm and answer the call.

"That took ages. I nearly gave up. What are you up to?" She's sitting on her bed with a bag of potato chips beside her. *That's my girl.*

"Not much. I'll just grab some chips from the cupboard and join you."

So many times we used to talk over the phone, even when we lived in the same town, sitting in front of our respective televisions and stuffing our faces with potato chips. It's nice that, sometimes, things are the same.

I walk into the kitchen, collecting the bag before returning to the bed. Tradition dictates that I'd be in my pyjamas for this, but instead, I just drop my jeans to the floor and crawl into bed where I perform the manoeuvre to remove my bra from under my T-shirt.

And then I let out a long breath.

"Better?" Delaney laughs as I fluff up the pillow and lean back.

"Much. How are things with you?"

She smiles. "Good. Josh is out tonight at some event, but I had a headache so I stayed home."

I frown. "That's not like you. Are you feeling better?"

"After some good painkillers and a ton of water, heaps better. And then I was thinking about how much I missed you, so here I am."

"I'm always happy to hear from you. How are things other than you feeling awful?"

Her contented sigh tells me everything I need to know. "So good. Josh has an idea for another movie, so he won't be leaving LA any time soon. I know we have a plan for if he has to travel, but I really didn't want to."

I grin. "He'll always put you first. You know that."

Delaney smiles. "Josh even offered to stay home with me tonight, but now he's got this production company going and they're making the movie, I think networking is more important than ever for him." She rolls her eyes. "Reece didn't go, but he waited until Josh left for the evening to show up."

I laugh. "Typical."

"He's actually been pretty responsible lately. Josh has been impressed."

"Really?"

She shrugs. "Well, better than he was. He was always reliable when it came to being on set, and he works hard, but when it comes to the business side of things, he's been pretty flakey. Things seemed to change after the wedding. It's like my baby has grown up."

I pop a chip in my mouth. It'll buy me some time before I say anything else.

But I end up not having to because the one thing I can rely on Delaney to do is talk.

"And then there were these stupid photos of him and Gabby on set. Gabby was so pissed. I mean, remember when they linked her to Josh? And now Reece. It's just ridiculous."

I swallow hard. "It must really suck for her."

"Right? I mean Antonio and her are joined at the hip most of the time." As if her and Josh aren't the same. "But, oh my God, Pania. The sex scene in the movie. Josh showed me and it is hot. Reece and Gabby are on fire on screen together. I'm not sure how they do it."

I eat another chip in an attempt not to think about *that*. Even on screen, seeing Reece with Gabby might just break my heart now. I'm a long way from where I was a few months ago when I watched the movie of his on the plane. I haven't seen one since.

"Oh, and Gabby's tits are to die for."

The chip goes down the wrong way, and I let out a choked cough, patting my chest as I try and recover from the chip and Delaney's words.

"I told Josh if I ever got plastic surgery, I'd get my boobs redone to look like Gabby's, and he took me seriously. He was all—"

"Delaney." I can't breathe for laughing.

Her eyebrows knit and she deepens her voice. "Delaney. You don't need new tits. I love yours the way they are."

Her impression of her husband is so accurate, all it does is make me laugh harder. "Of course he's going to say that. He loves you."

"And then of course Reece put his two cents worth in and told me it was a great idea. That just set Josh off all over again." She leans back on her pillows, tears in her eyes as she laughs as hard as I am.

"You do such a great impression of Josh."

Delaney's smile's as wide as I've ever seen it. "You should hear Melly. Her accent hasn't changed, but she's learned to imitate her father and it's so funny. I'll call earlier next time so you can hear it."

"I'd love that." I rub my neck. "I miss you guys."

"We all miss you. It's like I've lost a limb without you here." She wells up, and I know how deep Delaney feels things. She's always been the Robin to my Batman.

"It's weird not being around you. I'm just glad we have Skype, and one day I'll come and visit."

"I'm hoping once this movie's done, we can come for a holiday. We'll go to the house down south, but there's no way I won't be seeing you."

"I'd like that." I smile.

"Me too." She smacks her lips together. "Want to watch some TV together?"

"I'd love to."

I grab the remote and turn on the television before snuggling back against my pillows. We used to do this over the phone, but now it's a comfort to have my bestie on the other end of our Skype call while we kick back.

But my mind is not on whatever's on the television. Without even meaning to, Delaney just confirmed that Reece isn't with Gabby in any way. And it shouldn't, but it makes my heart sing.

Maybe I'm a fool to think he'd want more than friendship from me. When we kissed, we'd just spent two weeks in each other's company, almost exclusively for the first week. It was a different world to the one I usually live in.

My heart wants more.

My head tells me it meant nothing.

But that little bit of information about him gives me hope. Even if it shouldn't.

17

REECE

I don't know why I still come here.

I've kept up the tradition every year since my grandmother died. I'm not even really that sure why I never sold the house, but it's the last home I had before I moved to LA for my acting classes and career.

Tucked away in the Mariposa County hills in Northern California is the house that's been the closest thing to home I ever had—until I found my Hawaiian getaway.

I open the door and take a deep breath. There's a note on the kitchen counter, and I pick it up and smile.

Reece,

Mac and cheese is in the fridge as usual. Call us if you need anything.

Merry Christmas,

Marcy and Joel

WHILE I ONLY VISIT OVER Christmas, the rest of the year the property is maintained by Joel and Marcy Jackson, who live down in the township. Just like every other year, Marcy's made sure I have plenty of supplies to get through my time here.

And every year she leaves a huge dish of mac and cheese for me. There's no point in cooking much for Christmas when it's just me, and this will last me the next couple of days.

Opening the fridge makes me think of Delaney.

"What are you doing for Christmas?" she asks.

Josh grips my shoulder. "Reece always travels to see his parents for Christmas."

Her mouth falls open. "Oh, of course. I didn't think. When are we going to get to meet your parents?"

I swallow hard. "I'm pretty protective of them."

"I've never met them. One day ..." Josh drops his hand. "We're going away for Christmas."

I look between him and Delaney. "Where are you going?"

"New Zealand." Delaney smiles. "We're going to spend some time at our house there. You're welcome to join us."

It's tempting. So tempting. For the first time ever, I'm torn. They'll see Pania, and I want to see her. But I have an annual commitment to meet. I made a promise a few years ago that's important for me to keep.

"Maybe another time." It pains me to say it, but I have somewhere else I need to be—maybe someday I'll let my friends in on it, but I'm not ready for that yet.

I scoop a generous portion of food into a bowl and heat it in the microwave.

Nothing's changed in this house since my grandmother died—I prefer it that way. The multi-coloured crocheted blanket still hangs over the back of the couch, and when I'm here, I sleep in my old single-bed room.

Flicking on the television to channel surf, I stop on a Christmas movie with Jessie in it. Despite everything, I smile and settle back into my seat, downing the mac and cheese with a cold beer and watching the movie until I drift off to sleep in the recliner.

It's where I remain until Christmas morning when I wake and adjust the crook in my neck from sleeping at an awkward angle.

A hot shower and a change of clothes makes my aches go away, and then I grab the bouquet of roses I brought with me and head out to the car.

I drive toward the township and park outside the church. It's not a long walk from the sidewalk to the cemetery where my grandmother is buried.

Before she died, I made her a promise to come here and visit. She loved Christmas, and she was the one person in my life who always made sure I was spoiled on the day. This is my tradition—this is the most important thing I do today.

Her gravestone is immaculate. I only visit once a year, so Marcy comes down and takes care of this too. The marble gleams in the sunshine.

"Hey, Grandma." I crouch in front of the grave and place the flowers on the ground. "I'm here again, just like I promised." I swallow hard. "You'd be proud of me, though. I've settled down this year. Not with anyone yet, but there is someone special." I chuckle. "I've become more responsible. I know ... So not like the old Reece." I take a deep breath. "And I like it. I think I've been a lot like you and never wanted to stay still. But I'm finding me and realising how good it is to settle down. You'd like Pania, Grandma." I grin. "You'd love Delaney, too, and Amelia. I wish you were here to meet all of them." I press a kiss to my index finger and touch her name. "Love you. And I miss you so much. See you next year."

Standing, I tighten my coat around me and take one last look before I head back to the warm car to drive home.

Home.

I've talked about buying a house this year, but instead I've spent more time living at Josh's than anywhere else. The nomadic lifestyle

I've lead the past few years has been forgotten with Josh and I going into business together in LA.

I thought it would be a harder adjustment to make, but it really hasn't.

For the rest of the day, I watch television and graze on the mac and cheese. This is the one day I give myself to forget about everything else and just relax. Even when I'm not working, I've usually been on the go, but today I'm a vegetable on the couch.

It's so quiet, and by the evening, I drift off again, warm and comfortable.

My phone rings, and I startle, my heart racing at the unexpected call. No one knows I come here. And while I've had a heap of texts to say Merry Christmas, I don't usually get calls.

I pick up the phone and smile.

"Pania." My heart swells that she called me today of all days.

"I just wanted to wish you a Merry Christmas." Chatter's in the background of her call. It's a stark contrast to the quiet that surrounds me.

"Merry Christmas to you too." I grin. "Sounds busy where you are."

"Mum's house is full of family. There's a big tent in the backyard, but a lot of them are still in the house."

"Pania. Where are the clean glasses?" A man's voice booms through the phone, and Pania lets out a sigh. Jealousy ripples through me. It's ridiculous. It'll be a member of her family and not a boyfriend. Won't it?

"Look in the dishwasher if there aren't any in the cupboard." There's a pause. "I'm not your mother. Work it out for yourself. Maybe you should stack the dishwasher if you can't find any clean ones."

I swallow down a laugh.

"Sorry. My cousin is living with my mum at the moment and she dotes on him. He forgets how to take care of himself." She huffs. "Anyway, I thought you might want to watch some TV with me."

"Uhh."

"Delaney and I do it all the time. We'll both pick something to watch and then just talk to each other when we feel like talking."

I chuckle.

"If you don't want it, that's fine. I just thought—"

"I'd love it. What are we watching?"

She hesitates, and when she speaks her words are quiet. "Grey's Anatomy is our favourite show."

I fist my free hand and wave it in the air in excitement. "You're letting me in on your favourite show?" I frown. "Wait. Why aren't you doing this with Delaney?"

"She's having Christmas with her family. I mean, I am too but the house is full and I could do with some peace and quiet with a friend." She clears her throat. "I'm sorry, I should ask how your Christmas is going. Delaney said you're spending time with family?"

I swallow hard. "Uhh that's right. Okay. So, how do we do this?"

A door clicks closed and the background noise disappears at Pania's end. "I'm just going to grab my laptop and get comfortable. Oh, and I've got a bag of potato chips. Have you got snacks?"

I bite my bottom lip. "I can find something. How about I get ready and call you back so this doesn't cost you anything?"

"That'd be great. It'll give me a chance to get into my pyjamas."

I close my eyes. Holy shit. I really don't need an image of Pania in bed while we watch TV together. But I guess it's way too late for that.

"Sounds good," I croak. "Call you back in a few."

After retrieving a bag of potato chips from a kitchen cupboard, I walk to the bedroom and strip out of my clothes, pulling on a pair of grey sweatpants before climbing into bed. The one thing I did change about this place was putting in a new television a couple of years ago so I could watch TV in bed. Although, I've barely used it—the couch or the recliner have been the places I've fallen asleep.

I check my phone to find what streaming service Grey's Anatomy is on. And once I've confirmed I can watch it, I dial Pania back.

"Ready?" she asks.

"Sure. What do we do?"

"Just watch and keep each other company. Do you want to go with a new episode, or ...?"

"Should I start from the beginning?"

She laughs softly. "We can do. It'll mean fewer questions."

"Then let's do that."

I have no idea about this TV show, but I enjoy knowing Pania's on the other end of the line, and even though I can't remember falling asleep during the third episode, I think it's the best Christmas I've had in years.

18

REECE

Months later

I've never been to the Oscars before—let alone being nominated for an award. Tonight is the most special night of my career.

For the first time in a long time, I'm at my apartment. I wanted some time out to think about tonight and what it means. I've worked my ass off to sort my life out, and make myself feel worthy of the one woman I want to be more than just a quick fling.

The plan tonight is for me to go to Josh's place and we'll all travel together from there.

That's not going to work. I get as far as putting on my tux and Skyping Pania to try and kill my nerves.

"Hey!" Pania waves and bites her lip. It's glossy and plump, sheened in a gloss she doesn't normally wear. I like it. It suits her.

I wave back.

She points at the screen. "Look at you all dressed up. Are you going somewhere?"

I roll my eyes. "You know it. Don't tell me you didn't make Delaney's dress for tonight."

"I did!" Pania places her elbows on her table and rests her chin on her linked fingers. "It got there just in time. She sent me photos tonight. I can't wait to see her on the red carpet."

"I'm sure she'll look amazing. You always do good work." I suck my top lip. "It'd be better if you lived here."

She snorts. "I still have the rest of this year with dragon lady. You know I'm determined to see that out."

"I'm always unsure if it's because you're stubborn or just want to flout it in her face when you walk straight into a big design company." I shoot her a pointed look. "Or come here and take the fashion world by storm with your own."

Pania waves my words away, but the smile on her face tells me different. There's no way she doesn't think about a time where she moves here. I know she misses Delaney and Amelia, and maybe, just maybe, there's room in there for me.

"Give it a few years, and you'll be dressing half those women on the red carpet." I wink, and she blushes. I take a look at the clock on the computer. "Give me a minute? I just need to make a call."

She nods, and I grab my phone, heading for the bedroom.

Once I'm there, I dial Josh.

"Reece? Everything okay?"

"Hey. I know I was supposed to come over to your place for us to go together, but I'm tied up with something. Meet you there?"

Josh chuckles. "What's her name?"

I glance back into the room. "I'm on a Skype call, smartass. I'll see you on the red carpet."

"Sure thing. Ready to party?"

"Always." I grin. "What about you two?"

"I'm going to try and keep Delaney off her feet as much as I can. She's had swollen ankles the past few days, and I know she's putting on a brave face. But I think we'll be good."

"This must be unreal for her."

He laughs. "It's unreal for *me*. But I want her to have the night of her life."

"You're a good husband."

"That's what she tells me. I'll let you get back to your call, and finish getting ready."

"See you later."

After the call's ended, I pause for a moment to take a breath before heading back into the living room.

"Back." I smile.

"Don't you have to go?" I check the clock. If I give myself another fifteen minutes here, I'll still be there in plenty of time. "I don't have to leave for a while. And talking to you is calming my nerves."

Pania's lips twitch. "Since when do you have nerves?"

You still have no idea.

"I know you think I'm an overly confident asshole, but underneath is a pretty sensitive guy."

She leans back in her chair, and her tongue slides across her bottom lip, making me draw in a deep breath.

"It'd be good to see more of that." That adorable dimple on her left cheek pops up as she smiles. "Show the world who you really are. And for the record, I don't think you're any kind of arsehole."

"Not arsehole. Asshole. There's a difference."

Pania clasps her hands together as she leans forward again and laughs. "What's the difference? Apart from your terrible pronunciation."

"I'll have you know I once made an entire movie with an English accent. I know my arseholes from my assholes."

She flicks her long hair back, amusement all over her face. "I remember that movie. Your accent wasn't that great."

"Okay. Now I'm offended and I'm hanging up the call."

She does that thing with her tongue again, and I know it's an empty threat. I don't want to disconnect. If tonight wasn't so important, I'd sit here and talk to her till I fall asleep.

"I really love our friendship, Pania. I hope you know that."

She grins from ear to ear. "Me too. You're a good guy, Reece. Better than I think you realise."

"I'm glad you think so."

"Good luck." She grimaces. "Is it bad luck to wish you good luck?"

I fiddle with my bow tie. "I don't think so. I do appreciate it."

"Knock 'em dead, Reece. I'll be watching on TV. Gotta look out for my girl."

I grin. "I'll be sure to give her a kiss from you. And a hug. And maybe another kiss."

Pania rolls her eyes. "You're such a dick. Go and have some fun."

After the call disconnects, I sit and look at the blank screen for a minute. I'm never sure how I feel when I'm not with her, but even when we're talking on the phone, Pania has this way of making me feel good.

She's got just as smart a mouth as Delaney, but that helps me keep my feet on the ground.

I used to envy Josh that he had Delaney. We used to try and keep each other from getting big-headed, but she keeps him grounded in a way no one else ever could. Pania does the same for me, although I don't even know if she realises.

Delaney's now six months pregnant, and it's brought her and Josh closer than ever. I want what they have so much I can taste it, and for the first time in my life, I can see a path forward for me.

It's been easier than I thought it would be.

For so long I was hooked on the good life, cruising with no responsibilities. Now I want more, and I'm so close to feeling good enough about myself to reach it.

I look at the clock again.

Better get this show on the road.

DELANEY GLOWS. She has this radiance about her tonight, and it's hard to look away. Josh was always my best friend, but his wife is right up there with him. Her calmness soothes my soul even when it's not aimed at me. Delaney asked Pania to attend, but it's mid-term for her. I just wish more than anything she was with us.

I'm not even sure *I* should be here.

I never thought I'd be an award-nominated actor. Sure, maybe Teen Choice or something like that, but an Academy Award?

This is an event I might never get to attend again. But then again, this is a movie unlike any I've ever made before. Sure, I messed around in the beginning, but once we started filming, we all put our heart and soul into it. I've never believed in anything so much.

"Delaney, you look amazing."

She turns and meets my gaze. "You don't scrub up too bad yourself."

I peck her on the cheek. "Excited?"

She beams. "Terrified. But I'm here, and everything seems to be going well. We've stopped about five times for Josh to be interviewed, and my ankles will be mega-swollen by the time we get inside. But it's a wonderful night. Good luck."

I adjust my bow tie. "It's crazy to think we're even nominated. You're our good luck charm."

She laughs, shaking her head. "No way. You guys just needed to get your shit together."

I squeeze her arm. "That's why I love you. You're so upfront with me."

Blushing, she drops her gaze. "Always."

"Reece."

I shift my gaze to Josh, walking toward us. He slips an arm around Delaney, and she gives him that look of absolute devotion that I envy so much.

"It's good to see you, man. Let's head in," Josh says.

We get shown to our seats which are right near the front, close to the stage. Josh, Delaney, and I are at the end of the row, with Gabby and Antonio on the other side of the aisle. There are other production staff seated around us, and it feels so good to be part of a solid group that made such a wonderful movie.

We're up for a host of awards—our movie didn't just kill at the box office, but it got the critical acclaim we craved for it.

Even if we win nothing, we've achieved so much more than we ever thought possible.

My category is first up, and I feel as if I'm holding my breath while they go through the nominees.

"And the Oscar for best supporting actor goes to ..."

I clench my fists. There's no way I've got this—not with four other amazing actors who turned in brilliant performances. I'm in what's basically an indie film I made with my best friend.

"Reece Evans in *Coming Home*."

I lean back in my seat.

Beside me, Delaney lets out a yell and grabs hold of my arm. It takes a moment for my brain to register what I just heard, and I grin, leaning over to hug her.

Standing along with Delaney and Josh, I manoeuvre past her heavily pregnant bump and grip Josh's arm, pulling him into a hug.

"We did it," I whisper.

"This is just the start." He pulls back, his eyes so full of joy, and we're just at the start of the night.

On the other side of the Aisle, Gabby's clapping for me, tears glistening in her eyes. She's nominated for best supporting actress, but they're not presenting that until about halfway through the ceremony. And she deserves to win because I cry every time I watch our film. Although, that might also be because I was in the best condition I'd ever been in for our half-naked sex scene.

I head straight for her. She's the one who kills it in our scenes, and while she's up for her own award, I owe a lot to her for being such a great scene partner.

"Congratulations." Antonio slaps me on the back, and I give Gabby a quick hug before heading to the stage.

Accepting my golden statuette, I look over it in awe. "Err ..." I shake my head. "I never thought I'd ever be doing this." I run my fingers over my chin. "I was sure one of the other guys would win." There's a lot of laughter, and I focus my gaze on Josh. "From the first acting class we were in, I knew Josh Carter was special. He had this way of holding the audience in his hand, and we were immediately the best of buddies. I owe way more to that man than anyone will ever know, and, Josh, you are the person I have to thank for this. You pulled us all together, and you made this happen, and now look at us."

I shift my gaze to Gabby. "And to Gabby Reynolds for just being the best scene partner and making me look good."

She kisses her fingers and blows the kiss to me.

"I'd also like to thank the academy, and all those friends and family who have supported my career. You know who you are."

Waving the statuette in the air, I walk off the stage, my chest swelling with pride. I'd never been nominated for an Oscar before, and it took making a movie with my best bud to get this.

It's the best night of my life.

I'm GOING to get drunk. Very, very drunk.

I'm going to celebrate like I've never celebrated before and have so many regrets tomorrow.

"Give me that." Delaney grabs my statuette from me and shoves it into a bag.

"What are you doing?"

"I'm holding onto them because you're all drinking and I don't want any lost."

I grin. "You're the best."

"I know. It's why you love me." She waves me away. "Now, shoo and have some fun."

"What about you?"

She tilts her head to the side. "Josh is just securing a table." She looks down at her baby bump and runs her hand over it. "I need to get off my feet."

"Good thinking." I kiss her on the cheek. "Thank you for everything. I couldn't have done this without you and Josh."

"Bollocks." Her eyes shine.

"I've got a table," Josh says as he approaches us. "Let's go over here. Any sign of Gabby and Antonio?"

"I think they've gone to have a private party." I shrug.

He shakes his head. "Why doesn't that surprise me?"

Leading us through the crowd, Josh takes us to a table tucked in the corner and near the bathroom. For a moment, I wrinkle my nose before Delaney grabs his arm and kisses him.

"Thank you. It's perfect," she says before taking a seat.

"I thought you'd gone mad." I laugh.

"So does anyone when I say I want a table near the bathroom. But it makes it easier for Delaney, and it's worth the odd looks."

For the rest of the evening, Josh and Delaney hold court at the table. Josh watches over her like a hawk, and even though he's drinking, he keeps it to a minimum.

I'm not under any obligation to behave.

And the only thing I do is drink. I get at least two blatant propositions, and one that tries to be subtle, but I'm not about to throw nearly two years of good behaviour away. That's the life I used to lead.

Eventually, I stumble back to the table, and Delaney rolls her eyes as I sit beside her.

"I love you," I croon, leaning my head on her shoulder.

"I love you too." She leans her head against mine.

"Josh is such a lucky bastard," I slur. "I wish I had a woman like you in my life."

She chuckles. "I am in your life. Just in a purely platonic I-love-you-like-a-brother kind of way."

I raise my head. "Oh, I'm not coming onto you, Delaney. I respect you and Josh too much for that. But can we clone you?"

Delaney sighs and shakes her head. "That's a little creepy."

"Probably, but when has that ever stopped me?"

She's got that caring look on her face, where her expression's all soft and it tells me she's slipped into Mom mode. "One day you'll find the right person, Reece."

"Do you think Josh would be open to a time-share arrangement?"

"A *what*?"

"Come on, dude. Let's go home." Josh lays a hand on my arm.

"I think I might stay and have a few more drinks."

Delaney nudges my other elbow. "Come with us and I'll make mac and cheese for lunch tomorrow. You can have a whole dish for yourself."

"Really? I'd go anywhere for your mac and cheese." I smile. This is why she's perfect. She knows the way to my heart is through my stomach. So does Pania. *Pania.*

I want more than just friendship with her.

I want her.

Swallowing hard, I look at Josh. "I think I'm in love."

"Sure you are. Let's get you back to our place."

I sit between them on the limo ride home. Not that I remember much of the journey.

The cool night air bites when Josh helps me out onto the steps at the front of their house, and I'm not even sure how we make it upstairs.

Josh supports me, as I'm a bit loose on my feet. Reaching the bed, he pushes me onto it and shakes his head as I kick off my shoes and let them drop to the floor.

"We won. Come here you gorgeous hunk of a man and give me a hug." I lurch for him.

Josh laughs. "Now I know you've had too much to drink."

"Not enough if you ask me."

"Get some sleep. I'm going to go to bed with my wife. Sleep it off and she'll cook whatever you want tomorrow, I'm sure. I'm just glad you're here and safe."

I undo the top button of my shirt. "We won."

"We did. Get some sleep."

He walks to the door, flicking off the light before he walks out and closes the door behind him. I pull my phone out of my jacket pocket, then strip off the rest of my clothes, throwing them on the floor before climbing into bed and pulling the blanket over me.

I pick up the phone and squint at the bright light.

Me: *I wish you were here. We won ... everything. I fucking miss you.*

I toss the phone down beside me on the bed and close my eyes to try and stop the room from spinning. Tonight would have been so much better with Pania here. She's buried deep inside me now, and I don't know if she wants something more serious, but I know one thing for sure.

I do.

"You know, if it wasn't my house, I'd throw a bucket of water over you to wake you up." Delaney's voice breaks through my dreams, and I reluctantly open one eye.

She places a tray on the bedside cabinet, and I moan at the scent of pancakes.

"Take it easy on me. I'm delicate."

The sound of her laughter penetrates my brain. "You're hungover, that's what you are. I brought painkillers."

I open my other eye, wincing as my head thuds. "You're an angel."

The bed sinks as she sits on the edge, and I push myself up to grab the tray. Perfectly cooked pancakes are piled high on the plate, and there are side dishes of butter, syrup, and bacon. Two small pills sit beside the large mug of coffee.

"Thank you."

"You're welcome. We all had a pretty big night last night."

I blow out a breath. "It was one of the best nights of my life."

Her eyes dance. "Josh's too. I'm so proud of all of you."

I move the tray from my lap to the other side of the bed and clasp my hands above my head, stretching out.

"Can you please put your abs away?"

"Why? Do they do something for you?"

Delaney rolls her eyes. "I've got my own set out there, thanks. Yours are just distracting when I'm trying to talk."

I pull up the blanket and grin. "Sorry."

"You're trouble, Reece Evans."

"That's why you love me."

Delaney's cheeks pink up, and she meets my gaze head on. "I do love you. You were an unexpected bonus when Josh and I got back together. You're one of my best friends."

I grin. "How do I get that number one spot?"

"That's reserved for Pania." Delaney cocks her head. "But you're right up there."

Letting out an exaggerated sigh, I move the tray back to my lap. "Always second best."

"That won't always be true. You'll work yourself out one day." Delaney pushes herself to her feet and rubs her baby bump. "You're a better person than you think."

She turns and walks to the door.

"Delaney."

She pauses and looks back at me.

I swallow hard. I do love her, but not in a romantic way. In an I-always-wished-I-could-have-a-sister way.

Her brows knit. "Are you okay?"

"I just wanted to say thank you. For everything. You feed me, and you let me crash here when I need to, even though my apartment is five minutes away."

Her gentle smile warms my heart. "There will always be a bed here for you, Reece. Whenever you need it."

She winks and leaves the room, closing the door behind her.

Josh gets to wake up in the mornings with the one woman who will always be there for him. She laughs at my sometimes hare-brained ideas, but in her own gentle way, Delaney backs me, too, and I appreciate that more than I can say.

But I want that backing for myself with someone I know I can always rely on.

Pania.

Shit. I grab my phone from the bed. A new message notification sits on my screen, and I close my eyes. What did I send her?

I take a peek at the screen.

Pania: *Have you been drinking? Miss you too, doofus. Congratulations.*

I grin.

She misses me.

My head's still pounding, but it doesn't matter. Pania misses me. I'm such a pussy when it comes to her. What I should do is just tell her how I'm feeling, but I'm scared she'll laugh.

Tomorrow, I start work on another movie—there's no downtime for me for the next three months. When that's done, I'm due a break.

And then I can plan for my future.

19

REECE

Three months after our Oscar win, and I'm about to wrap another movie. Being here is hard. What I want to do is take off to New Zealand and put it all on the line for Pania. But I'm also well aware of all my flaws. Including the fact that I've never put down roots, and she's the kind of woman who would want that.

I need to know I can do it before I make a move.

But that doesn't mean I can't still pursue whatever this is between us.

Me: *Still miss me?*

Pania: *Are you still going on about that?*

"Reece." I look up into Jessie's green eyes. She's got a small part in this movie, and has been driving me nuts wanting me to somehow influence the director and make it bigger.

"I'm sorry. What?"

"I asked if you wanted to sneak off to your trailer. I'm only here for a couple of days and I could do with getting laid."

I shake my head. "Sorry, Jess. I'm not in the mood."

One of her perfectly curved eyebrows rises. "Since when?"

It's been about three years since we last hooked up. I hadn't thought of just how long it had been until this moment. And I smile to myself at the pride I feel in not hooking up with anyone in that time.

It's not even been as difficult as I once thought to focus on myself for a change.

"Reece?"

I blink and refocus. "Since I decided to take myself more seriously. I'm not screwing around anymore."

She scowls. "Let me guess. That's Josh's wife's influence."

"Her name is Delaney."

Jessie flicks an auburn curl over her shoulder. "Whatever."

"No, not whatever. She's a good friend, and I'm not going to let you disrespect her."

Her eyes widen. "But it's okay for her to disrespect me?"

"When did she ever disrespect you, Jessie?" I stand and turn to face her. "The only thing she ever did wrong in your eyes was exist. Josh loves her more than anyone or anything else on this planet. And you know what? She's such a good person and doesn't deserve your bitchiness."

Jessie clamps her lips together and looks away. "So, she's got you too."

I run my fingers through my hair in frustration. "She's a good friend, and her and Josh inspire me to want to be a better person. I owe it to myself."

"And being a better person means we don't hook up?"

"I'm not hooking up with anyone."

She drops her gaze, and I take her hands in mine. "You know we make better friends than anything else. And it's still not me you really want."

Jessie takes a deep breath. "I just never got why he didn't see me."

I drop her hands and reach for her chin, raising her gaze to mine. "Someday you'll find someone who does see you. You're so much more than you think you are. I always knew that."

She bats my hand away, a wry smile on her lips. "Stop it."

"You're a good person, Jess. You just let that inner bitch out way too often."

Jessie laughs and pushes herself to her feet. "Probably. Want to go and get coffee?"

"That I can do."

I tuck my phone into my jacket pocket and follow her, away from the trailers and across the set to the catering trucks.

Picnic tables are laid out for people to eat at, and we find an empty one with our coffees in hand.

Jess traces patterns on her cup and sips at it occasionally. I know her well enough to know what's still on her mind.

"You could just bite the bullet and apologise, then this stops being an issue. They've been married for two years." I take a sip of my coffee.

She stares at her cup. "I know. Every time I think about doing it, I just feel embarrassed about the way I behaved."

"You're still bitching about Delaney, though."

She fixes her green eyes on me. "It makes me feel better about what I did."

Reaching across the table, I put my hand on hers. "Seriously, spend some time focusing on yourself instead of other people. You'll be happier for it."

Jessie wrinkles her nose. "Is this the new Reece philosophy?"

"I feel settled. Like I finally really know what I want from life, and I just have to work out how to get it. Instead of that haphazard mess that has been my life so far."

Her brows knit. "Who are you and what have you done with Reece?"

I laugh. "You should try it. My life's so much better for it."

She squints as if examining me closer. "I'm serious. You always seemed happy with your life."

"I was." I take another drink of coffee—longer this time to think first before I say it. "I didn't realise how empty it was. Travelling from place to place, never putting down any roots. I'm still working out who I am, but I'm much happier for it."

A couple of extras greet us as they sit at the other end of the bench.

"We should go for a walk to finish this off," Jess says.

"I *was* on my way to my trailer before you derailed me. I have scenes to shoot later today."

"I'll escort you back." The smug smile on her face says it all. She might not have a big part in this movie, but she's going to make sure people are aware she's good friends with one of the leads. I know her a little *too* well.

I suppress an eyeroll and stand, stepping out of the seat and waiting for her to pull up to my side.

We sip our coffee as we make our way toward the trailers, and when we reach my door, I drop my cup into the bin beside the trailer. Jessie follows suit.

"Delivered to your door."

"Thank you."

She sucks on her bottom lip. "I'll think about what you've said. I've been trying really hard not to obsess over everything, but maybe I need to find a hobby."

"Or get a pet."

She laughs. "Maybe. Thanks for always being here, Reece."

"You're welcome." I tap her under the chin, then open my door. "See you later."

Once I'm in my trailer, I pull out my phone.

Me: *Yes, yes I'm still going on about you missing me. It's my favorite topic.*

Pania: *LOL I wouldn't have said I missed you if I didn't mean it.*

I trap my tongue between my teeth and grin.

Me: *I'm glad to hear it. I'm on set today and bored.*

Pania: *You're always bored. And I'm just about to finish my break. I need to stop texting before I get in trouble. Again.*

I chuckle, and pocket my phone.

It's not just that I'm not in the mood for sex with Jessie. It's that I'm still not in the mood for anything with anyone other than Pania.

I just have to work out how to tell her.

Me: *Talk tonight?*
Pania: *I'm working tonight. Will be home after eight, my time.*
Me: *Talk to you then.*

LATER, in my apartment, I watch the clock until I see her Skype status change.

Pania: *Call me now if you're ready.*

I press call, and she accepts.

She rubs her face as the video comes up.

"Hey," I say.

"Hey. I just got home from work and I'm beat. I just want to say hello, but I need some sleep …"

She's just as beautiful as ever, but her eyes are tired. I'd be selfish to keep her up. If I made her my world, she'd never have to work again. My heart beats hard at the thought of that, but I know it'd be a tough thing to get her to accept.

"Maybe we can talk tomorrow?"

Pania sucks in her bottom lip. "I've got a date tomorrow night."

My chest aches. I should have known this would happen at some point. Hell, it could have already happened—I don't know if she tells me everything. But the fact she's telling me surely is a sign this is the first one in a while.

"Really? I thought you didn't date." I croak and then reach for my water bottle, hoping she didn't notice.

"Sam in my class wanted to set me up. I especially hate blind dates, but she's been my friend in class the past two years, and she tells me this guy is really nice." A smile graces her lips, but it doesn't reach her eyes.

My tension eases a little, even if the thought of her being out with someone else is painful.

I have to remind myself that she's not mine.

What if this guy sweeps her off her feet?

"Just be careful. Even nice guys can be trash."

Pania tilts her head forward a little. "I know. There's a reason why I don't date." Her smile widens. "You know me. I won't let myself be treated badly."

I swallow, even though there's a lump in my throat. "Good. You're a queen. Remember that."

"Sometimes a girl just needs to hear that."

After I've said goodnight to her and we disconnect the call, I sit in the dark and take deep breaths.

Shit.

20

———

PANIA

It's been more than two years since I've been on a date. Between school and working and spending my evenings talking to Reece or Delaney, I just haven't felt any inclination to pursue anything.

Not to mention my long unresolved feelings over Reece.

There's a knock on my door a few minutes before six.

"He's early. That's a good start," I murmur to myself.

After opening the door, I have to step back a little just to see the top of Devon's head, which I swear nearly collides with the ceiling lamp above my front porch.

"Hi," I say, unable to hide an awkward giggle.

Devon's deep brown eyes drink me in. Standing there in dress pants and a collared shirt, he looks like he could be a cover model.

"Pania?"

I smile. "That's me."

"You look great." He leans in and kisses my cheek.

He'd told me to dress smart casual, so I'm wearing a long black, flowing skirt and short-sleeved shirt. For the first time since Delaney's wedding, I'm wearing makeup, which is the weirdest feeling. But it's worth it for one night out.

"Thank you. I'm ready to go if you are."

He smiles. "This way."

Leading me down the driveway to what looks like a reasonably new Toyota Corolla, he opens the passenger door for me and I step in.

So far, so good. But he's not Reece.

"So, you're at tech with Sam," he says as he climbs into the driver's side.

"I sure am."

But not for lack of trying on my part, that's the last of the conversation until we arrive in the city and pull up outside the restaurant. I'm unfamiliar with it, but I've never been one to try something new.

Devon rounds the car and opens the door. I guess at least he's a gentleman even if he's impossible to converse with.

We walk into the restaurant, and while he sorts out our table, I admire my surrounds:

Circular tables with starched-white tablecloths, cloth napkins, and silverware that doesn't look like it came from the discount stores I shop from. It's a decent enough looking place.

"Right this way," a waiter says, and leads us to our table before presenting us with menus. "I'll be back shortly to take your order."

We both say, "Thank you" before Devon asks, "Anything look good?"

"Oooh, they have steamed mussels. That sounds like me."

Devon screws up his face. "I think I'll just have a steak. The food here is apparently quite good."

"I hope so." I laugh.

Once our order is taken and the drinks arrive, he takes a sip of his beer and shuffles in his seat.

"Shit," he mumbles.

I cock an eyebrow. "What's wrong?"

He looks up at me, his mouth a tight line, his expression so sheepish I can't wait to see what comes out of his mouth. "I've left my wallet at home."

Oh.

"Oh, that's a shame."

He raises his shoulders in an attempt to look, I guess, cute? But I'm no fool and there's a reason why I don't date much.

I don't say anything because there's no way I'm offering to pay for this. While I would have been happy to go halves, I should have clarified that before we came out. This is the dumbest trick this guy could have tried to play on me.

I scrunch up my napkin and place it on the table. "I just need to go to the bathroom. Be back in a tick."

Before he can respond, I stand up and walk away. There's a young woman behind the bar in the corner, so I approach her.

"Excuse me. Do you have a back door I can sneak out of?"

She snorts, clapping her hand over her mouth.

"I'm on a blind date, and the guy is a total dick."

Her lips curl. "I totally understand that. Come this way."

I glance over my shoulder. Devon's picking at his nails and looking around the room. His gaze finds mine, and I give him a quick smile before heading past the bathrooms and to a door marked exit.

"Here you go. Can you get home safe, or do you need me to call a taxi?"

I pluck my phone out of my bag and hold it up. "I'll get an Uber. Thank you so much."

She smiles. "You're welcome. We've all been there."

I step through the door and into a car park. There's plenty of street lighting, and it's not like I'm escaping into the dark. I make my way to the footpath and pull up the Uber app to request my ride.

This has to be some kind of record for me. I've escaped bad dates before, but this is the earliest I've taken off.

I wonder how long it'll take for him to realise I'm not coming back?

Swiping out of the app, I bring up my contact list and block his number. At least now he can't call me when he realises I've gone.

I'm not disappointed. It's sad, but at least I know how to take care of myself. And it's not like I knew him well enough to be heartbroken by what's happened.

I could have done without having to pay for an Uber, but I'll know better than to go on a blind date next time.

It's still early when I get home, and I tug off my clothes, slipping on my pyjama shorts and tank top before climbing onto the bed.

Opening up the computer, I ponder Skyping Delaney. But it's after eleven at night over there, and she needs all the rest she can get when the baby's due any day.

I flick off a message to Reece.

Me: *You awake?*

Reece: *Want to talk?*

Me: *I don't want to bother Delaney.*

Reece: *She went to bed early tonight. I'll Skype you.*

The call comes through on my laptop, and I take a deep breath before accepting. Reece's face fills the screen. I swallow hard. He's sitting in bed, too, with no shirt on. I can't see below his pecs, but I know what the ripples of his abs look like.

It still makes it hard to concentrate when those spring to mind.

"What's the time over there?" Reece's gaze shifts for a second. "It's still early. Didn't you have a date tonight?"

I brush an errant piece of hair off my face. "I did."

"Look at you all prettied up. Not bad." He winks, and my heart leaps. Why did I even accept the stupid date when I'm head over heels for Reece?

"So, why are you home?"

I shrug. "He was a dick."

"Good." His expression straightens as his smile disappears. "I mean, not that he was a dick to you. Good that you're home."

My eyebrows creep up as he seems to scrabble for words for a change.

"I told him I was going to the bathroom and then left through the back door."

He laughs. "What did he do? Do I have to come all the way there and kick his ass?"

I shake my head, though my heart is pounding at the thought. "We got there, ordered, and then he tells me he can't pay."

Reece's mouth falls open. "He did not."

"He did."

Reece facepalms "Man, I have done some dumb things in my life, but nothing like that."

"No, because you're actually a decent person."

He peeks out between his spread fingers. "Thanks."

I lean back on my stack of pillows. "I left through the back door and caught an Uber home. I'm just wondering now how long it took for him to work out I'd left. And whether he ended up paying for the meals or pleading poverty."

Reece chuckles. "What a dumbass he must be to think he can pull one over you."

I wriggle to get comfortable. "I thought about calling Delaney, but I know it's late over there and she'll need all the sleep she can get right now."

He nods. "Yeah, I was over there earlier but decided to come home and let them have some space. Things are pretty dire. Josh cooked dinner."

I clap my hand over my mouth. "What?"

"Delaney had a headache so she went to bed early. I told him we should get pizza or something, but he was determined to make her something to eat."

"Let me guess ... grilled cheese?"

He shoots me some side-eye. "How did you know?"

"Because it's the only thing he knows how to cook. Did he manage to make it without burning it?"

Reece laughs. "It was terrible, so I got on my phone and ordered pizza while he was distracted. Amelia loved it."

Such a big part of me wishes I was there. I was with Delaney through her first pregnancy, when her mother wouldn't stand by her. From morning sickness to holding her hand when she gave birth, I was by her side.

And Melly, even if she's not so little anymore, holds a special place in my heart. She's the reason I worked so hard with Delaney to get the diner up and running. That was for the two of them. It's why I diverted from my dream to become a cook, and I loved doing that with my best friend so much.

And now I'm following another dream but hating what I'm doing and missing them more than ever.

"Pania? Are you okay?"

I look up to see Reece's brows knitted together in concern.

"I'm fine. Just missing my girls."

"You know, any time you want to come over here, I'll make it happen."

I shake my head. "No. This time belongs to Josh. He missed it with Melly, and this has to be his and Delaney's time together."

"Doesn't mean you can't visit."

Blowing out a long breath, I take a moment to compose myself. "Maybe I will at the end of the year."

"I'll help you if you need it. Delaney would love to see you." His tone's so gentle, it almost makes me tear up. Almost.

"I miss her a lot. You know, I'm not sure what I'd do if I didn't have things like Facetime to talk to her." I swallow hard. "And having you to talk to makes things easier. I know you're watching out for her."

He smiles. "Always. I try and do the same for you too. You mean a lot to me."

"The feeling's mutual."

My heart pounds at the affection all over his face. I've seen Reece acting, and he was so annoying when we first met, but the last two years, I've seen a change in him. There's nothing in particular I can put my finger on, but he seems to have softened. We joke, but the edge has been taken off as we've eased into a good, solid friendship.

"Anyway, I should let you get some sleep. And I need to wash all this make-up off my face. It feels weird."

Reece laughs. "You look beautiful. That guy is an idiot for screwing you around."

"You always make me feel better about things."

He winks, and my heart does flips. "That's what friends are for, sweetheart. Talk to you later."

"Later, 'gator."

Reece narrows his gaze. "That's a Delaneyism."

"I borrow from her sometimes." I shrug.

He laughs. "Goodnight, Pania."

"Night, Reece."

With the call disconnected, I head into the bathroom and scrub my face clean. My stomach grumbles for some dinner, but even cooking now feels like too much effort. Instead, I grab a bag of potato chips and head to bed to indulge. It's usually at this time that I call Delaney to watch TV together, but that's a no-go. And I'm not calling Reece back for him to listen to me eat potato chips while he lies in bed with those ridiculous abdominal muscles of his.

So I lie back and imagine balancing a bag of potato chips on those abs—the best of both worlds.

My eyelids grow heavy, and what's on television doesn't even register as I drift off.

I wake up just as my phone vibrates beside me in bed.

Flicking my finger up the screen to unlock it, I grin at the screen full of messages.

Delaney: *This is it. We're on our way to the hospital*

Delaney: *Oh my God! Josh has got us lost AGAIN*

Delaney: *This is the end. I'm divorcing him*

Delaney: *We're in some street called Addison Street. I just told him I'm naming the baby Addison. LOL*

Delaney: *I'm serious about the divorce*

Clapping my hand across my mouth, I laugh so hard. This is so Delaney, and I wish more than ever that I was there.

And then I scroll to the latest message. And this time, I tear up because Delaney's sent me a photo of her, Josh, and her newborn baby. I assume she got someone else to take it because she's cradling the baby, and Josh is well in frame. And the awed look on his face makes me sigh.

This is why, even if I didn't have other commitments, I stayed away. Josh deserves this. The love is there for all to see, and I'm so happy they got their little family together. And now that family has a new member.

Another message pops up.

Delaney: *We've named her Addison. Addison Montgomery Carter. Josh has no clue about Grey's Anatomy, and I had to tell him where it came from. But he likes it.*

Me: *Congratulations, my friend. I love you guys. Let me know what Melly thinks of her little sister*

Delaney: *She's so excited. I'm looking forward to taking her home. Everything went well, except for Josh getting us lost. I'm pretty sure I'm not divorcing him now.*

I laugh out loud. That's my girl.

Me: *Love you. Call me when you're ready.*

Delaney: *Will do.*

It's mid-afternoon when Delaney's name pops up on my phone screen.

I grin as I answer. "Hey."

"Hey."

"You sound tired."

She sighs. "Very. But Josh has gone home for the night and I'm here by myself with Addison. We'll be going home tomorrow, probably."

"I'm surprised he's not there."

Delaney laughs softly. "Hospital rules. And I'm okay with it. I've got a night to myself with my beautiful baby. When I get home, Josh's parents are there, and no doubt Reece will show up, so we'll have a bit of a full house."

I suck on my bottom lip at her description of that massive house being full. She could park herself away and not see any of them if she wanted to.

"How is Josh?"

"He's over the moon. And Addison looks so much like Melly when she was born. I'm wondering now if she'll have brown eyes like Josh and Melly or if she'll take more after me."

"You two make beautiful babies, Delaney, no matter what colour eyes she has."

There's silence for a moment, and I hear a bleat in the background.

"She's already found her voice." Delaney chuckles. "Give me a second, she'll want some food. I'll put you on speaker."

There's a rustling noise in the background, and a clunk which I assume is her setting the phone down.

"Remember how hungry Melly was? Addison's even worse and she's only a few hours old."

I laugh. "I remember all the sleepless nights we did together when Melly was born."

Delaney lets out a loud sigh. "I'm not looking forward to those again. Josh is so excited about everything, though, so he'll probably be up to get her before I can."

"Make him do the work. He half made the baby."

"He'll take good care of us. Not sure about the cooking, but he can do everything else." She chuckles. "Tell me what's going on with you. It's nearly the end of term. What are you doing for the holidays?"

"Going to see Mum as usual."

"Give her my love. I'll send you a ton more photos of Addison because I know you'll both want to see them."

"Send me all of the photos."

Delaney yawns. "Excuse me. I think she's sucking all the energy out of me."

"I remember what you were like with Amelia."

"Breastfeeding is exhausting." She sighs. "Anyway, this one has fallen asleep with my boob in her mouth. I'm going to try and get some sleep for myself until she wants more food."

I laugh. "I hope you get some rest."

"Tomorrow, Josh's mum will help out. I'm so glad to have them. I miss you and your mum, though."

"We miss you too. Go get some rest."

Once the call's disconnected, I drop the phone on the table and flop onto the couch.

I couldn't be any happier for Delaney, but it leaves me feeling a little empty. I've never been a woman who thought she needed a man to complete her, and I still don't feel that way, but it would be nice to find one who would just love me as I am.

I know we're good friends now, but I still wonder if that person is Reece.

21

———————

REECE

Delaney looks up as I walk into their living room. Josh bought her a rocking chair, and she sits in the corner of the room, nursing the baby and smiling a hazy, contented smile.

"This is no excuse for you to look at my boobs," she says.

I shrug. "Would I do that to you?"

"Yes." She laughs.

"She's got you there." Josh walks into the room from the kitchen and places a mug beside Delaney's chair.

"You're so good to me."

He pecks her on the lips. "Anything to take care of my babies."

I fake a gag, and he glares at me.

"Reece." Amelia runs into the room. "Did you see the baby?"

I nod. "I did. She's beautiful. Just as beautiful as you."

She smiles as she twirls and then falls onto the couch beside me.

I hold open my arm and she snuggles into my side. Planting a kiss on the top of her head, I smile. "You're so lucky. You have a mom and dad who love you very much, and now a new baby sister who'll grow up and be able to play with you." I swallow hard.

"And Gran and Poppa. I have them too."

I nod. "Yes, you do."

"And you and Pania. I haven't seen Pania in a long time." She pouts, and my heart melts at the sight.

"You and me both. I bet you miss her."

Amelia nods. "She used to be at the diner with Mummy all the time."

"Maybe we could talk to her and see if she'd come for a visit."

Her mouth falls open. "Can we?"

"I can't see why not. I'm sure she's missing you too."

"I spoke to Pania last night," Delaney says. "It's nearly the end of term and she'll be visiting her mum. But I'm wondering if we could persuade her to come here for Christmas."

Amelia punches the air. "Please. She can read Hairy Maclary to Addison."

I look back at Addison and smile, thinking of the time I stood in the doorway and heard the whole story as told by Pania. And how much Amelia loved it.

I'm in love with Pania.

I wanted to be a man she could be proud of, and a man who would love her the rest of her life. Two years ago, I wasn't that man.

Now I am.

I want to be with her when I tell her how I feel. This isn't something I want to do over the phone or Skype or any other medium.

I need to see her.

Two days later, I'm boarding a plane to New Zealand. It's surreal. I've never done anything quite this spontaneous, and I've done a lot of dumb stuff in my life.

I lean back in the seat and close my eyes. I'm not a fan of long-haul flights, but this one I'll happily take on.

All I can do is hope that at the other end is a woman who wants me as much as I want her.

22

REECE

By the time we touch down in Auckland, my nerves are all on edge. I'm still not even sure what I'm doing despite planning this for two days. All I can think about is how Pania will react.

I've flown across the world to lay my heart on the line, and for all I know she could still reject me.

Once I've cleared customs, grabbed my bags and walked out of the airport, I pause outside to text her to find out where she is. It's early afternoon here, and I'll find a hotel for the meantime if I have to.

As soon as I turn my phone on, a dozen missed calls come up on screen.

Sara.

I bring up one of them to call her back, but she beats me to it.

"Sara—"

"Where are you?" she shrieks down the phone.

"Why?"

"You're supposed to be on the set of the Western Banks commercial."

Shit.

"I forgot. Sorry. Something important came up."

"Something or someone?"

I can't lie to her. She knows me too well.

"Someone, but—"

"Reece Evans, you are way more professional than this. Usually. How quickly can you get to the set?"

I blow out a long breath. "Well, Sara, the thing is ... I'm in New Zealand."

"You're what?" I think her anger just hit level twenty-five on a scale of one to ten. Smoke is close to pouring out of my phone.

"I'm so sorry. I came here to ..." What? Persuade Pania to run away with me? Maybe settle down. What on earth was I thinking flying halfway around the world for a woman who's never even slept with me?

"I'm waiting, Reece."

"I think I'm in love."

There's silence for what feels like forever before Sara's laughter roars down the phone. "Who are you, and what have you done with Reece?"

"You're the second person to ask me that. I'm serious."

She lets out a big sigh. "What the fuck am I supposed to tell these people? You have a contract."

Guilt floods my system. I was so preoccupied with tracking down Pania, everything else flew out the window. I'm so screwed.

"I'll tell them you're in a coma. Because you will be when I get hold of you."

I'm such a terrible client. I flirt with Sara, and I'm easily distracted on the job. She makes a lot of money out of me, but she deserves better.

"I don't know what to say, Sara. I'm so, so, sorry."

"That's the first time you've ever said that." She still sounds pissed, but her tone's a little softer.

"What do you mean?"

"You've never run off halfway around the world to screw up, but that's the first time I've got what sounds like an actual apology. You're good at running from things, Reece. Not so good at saying sorry."

I fist my free hand. Sara's hard on me because she has to be.

"I don't think you mean to be inconsiderate, and I wouldn't put up with it if you weren't Reece Evans. But you need to pull yourself together. You're not a teenage star anymore. You're a serious Oscar winning actor."

Shame takes over. If I could dig myself a hole in the ground I would. She's one hundred per cent right. I've always been good at going off on a whim, and not stopping to think about what it means.

And Sara cleans up behind me.

"I feel really bad."

"You should. I'll sort it, but don't you ever do this to me again or that's it. I'm not doing this anymore."

I swallow hard. "Let me know what I need to do and I'll make it happen."

"You had better." She pauses. "Are you seriously telling me you flew across the planet for a woman?"

I blow out a long breath. "Sure did."

"Wow. That is insane. *You* are insane. And you're very lucky I adore you."

"Now you tell me." I run my fingers through my hair.

"Not enough to sleep with you, but yeah. And it sounds like you've finally worked out what you want."

I clutch the phone to my ear and look up at the clear blue sky. "I have."

"Leave it with me and I'll see what I can do."

By the time I've sent a text to Pania asking for her address, there's a message from Sara.

Sara: *You've got two weeks. The shoot's being rescheduled, and they're not happy. But, thankfully, they have to wait for the site to be available again. I had to sweeten things a bit so your deal isn't quite what it was, but it's workable. And I did it on the assumption you'll be fine because you screwed up.*

Me: *Thanks, Sara. I owe you everything.*
Sara: *You'd better get the girl, then.*
I grin. Yes, I'd better.

23

PANIA

"I'm so glad this term is nearly over." Sam nudges my arm, and all I can do is nod.

"Me too. I'm so tired. And I'm not sure I can do the rest of the year."

She laughs. "If I can, you can."

My phone buzzes in my jacket pocket, but I do my best to ignore it. I shouldn't be texting during the day, but it's early evening in LA and the best time for Delaney or Reece to talk.

I wait until Judith's got her back to me and slide my phone out of my pocket.

Reece: *Where are you?*

I look up. Judith's busy talking to one of the other students.

Me: *In class.*

Reece: *Send me the address. I'm coming to see you.*

I gasp and slide my phone back into my pocket.

"Pania?"

I turn toward Sam, who's looking at me with a crooked eyebrow. Feeling more eyes on me, I look around the room, plastering a faint smile on my face.

"I'm fine," I say quietly.

Judith approaches me, and I straighten up. "Is there something you want to share, Ms Wilson?"

"I just pricked myself with a pin. Sorry for the disturbance."

She snorts and walks back to the other student.

I slip my phone back out and hold it under the table.

Me: *What do you mean?*

Reece: *I need to know what address to give the taxi driver.*

I stare at the screen, and before I know it, I've tapped in the address and sent it.

Reece is here? My heart thuds. He's said nothing in previous days about arriving. I thought he'd be with Delaney and Josh, maybe even helping out because of the baby arriving.

Instead, he's in Auckland and texting me.

My heart wants to believe he's here for me, but my head tells me I'm being stupid, and Reece is filming something and forgot to say anything. It's entirely possible.

I can't focus enough to get much more done, and I drag through the bare minimum before it's time to go home. I'm just glad tonight isn't a work night as it appears I'll be catching up with Reece instead.

"See you all tomorrow," Judith says.

For a moment, I just sit there.

"Pania, are you okay?" Sam asks.

I nod even though I'm not sure I am.

Grabbing my bag, I stand and make my way out of the door. I reach the exit and lay eyes on him. He's leaning against one of the pillars outside, his arms folded and his ankles crossed. I'm sure there are all kinds of curious looks at him, but he's all I see. My heart thrums at the sight of him, in the flesh, right in front of me.

I come to a halt, and a body slams into me from behind, jolting me forward.

"What the ..." Sam's voice sounds right near my ear. "Is that ..."

"Reece," I whisper.

I walk toward him, our gazes locked together as if no one else is there.

He straightens up. "Hey."

"Hey. What are you doing here?"

He wraps his arms around my shoulders, and I fold into his embrace, closing my eyes. We might not have been face to face for two years, but he means so much to me. Hope grows inside me that this means I mean the same to him.

A smile sweeps his handsome face, and he presses a kiss in my hair. "I came to see you."

"Me?"

"There's a lot I want to say, and it didn't feel right doing it over Skype."

I lean back, letting go of him. "Stop. Are you here making a movie?"

He shakes his head. "No, Pania. I flew halfway around the world just for you."

I choke down what feels like a golf ball-sized lump in my throat. "What are you talking about?"

Reece looks into my eyes. I've never seen such an earnest expression on his face—not even in any of his films. "Can we go somewhere more private to talk?"

"I ... I'm just on my way home. We could go there."

His lips quirk. "Well, I do need somewhere to stay."

I gape at him. "You really didn't plan this well, did you?"

His smile widens to a grin. "Not at all."

I shake my head. "What am I going to do with you, Reece Evans?"

"Once we get to your place, anything you want."

Swallowing hard, I try and smile, but my head's spinning from his words. Where has this come from? I'm not complaining—hell, thoughts of Reece have often kept me warm at night, but this is unexpected.

"I thought ..." Tears prick my eyes. *I don't cry.*

"We've got an audience. Let's go," he says gently.

I turn my head. Behind me, Sam and about two dozen other people have gathered to watch us.

Turning back, I shake my head rapidly as if waking myself up.

"We have to catch a bus and then it's a bit of a walk to my car. It's not parked near here."

He shrugs. "I've been on a plane for hours. I could do with stretching my legs."

"Come on, then."

Reece picks up two duffel bags and nods. "Right behind you."

I take a deep breath and lead him down the steps and onto the footpath. We walk down to the end of St Paul Street and cross Symonds Street to get to a bus stop that will take us to Mt Eden Road.

He's dressed casually in jeans and a T-shirt, and we get the odd curious look but no one approaches us.

"It's good to see you," he says.

I'm not sure I want to have this conversation at a bus stop, surrounded by other people.

"You too."

He takes my hand in his, and I look down as he runs his thumb over my knuckles. I gaze at him, my stomach fluttering as he does it in front of a crowd. I'm not even sure anyone notices, but this is Reece staking his claim. I think. It's so confusing right now.

"Do you need me to carry one of your bags?" I ask.

He's carrying two duffel bags, and although he has both handles gathered in one hand, I want to help.

"No, I'm good." He squeezes my hand.

I use my bus card to pay our fares, and we take seats near the front because it's not a long trip, and there's room for his bags.

He leans against me. "I don't know the last time I was on a bus."

"Welcome to my life."

Reece smiles. "I'm glad to be in your life."

I swallow hard. This isn't like him. There aren't any jokes or making fun of me, and I don't have the heart to do it in return when he seems to be so earnest.

Looking out the window, I try and focus on making sure I press the button in time to get off at the stop nearest my car, but it's not easy when Reece is right next to me.

Reaching the right spot, I press the button and smile at Reece as the bus pulls to a stop. He gives me a quick nod, and moments later, we're alone on the footpath.

"Now where?" he asks.

"It's just around the corner."

"You do this every day?"

I slip my arm into his. "Uh huh."

"It must be tiring if you still have to drive home."

I lean my head on his shoulder. "I'm not working today either. That's tiring."

He's quiet for a moment. "Let's get to your car."

It's not a long walk. Reece rubs his hands together. "It's much cooler here than it is back home." Reaching my car, I open the boot and he places his bags inside.

"It's the middle of winter. You're lucky today is mild."

He nods toward the car. "You weren't kidding about how far to your car. Why don't you park in town? I saw parking buildings."

I laugh. "There are buildings, but I can't afford to park my car in the city. The price is insane."

He just stands there and blinks as if the thought never occurred to him.

"We live in very different worlds, Reece. It's why I'm kinda surprised you're here."

Reece captures my wrist. "Maybe now we do, but I don't come from a rich family. I get it more than you know."

"Maybe now you're here you can tell me all about it."

He lets me go. "In time."

There's something so awkward about him. The way he drops his gaze and how his Adam's apple bobs as if he's swallowing hard. But I won't press him. He'll tell me whatever it is when he's ready.

"We'll take the motorway. Not really much in the way of sightseeing, but it'll get us there faster." I walk around the car and open the driver's door. He climbs into the passenger side, and I take a deep breath as I drop into my seat.

"The sooner I get you alone, the better."

"You're being awfully presumptuous." I slide the key into the ignition, start the car up and then put it in drive.

"I hope not."

I roll my eyes, and pull out onto the road, driving back the way we came from to get onto the motorway south.

It's a quiet ride home, and the traffic's not too bad this time of day —another half hour and our trip time would easily be doubled, and I'm still relieved to turn down the driveway and park in my carport.

Climbing out of the car, I pop the boot for Reece to retrieve his bags, and then he follows me into my flat, dropping his bags inside the door.

"This is your apartment?"

I wave my arm around. "For comfort's sake, the bathroom is just over there, and the exit is back the way we came. The living room doubles as my bedroom."

He laughs. "The place Josh and I first had in LA wasn't much bigger. We had bedrooms, but the rest of the place was tiny."

"And now look at Josh's house. I'm sure your apartment is bigger than this."

His lips twitch. "Just a little."

"Uh huh. Anyway, you said you were here to talk, but I'm starving. Want to eat first?"

He grins. "I'd love to. The food on the plane was fine, but it feels like hours ago."

"It won't be anything too exciting."

Reece shrugs. "I've eaten your cooking. It's not as good as Delaney's but it'll do."

I gape at him, slapping his arm. "Hey."

"I'm kidding." He laughs. "Tomorrow I'll take you out to dinner to say thank you."

"For what?"

"For not freaking out too much when I arrived."

I roll my eyes and turn toward the kitchen. "Oh, I freaked out alright."

"I doubt you ever freak out."

Opening the fridge, I pull out the chicken breasts I'd taken out to defrost this morning. My plan had been to make enough for lunch for my final day of school, but I might treat myself to a bought lunch instead.

"You surprised me. I nearly got in trouble for texting in class."

He laughs. "Sorry."

"It's okay. I told dragon lady that I gasped because I'd stabbed myself with a pin."

"Did it work?"

I shrug. "Probably not, but she doesn't like me that much to start with."

Reece frowns. "I don't get how anyone doesn't. You're smart, talented, and I'm your best friend."

I pat his cheek. "Second best."

He captures my wrist, his eyes sparkling. "Can't blame a guy for trying."

I chop up some vegetables and turn the element on, heating up my wok to cook a stir fry. It doesn't take long until everything's sizzling away, and Reece comes up behind me.

"That smells good."

"I hope you like it."

He kisses my temple. "I'm pretty sure I'll like anything you cook."

My heart thuds. "It's so weird that you're here."

Reece turns me around. "I don't want to be anywhere else."

I gaze into his eyes. It's so hard to wrap my head around the fact that he's here—here for me. Butterflies take off in my stomach as his eyes drink me in. "Don't make me burn the food. Sit at the table and I'll bring some over soon."

"Yes, ma'am," he says softly.

I turn back to the food. It's nearly done, so I grab a couple of plates from the cupboard and dish up the food.

After stashing the leftovers in the fridge, I carry the plates to the table and place them down before returning to grab some condiments and forks.

Sitting at the table, we both start to eat.

Reece lets out a moan that makes my toes curl.

"Oh my God, this is good."

"Better than Delaney's?" I tease.

He stops, puts his fork down and raises his eyebrows. "You'll get me in trouble."

"I'll take that as a yes." I smile smugly at him, even though I know Delaney and I had the same cooking training by the same tutor, and we were always able to cover for each other in the diner because we were so in tune.

"Don't you make me choose."

I press my lips together to stop myself from saying something else smart. The words on the tip of my tongue will only get me into trouble.

He eats like a mad man, cleaning his plate so fast I'm sure he'll be like Oliver Twist and asking for more any minute. Instead, he leans back and groans. "I might have to employ you to cook for me all the time."

"I'll do it for free if you play your cards right."

His eyebrows rise. "Is that right?"

"While you're staying here, that is."

He leans forward, studies me closely, and then picks up his plate. "Want me to wash the dishes?"

I shake my head. "Just leave it on the bench. I'll throw it in the dishwasher."

Doing as he's told, he takes a seat back at the table.

"Are you going to watch me eat now?"

He smiles. "I'm just waiting for you to finish so we can talk."

I put my fork down. "I guess you have something to say."

It takes a few moments before he narrows his eyes. "Are you going to start eating again?"

"Not if you keep watching me like that."

He turns his chair around. "There you go."

I chuckle to myself and pick up the fork. As much as I'm dying to know what he has to say, torturing him by making him wait is so much fun.

But I might just swallow the rest down without chewing as much as I usually do.

After the dishwasher's loaded, we make our way to the couch.

The silence is deafening. He clasps his hands together and opens and closes his mouth like a fish a few times.

"Are you okay?" I ask.

He looks away. "I'm fine. This … just worked a lot better in my head."

I place my hand over his, and he raises his gaze to meet mine. "Just tell me, Reece. It can't be that bad."

"Depends on whether you agree." His blue eyes seem to look into my soul. I've seen him a million times on Skype, but never felt him looking at me like this before.

I swallow hard. "Agree on what?"

He pauses, sucking on his bottom lip for a moment. "I know we haven't seen each other in person since Hawaii, but I feel like … we've really got to know each other."

"We have."

"And "—he takes a deep breath—"I like you. Really like you. I was always jealous of the way Delaney keeps Josh grounded, and I don't think you know just how much you do that for me."

Oh.

"I'm glad to hear it."

He lets out a nervous laugh and runs his fingers through his hair. "Women don't usually make me nervous."

I raise an eyebrow. "And you are now?"

"*You* make me nervous." He runs his tongue across his lower lip, and I can't take my eyes off it. I blink, look up, and meet his gaze, expecting to see him smirking in that Reece way. Instead, his eyes search mine.

"Why? It's just me." I place my hand on his hand.

"You're not just you. That's the problem." He swallows. "I suck at this so much."

I hold my breath for a moment. The strain is clear from his furrowed brow and inability to drive this conversation forward, but it's clear to me where he's going with it.

"I really like you too, Reece. More than our friendship."

"You do?" His brows straighten, and his eyes search mine.

"It's weird. It's almost as if we've reversed roles." I bite my bottom lip. "When we met, I was a little starstruck and you made *me* nervous."

He laughs. "I would never have been able to tell."

"And then I thought you were annoying. But it was clear to me that you'd become friends with Delaney, and if she can put up with you, anyone can."

He raises his free hand to his face and covers his eyes. "Am I really that bad?"

"No."

He drops his hand.

"You're so much worse." I bite down a laugh.

His eyes narrow. "I didn't think I was *that* bad."

"There are times when I don't know what to make of you. But you're a good man underneath all that bullshit. I can see that. And I've loved this friendship we've cultivated."

He grimaces. "You're about to give me the friendzone speech, aren't you?"

I shake my head. "I already said I like you ... more than a friend."

"That's how I feel too." He pauses. "Now what?"

I shrug. "I don't know. You started this."

Reece chuckles. "There, that's why I like you. Well, one of the reasons." He raises his gaze to the ceiling. "I want more with you ..." His blue eyes fix on me. "And I'm not just talking about a quick fuck."

"I didn't think you'd flown all the way here for *that*." I sit up straight. "Besides, I'm just not that kind of girl."

His mouth falls open. "I didn't think you were."

I shrug and lift my hand to brush my hair off my face. "I could be, given the right circumstances."

Reece laughs again, shaking his head as he leans back. "This conversation is not going the way I thought it would." His eyes shine with amusement. "But then, nothing with you ever goes the way I think it will."

"What do you mean?"

"I was attracted to you from the start." He leans forward, knitting his fingers together. "And then I loved how honest you were with me. I realised it's not something that happens much anymore."

My head spins. I'm still not sure what he means, but I raise my eyebrows again and his lips twitch.

"I never noticed that with fame comes the ass kissers."

I snicker.

He smiles, the dimples in his cheeks coming into view. This is one gorgeous man, and he's laying his heart on the line for me.

"I mean, I have people who work for me, and they're honest with me because I get to know them as friends, but the rest of the world can be a little … I'm not even sure what the word is."

"Sycophantic?"

He tilts his head. "I'm not sure I'd go that far. But I mean I do treasure people who don't let my ego get away on me, and that happens sometimes."

"Only sometimes?" I cock my head.

"And that's what I'm talking about." He looks down at the table. "I like it when you do that."

"You're a glutton for punishment, just like Josh."

His gaze meets mine again. "I guess I am."

My heart pounds, so hard and fast that, for a second, I'm not sure I'm breathing. The taut muscles in his neck, his locked jaw, the way his eyes settle on my lips, everything feels different now.

We joke a lot together, but I've never seen him so open as he is now, even if he's having trouble finding the words.

"So, what now?" I ask.

"It's up to you. I want to be with you, Pania. More than friends. I don't know how to do this, so I need your help."

I rise from my seat and walk around the table. He turns to face me, and I take his hands in mine. "I want more too."

"Really?"

"When we were in Hawaii, and you kissed me, I wrote it off as a once-off. I thought it might have been because I was there, and maybe you felt obligated to spend time with me because I was Delaney's friend."

He shakes his head. "I spent time with you because I liked you."

I squeeze his hands. "Maybe. I wouldn't be upset if it started that way. It shows me how good a friend you are to both of them."

Letting his hands go, I turn and walk to the couch, dropping onto it.

"I was surprised when you first got in touch. Your messages meant a lot to me." I rest my palms on my thighs. "You make me laugh, and I feel we've grown close."

Reece stands and makes his way over to the couch and sits beside me. "I feel that too."

I swallow hard. "I guess that's why you're here."

He reaches for me, cupping my cheek and tilting my face toward him. "I've done a lot of thinking lately, especially since the whole award thing. I want someone to share all the good times with. I can't promise there won't be bad times—I don't think anyone can predict what the future holds—but I want to share it all with you."

"Reece," I whisper.

He leans forward, pressing his lips to mine. I open up to let him in, and his tongue tangles with mine. It's just as good a kiss as it was back in Hawaii. I sink into him, and tremble as he grips my arms.

Pressing his forehead to mine as the kiss ends, he takes in a deep breath.

"I feel like I've waited forever to do that."

"I never thought you'd do that again."

He pulls away. "The problem is that I want to do it all the time."

"And how is that a problem?" I raise my hands to cup his face. "Sounds good to me."

Reece kisses me on the nose. "Sounds good to me too, but I just had to fly all this way to do it."

I fight a smile and lose. "Sounds like a you problem rather than a me problem."

He laughs, and before I can say anything else, his mouth's on mine again.

I'll have to be a smart arse more often.

24

REECE

"Now what?"

Pania draws in a deep breath. "Now we watch TV and then get some sleep. That's how exciting my life is."

"But I'm here." I hold up my palms.

"And I still have a class tomorrow. It's Thursday today." She leans forward and picks up the remote. "But it's also the last class of the year before we break for the holidays." Flicking on the television, she pushes some buttons to get the right network and drops the remote again. "How long are you staying for?"

You've got two weeks. Sara's words echo in my ears.

"A couple of weeks. I've got no other plans."

She smiles. "Cool. Hope you're happy to dive into the deep end and meet my mum."

"Your mom?"

Pania nods, turning back to look at the TV. "I was planning to drive to Whakatane on Saturday to spend the holidays with my family."

Woah. I gulp. "Sure. What the hell."

She laughs. "Are you really ready for that?"

"Do I have much of a choice?" I wrap my arms around her as she snuggles up against me.

"No."

I laugh, kissing her temple. "I guess I'm joining your family for the holidays, then."

"They won't bite." She wrinkles her nose. "Well, Mum might. She thinks you look charming. Not that she knows the real you."

I hold out my hands. "I like your mother already."

"She'll love you." Pania nuzzles my neck.

"So ..."

She raises her head. "So ...?"

"What do we do about sleeping arrangements, if you're so intent on going to sleep?"

"Well—" Pania pushes down on the cushion she's sitting on. "—the couch isn't comfortable, and it creaks. So, I guess my bed."

"Are you ready for that?"

She leans her head against mine. "I need to get some sleep tonight, but I want to be with you."

"If I'm in bed with you, we're not getting much sleeping done."

Standing, she bends over and pecks me on the lips. "I'm going to get my pyjamas on. The alarm's set for six."

"Six? Are you crazy?"

She walks toward the bed and picks up some clothing from on top. "I'll never beat the traffic if I sleep in. Today was easy."

I grab the remote and turn off the television while she heads into the bathroom. If I'm honest, I'd hoped we'd be rolling around in bed already, but this pace is comforting in some ways. She wants me as I want her, and I guess if I was impatient, I wouldn't have waited so long to tell her how I felt.

But now I'm so much more confident I can be who she needs me to be.

Stripping off my shirt, I make my way to the bed.

The bathroom door opens, and Pania stands there in her pyjamas. She's wearing shorts and a tank top, and her long hair is down.

"Bathroom's all yours."

Her hazel eyes drink me in. I've been shirtless—even naked in movies before—but never been self-conscious the way I am right now. My heart thuds as I cross the room. Maybe because it knows it's all hers.

It's never belonged to anyone else before, but now it does.

"Thanks." I grab my toothbrush from my bag and head inside the bathroom. As we pass each other, my arm brushes hers. Electricity flares through me, and she comes to a stop, her eyes scanning mine. My stomach flips.

This is stupid. I've never struggled with confidence, but Pania undoes me.

After I've brushed my teeth, I take a moment before joining her, dropping my pants to the floor, pulling back the duvet and climbing into bed.

A pillow practically smacks me in the face. "Wh-what are you doing?" I ask, pushing it out of my way.

Pania places it between her pillow and mine, then pops her head over the top. "If I don't put this between us, you know what will happen." She bites her lip, her eyes skating over my shoulders.

Warmth rushes through me, and I grip the sheets. Staring her down for a second or two, I then flop onto my back and groan. "Yes. Fine. You're right. I could always go and stay at a motel."

Her eyes fill with amusement. "To be honest, I wondered why you didn't."

"A motel doesn't have you in it."

I'm distracted by her tongue which slips out and slides across her bottom lip.

"You're being sweet again," she says. "What's going on?"

I look up at the ceiling. "I could say I'm trying to get you into bed, but that achievement's been unlocked."

Pania picks up the pillow between us. "I should just suffocate you with this right now and put us both out of our misery."

I catch her wrist, wrapping my fingers around it. "You wouldn't dare."

Her eyes light up. "Watch me."

She laughs as I grab hold of the pillow and throw it across the room. It hits the wall behind the couch with a dull thud and falls to the floor. "Now try it."

Pania shakes her wrist free of my grip, lies back on the bed and stretches out. Her tank top rides up a little, and I can't stop looking at her smooth skin.

I flex my hand, resisting the urge to touch it. "I think I'll go to sleep instead."

"You're no fun."

She rolls onto her side. "I'm lots of fun. Just not tonight because I have to get up early in the morning."

"It's not that late yet."

For a moment, she just stares at me before blushing and looking away.

"Maybe I just want to kiss you some more."

She looks at me from under her long eyelashes. "I'd like that."

I scoot over to the middle of the bed, and she moves forward. I look into her eyes. Her cheeks are flushed, and her breathing seems a little heavy.

"Touch me," she whispers.

I hesitate. She takes my hand and guides it to rest on her stomach.

"I want to kiss you more first."

Pania's lips twitch. "I guess that's really the first step."

I press my lips to hers, and she opens up. For a moment, I'm lost as my brain stops working.

I slide my hand up her shirt as I kiss her again. Her breast is firm beneath my hand, her nipple pebbled under my fingers.

She rolls onto her back and I follow, squeezing her breast, my mouth on hers.

Pulling away, she gasps. "You cheated. I thought you were kissing first, touching later."

I nuzzle her neck. "I have the rare male ability of multitasking."

Pania throws her head back and lets out a throaty laugh that's so sexy, it drives me wild. "Prove it."

I kiss her again, and this time as our tongues do battle, I slip my hand into her pyjama shorts, pushing aside her panties and moaning as I touch her smooth pussy.

"Reece," she whispers.

I slide one finger into her, and she battles to keep her eyes open as I slide it back out and over her clit.

"Please." She arches her back, and I pull up her tank top with my other hand, exposing her breasts. She's so beautiful. Her nipples are a darker shade of brown, and I lean over, taking one in my mouth as I keep working her clit.

"This isn't happening," she whispers.

I raise my head. "It is."

"You can't be real." She reaches out and strokes my face, her hips moving in rhythm with my hand.

"I'm real, sweetheart." I turn my head and kiss her palm before kissing her again. And then I'm lost in her, the woman I've wanted for so long. She's in my arms, and her body tenses below me.

"Pania." I nuzzle her cheek. "I'm right here."

She explodes in my arms, shuddering, her hips thrusting upward before stilling. The hazy way she looks at me makes me smile.

"I need you inside me," she says.

"Don't you want me to—"

Pania presses an index finger to my lips. "I just want you. Have you got a condom?"

I freeze. Do I? I haven't used one in a long time, but surely there must be one in my wallet.

"Umm ..."

Pania cocks an eyebrow. "I don't have any, so if you don't, then you're shit out of luck tonight."

I've never scrambled off a bed so fast, reaching for my jeans and rifling through everything to see what I can find.

"Would you kill me if I said no?"

She laughs—*laughs* at me.

"No. I'm just going to roll over and go to sleep. Are you coming back to bed?"

I hold out my hands. "What am I going to do with *this*?"

Pania shrugs. "That looks like a you problem, not a me problem."

"Really?" I stare at her in misbelief.

Her wicked smile makes me even harder. "Get over here, and we'll see what we can do to alleviate it. But you owe me."

"I can't believe I fucked this up."

She laughs again. "I can. Come back to bed."

I drop my jeans on the floor and cross the room, sliding back into bed beside her. "What do you mean, *you can*? You have so little faith in me."

Pania takes my cock in her hand, stroking it and making me gasp. "You were clearly in a hurry."

"I was." I grit my teeth as she runs her thumb over the tip.

Her expression softens as she looks into my eyes. "You flew all this way for me."

"Only for you."

She lowers her head to my cock, licking it from top to base.

I let out a groan. "I'm not sure I'm going to last long."

"If you don't, that's two you owe me." She chuckles, taking my length in her mouth. I close my eyes and shudder as the wet heat of her engulfs me. It's not how I wanted to spend our first night together, but being inside her one way or another makes me feel so good.

I moan as she works my shaft, her tongue flicking up and over.

"Pania," I whisper.

She doesn't respond, picking up the pace, tightening her grip on me. I swear my eyes roll in my head as I sink into the mattress and just enjoy her attention.

My whole body is alive. It's not just that I've been without a woman for so long, it's Pania. The only woman I've fantasised about these past couple of years.

"Pania, I ..."

Heat spreads from my toes to my face as I come in her mouth. She slows, still using her tongue until my cock stops pulsing before she swallows and raises her head.

"That was incredible."

She smiles. "I'm glad you liked it."

I want to tell her that I love her, but I also don't want to move too fast. I've not said that in a romantic way to anyone, but Pania's different.

We spent the past two years getting to know one another. Now we get to spend time together.

"Now, I really need to get some sleep."

She rolls onto her side, facing away, and I snuggle up, spooning from behind.

"This bed gets warm. It'll get way too hot overnight to do that."

I kiss the back of her neck. "I'm happy to get hot and sweaty if it means being next to you."

"You're a big softy, Reece Evans."

"I'm just appreciative of getting good head."

She laughs, and while I can't see her face, I can just imagine the broad smile that graces it.

"Goodnight," she whispers.

"Goodnight."

25

PANIA

I rub my face and try my best to ignore the blaring alarm in the morning.

It doesn't work.

Reece nudges my arm. "Last day."

I reach over to the bedside cabinet and touch my phone screen, switching off the noise.

"It's not so easy to get out of bed this morning."

He kisses my ear. "I know. I'd be happy to stay here too."

I sit up and laugh. "You are staying here. The moment I'm gone, you'll roll over and go back to sleep."

Reece shrugs. "I am still tired after my flight."

Leaning over, I kiss him on the lips. "I'll be back about two-thirty-ish. We finish at two today."

He grabs my arm as I turn to climb out of bed. "Come back here. I want more than that."

"I don't have time," I whine, but I still lean back again and linger on his lips.

"That's better. I still don't know how I'll go a whole day without seeing you." He lays his palm flat on his pecs, the other hand, palm up, on his forehead.

"How on Earth did you win an Oscar with *those* acting skills?" I stand up and move away from the bed before he can grab me again. "You'll be fine. After today, you get to spend two whole weeks with me." He doesn't respond, and as I get to the bathroom door, I turn. "And, you might even get to have sex with me in that time."

I grin at the sound of his laughter and look at myself in the mirror. This is all still so unreal. I got used to our banter, but now it's taken on a whole different meaning.

But none of this pondering is helping me get to class, and I flick on the shower and wash myself quickly before drying and wrapping a towel around my body.

Reece is still lying in bed, his eyes following me as I cross the room.

"Now we're talking."

"Hush, you." I grab a pair of jeans and a shirt out of my drawers before returning to the bed and grabbing clean underwear from the bedside cabinet.

He's surprisingly well behaved as I drop the towel and pull on my clothing, except for when I sit on the bed and he lazily drifts his hand up and down my back.

"Do you really have to go on the last day?"

"She's making her announcement today about whose designs will go on display in her store." I tug on my socks.

"Do you think she's going to choose you?"

I shrug. "Doubt it. She hates me. I missed out last year and the year before. And in my opinion, my dresses were the best."

Reece pulls me round until I'm facing him. "Why are you still doing this, then?"

"Because I made a promise to myself to complete the course. She's just pissy because Delaney keeps mentioning me in interviews. I could ask Delaney to stop, but I kind of enjoy it."

He grins. "You're such a masochist."

"I could have dropped out, but I'd still have a student loan to deal with. I've learned a lot. It's not all been a waste."

Reece squeezes my arm. "I'm sure. You're so talented. It's not surprising Delaney sings your praises."

My cheeks burn. "Stop it."

"It's true. Everything I've seen, from her wedding dress to the dresses she wears to events, are amazing. You've got a huge career ahead of you. Shame that whatever her name is doesn't want to nurture that."

I lean over and brush my lips against his. "You're the best for my ego."

"You're just the best. Period."

I pull away. "I need to get going or I'll be late. Last day. I finish at two, so I'll be home after that."

"I'll go and buy some condoms."

Laughing as I stand, I turn to face him. "Good thinking. I'll leave my spare key on the coffee table if you do want to go out."

I grab the leftovers from the fridge, pick up my bag and head out the door, blowing him a kiss before I close it behind me.

It'd be so easy to stay in bed today, but I have to see this through.

I GET a ton of curious looks in the morning, but no one says anything.

Thanks to Judith, they're all aware of my relationship with Delaney, and if any of them are fans of Josh or Reece, they'll know how we're all connected.

Even Sam, who I was anticipating an interrogation from, says nothing. It makes me self-conscious, but with it being the last day of term, we're not doing much actual work. It's good because I wouldn't be able to concentrate, but at the same time it makes the day drag.

At lunch time, I head out alone and go for a walk around the block. I'm still not sure how to process the events of the past twenty-four hours, and when I think of the way Reece touched me last night, my cheeks get hot.

I can't believe he's here—in my flat, in my bed. I've dreamed about him for so long, and he has feelings for me.

It's so hard to wrap my head around.

By the time I return, there's an hour left to go. Everyone's back at their tables, and I join Sam, who smiles at me.

"You okay?" she asks.

"I'll just be glad when today is over."

Judith starts talking about plans for next term, and I lose interest as she drones on. And of course because my eyes are firmly on the wall clock above her head, the hands move slower than a sloth.

"There's one more thing I need to do before we finish for the term, and that's to tell you who will have their works on display in my store." She smiles, and I blink a few times, waking myself up to listen to her. "There are some outstanding designs this year, and I'm so proud of all of you."

I hold my breath. I'm positive she won't pick me—she never does, but a girl can hope.

"It's been such a hard choice, but the designers on display will be —Caitlyn Ruddock, Aroha Potu, and ..." She fixes her gaze on me. My heart leaps. "Samantha Crew."

I blow out a long breath.

"I can't believe she didn't pick you. *Again*. You're so much better than I am," Sam says.

Swallowing down my disappointment, I turn to her. "Thank you. And congratulations. It's so awesome for you."

"Thanks." She puffs. "I really wasn't expecting it. And I don't know about Caitlyn's work being on display—there's a good chance a seam will fall apart."

I bite my knuckles to stop myself from laughing. "Stop it."

"You know it's true." She runs her tongue across her upper lip. "I didn't want to say anything because I'm sure you don't want to be hassled, but ..."

"You want to know about Reece."

She nods, her eyes crinkling at the corners as if she's reluctant to say the words.

"Hey. I think I'm early."

Reece's voice comes from the doorway. My heart speeds up as I raise my gaze to meet his.

Sam nudges my arm. "He's here to see you, right?"

"What are you doing here?" I mouth.

His lips curl into a mischievous smile. "You said you'd be done about two."

"It's not two yet."

I shift my gaze to Judith and clamp my lips together. From the wide-eyed expression on her face, you'd think it was the second coming of Christ in the door.

Reece knows the effect he has on women. I have no doubt about that. As I cast my gaze around the room, there's plenty of similar expressions on my classmate's faces, including Sam.

But his eyes are firmly on me.

"Mr Evans." Judith shakes herself out of her stupor and smiles. "I'm Judith Brookes."

"Please, call me Reece." He crosses the room to shake her hand. "I apologise for interrupting."

"Not at all." Her tone's so soft, and I press my lips together even tighter to stop myself from laughing. "We're just about to finish for the term."

He nods. "Pania told me." She bristles, and he looks back at me. "I'll wait outside."

"No, please. We'll be done in just a moment." The most dazzling smile appears on her face, and I snort, then cover my nose in embarrassment.

"I'll just grab a seat," he drawls.

I've noticed his accent changes a little when he's putting on the charm. It's like it slows even more. He's such a flirt.

Wait. He uses that on me all the time. Did I not notice him flirting with me *at all*? How did I miss that?

Awareness rockets through me as I look toward him and meet his gaze. He winks, and Sam nearly melts beside me.

"Are you two ...?" she asks.

"I'm not sure what we are yet. But he's in so much trouble for this."

She laughs. "He's got Judith eating out of the palm of his hand."

I knit my fingers together and squeeze. "I'm not sure if that's a good thing or not."

Judith claps to get everyone's attention seeing as they're all now focused on my interloper.

"Have a good break, everyone. Relax and come back refreshed and ready for new challenges."

This time, I have to apply pressure with my hand to stop myself from laughing; she sounds like an entirely different person.

And then I wait as the class empties, but not before some of the women ask Reece for selfies. He obliges every single one and then saunters toward me.

"Ready to go home?" he asks.

Sam's still standing nearby, staring at us.

"What are you doing here?"

"I forgot to take the key with me when I went out. So, I took an Uber."

I grin. "You knew damn well you were making a scene."

He places his palm on his heart. "Who, me?"

"Yes, you, Reece Evans. You shit stirrer." I laugh. "There's someone I want you to meet."

I hold my hand out toward Sam. "Sam has been with me through my whole training, and she's a friend."

He smiles. "How's it going, Sam?"

"Great." Her face tightens, but her eyes are bright. I'm not sure she knows how to handle this situation.

He holds his hand out to shake and she takes it. It makes me think back to the day we met. He didn't intimidate me, but I was a little starstruck. I can empathise with how she's feeling.

"It's good to meet you. Any friend of Pania's is a friend of mine." He lets go of her hand and slips his arm around my waist. "Ready to go?"

"After I take a photo of you and Sam." I turn to her. "Give me your phone."

Sam's eyes widen as I take the phone from her and Reece moves next to her. He talks softly to her, and she giggles before his arm goes around her waist and they pose for me.

I take a bunch of photos before giving her the phone back.

"Thank you," she says to both of us.

Reece winks. "You're welcome."

She grabs her bag and smiles at me. "See you after the holidays."

I wave. "You bet."

Picking up my bag, I take Reece's outstretched hand and we walk toward the exit.

Reece plants a kiss on my temple. "You're a good person, Pania."

I let out a contented sigh. "I know. Just don't tell anyone."

"Your secret's safe with me." He grabs my hand and laces his fingers with mine. "Now, where's this famous dress?"

"You want to see it?"

"You know I do." His eyes shine with pride, and I draw in a deep breath and give him a sharp nod.

"It's over here." I lead him to the back of the room where our designs are set up on mannequins. My skin prickles as Judith's eyes follow us, but I don't care. Reece has seen the dresses I've made Delaney, but this is my chance for him to see something I've made for me. "This is it." I brush my fingers down the soft fabric. Every time I see the deep blue of it, I fall in love all over again.

"Woah." Reece's tone softens. "It's beautiful. Tell me this is going on display in her store."

My cheeks burn. "No. I didn't get a spot."

"What?" He shakes his hand free of mine and holds up his palms, and his voice is way too loud, but there's a part of me that doesn't care because I wanted this so badly. "You're wearing this next time you're in LA."

I don't dare look away from him. "I don't know—"

"This is a red carpet dress."

His devilish smile makes me dizzy. He knows exactly what he's doing.

Reece dips his head and kisses my ear. "I mean it."

A cleared throat behind us makes me turn. "Ms Wilson, I'm about to lock up, so ..." Judith's icy tone is back, and when Reece turns, her lips curl into a smile. "Have a lovely holiday."

"Thanks."

Reece grabs my hand again as I walk back to the bench to pick up my bag, and we leave the room, hand in hand.

"She would have heard all that," I mutter.

"That was the plan. She's a fool. You're meant for bigger and better things, Pania Wilson."

"You say that as we walk to the bus stop." I laugh and lean my head against his shoulder.

"Let's Uber instead."

"That sounds way too luxurious for me."

COMMUTERS out of the city honk their horns as they fight to gain more distance and time, but none of us are really going anywhere.

Despite being earlier in the day, I didn't anticipate the stampede out of town before the holidays as people decide to take off early.

It's nearly four by the time we get back to my flat.

"So, now you're all mine for two whole weeks?" Reece asks.

"And Mum's." I laugh.

"I'm looking forward to meeting her."

I drop my bag beside the couch and throw myself on my bed.

Reece sits beside me and places his hand on my back. "Tired?"

"Yes, but glad to be on holiday." I roll over and push myself up to sit. Thank you for what you did for Sam. It was really sweet."

His eyes meet mine, and for a moment he just gazes at me. "I'd do anything for you."

I reach up and cup his cheek. "*You* are really sweet. Did you buy condoms today?"

"I bought three packets to be sure."

I bite my bottom lip and snort at the thought of some poor checkout operator serving Reece Evans buying three boxes of condoms. "Three?"

"I bought some other things to make it look like I wasn't just buying condoms. All the shopping's in the kitchen. Nothing that'll spoil while we're away."

I snort again. "I thought you forgot the key."

"About that ..." He shrugs. "I just wanted to see this woman who has you tied up in knots. And maybe a little of that shit stirring you were talking about." He slides his arms around my waist. "Now, I'm way overdue kissing you, so pucker up."

"Is that right?" I purse my lips.

And then he kisses me, and all is right with my world.

Even if he just pissed my tutor off even more.

26

REECE

Pania's bags are packed, and we're ready to leave for her mom's tomorrow. My stomach churns at the thought of taking this step. I've never met anyone's mother before. But there's also something about it that feels right. If I was going to take this step with anyone, it'd be Pania.

She slides her arms around my waist from behind. "Ready for bed?"

"Thought you'd never ask."

"The Imperial March" from *Star Wars* burst from the speaker of my phone and echoes through the room.

Pania laughs. "What on Earth ...?"

"That's Josh. I changed his ringtone when he took charge of our movie."

Grabbing my phone from the edge of the bed, I accept the call. Pania lets me go and walks over to the couch, dropping onto it.

"Josh."

"Where are you? We haven't seen you for three whole days and Delaney's worried."

I chuckle. "Is it just Delaney who's worried, or do you miss me too?"

Pania's eyebrows rise as she catches my gaze.

"It's just not like you to not turn up to be fed. I know you're not working."

I run my tongue over my bottom lip. "Uh yeah. I'm in New Zealand."

"New Zealand? What are you doing there? Oh …"

It takes a moment longer for Delaney to squeal in the background.

"Is he with Pania? Please tell me he is."

"I don't know. Give me a minute to find that out." Josh laughs.

"Yes, I'm with Pania."

Pania bites her bottom lip as her mobile starts jiggling on the bed. She crosses the room and picks it up. "Delaney."

Delaney makes so much noise, I can hear her from across the room.

"Yes, he's here. Yes, he came for me."

"Not tonight, I haven't." I grumble.

"What was that?" Josh laughs.

"Shit. I forgot you were on the other end of the call." I look over at Pania. "This isn't confusing at all with us both on the phone to the two of you."

Pania holds up one hand and walks straight into the bathroom, closing the door.

I laugh. "Pania's just disappeared into the bathroom with Delaney."

"Delaney's just headed to our bedroom."

I blow out a breath. "Thank God because that was nuts."

"So, where did this come from?" he asks.

I'm lost for words for a moment, unsure how to tell my best friend everything that's happened within the past two years.

"Dude, I'm sure as shit not judging you. I think it's great."

I swallow hard. "I'm glad."

"I have noticed you've worked hard on yourself. Remember when we first started our company and you'd disappear to make food videos with Delaney?"

I chuckle. "That was much more fun than any actual work."

"Yeah, but then you put in the work. You got the rewards and now you have the girl. And we both definitely approve of her."

I look at the ceiling. "I don't know if you remember, but before your wedding, you warned me away from her. Told me not to fuck and ditch her."

"I'm so sorry. I should have given you the benefit of the doubt."

Drawing in a deep breath, I take a moment to answer. "You were right. At that point, if things had taken that turn between us, I would have hurt her. But I wanted to be better than that."

"You've always been better than that, Reece. You just didn't know it."

The bathroom door opens, and Pania walks out. She drops her phone on the coffee table and then sits on the end of the bed.

"Thanks, Josh. I really appreciate it."

"Delaney's just walked back in, so I'll leave you guys to it. Have fun."

After saying goodbye and disconnecting the call, I look at Pania.

She stands and walks toward me. "Delaney says you're a true romantic and she didn't think you had it in you." Pania raises her palm to my chest. "She says she's very proud."

I grin. "They're both pretty happy about it."

"It's not really surprising. They love us."

I drop my phone on the coffee table alongside hers. "They do."

"So, now what, Mr Evans?" Her eyes shine with happiness.

"This." I lean in and kiss her, starting soft but deepening the kiss until she sighs in my mouth.

Pulling her in tight against me, I run my hands up and down her spine.

"You know I'm not like the women you usually date. I have cellulite, and my boobs are natural," she says.

I laugh. "Why don't you let me worry about what I want? I want you."

She pouts, and it's the cutest thing ever. "I just worry—"

"Have you ever worried about it with any other man?"

Pania blinks rapidly then drops eye contact. "No."

"I'm just a man." I kiss her just under her ear. "A man who's crazy about you."

I pepper kisses down her neck and across her throat before kissing her lips again. She kisses me back, her tongue seeking entrance, and I open up and let her in.

This woman owns my heart.

I reach for her shirt and pull it over her head before unhooking her bra. She grips the front of my T-shirt and laughs softly until I kiss her again. Her hands are on my waist, and she slides her fingertips underneath my shirt.

Her touch is soft, and I strip the shirt off while she unbuttons my jeans.

"Pania," I whisper.

"Take me to bed."

"It's right there." I point to it. "Let's go."

She laughs as she pulls away from me. I drink in the sight of her, but she's still wearing way too much.

Pania unbuttons her jeans and pushes them down, taking her panties with them and then turns and leaps under the blankets.

"I got about a two-second show just then." I shake my head.

"Get your butt over here."

Dropping my jeans to the ground, I do as I'm told before slipping off my boxers and climbing into bed beside her.

"What was all that about?" I ask.

"I'm shy." She flutters her eyelashes.

"Why do I find that hard to believe?"

Pania opens her arms. "Does it really matter?"'

I fold into her embrace, my naked body pressed against hers. I'm as hard as a rock, and she drops one hand to my cock, gripping it tight.

"Oh no you don't." I kiss her throat.

"What?" She laughs.

"I'm not coming until I've been inside you."

"Sweet talker." She sighs and lets me go.

I nuzzle her breasts, sliding my hand down her body until I slip a finger into her, just like last night. Only this time, I can follow through.

"God, I thought about this so many nights when we were talking on Skype."

"You did?"

I raise my head. "You didn't?"

Her eyes dart from side to side. "Maybe."

She arches her back to meet the rhythm of my hand again, but I have other plans tonight.

I drop my head so I can whisper in her ear. "I've thought a lot about eating your pussy."

Her eyes widen.

I kiss my way down her body, across her stomach, and down to where my finger still strokes her clit. She parts her legs, and I crawl between them.

Her chest rises and falls rapidly, her eyebrows twitching in anticipation.

Leaning over, I tongue her clit, and she lets out a long breath, clawing the sheets as I tease her.

"Reece," she cries out.

"You were worth the wait." Sucking gently on her clit, I lap at her, enjoying the way she pushes toward me, riding my tongue until she arches high and drops back down, her whole body trembling.

"Hurry up," she whispers.

"I'm going as fast as I can." I laugh against her skin. "No one's ever told me to hurry up before."

"No one's ever waited two years for you to get your shit together." Her eyes flash with amusement, and I laugh again.

"I love being with you. Even when it was just virtually, the moments we were together were everything."

Pania stops and looks into my eyes, blinking a bunch of times like she's fighting back tears.

"I don't cry, Reece. Don't make me."

"Even happy tears?"

She shakes her head. "Especially happy tears. Just love me."

"That's the easy part."

I roll on the condom, and without another word lean over and slide into her. She raises her knees, and I drive in deep.

"Oh God! That feels so good." She moans.

It's all I need to fall for her all over again. We're the perfect fit.

We move together with my mouth all over her body. I kiss her breasts, her nipples, her throat, her face. And then I kiss her deeply, gripping her hips and pulling her as tightly against me as I can.

She lets out a strangled moan, and I slip one hand between us, rolling her clit under my thumb until her pussy squeezes me as she climaxes again.

Placing my hands either side of her, I ride her orgasm until my body tightens, and I let out my own groan as my body soars and I come.

Pania pants as I slow. "Is that all you've got?" she teases.

"There are still thirty-five condoms to go." I shrug.

She laughs as I pull out of her slowly and roll to her side.

Turning toward me, she lays her palm on my chest. "It wasn't too bad."

I narrow my eyes.

"Okay, okay." Her grin makes my heart leap. "It was wonderful. You *are* wonderful."

"Let me just go get rid of this condom."

"There's a bin in the bathroom." She pecks me on the lips.

Once I've returned, she climbs out of bed to use the bathroom and returns to the bed, naked.

"We've got an early start in the morning." She kisses me on the nose. "And all that sexy time has left me tired."

She rolls over and I nuzzle her neck. "Really? You're not keen on another round?"

Leaning her head back, she sighs. "Yes, but ..."

I pull her onto her back, and she smiles. "Just a little bit more sexy time?" I ask.

Pania strokes my bicep. "Well, maybe you could convince me."

And then I kiss her, and try to make her forget for a while that we ever have to leave this bed.

It works.

27

REECE

"Reece." Pania shakes my shoulder, and I bat her hand away.

"Hmmm?"

"It's time to get up."

I open one eye. "It's still dark out."

"Yes. You can sleep in the car. I want to get out of the city early because it's school holidays and the traffic will be awful if we leave too late."

I yawn and sit up. My phone's all the way over on the coffee table. "What's the time?"

"Just after five. You need to get dressed, then we'll be ready to go. We can grab something to eat once we're off the motorway."

Rubbing my face with my hands, I push myself to my feet. "Do I have enough time for a shower?"

"If you only take five minutes, yes."

Groaning, I walk to the bathroom and turn on the water. My eyes want to close, but being under the shower wakes me up, and I wash myself off. Pania has some coconut scented shampoo, and I have nothing else, so I just use that to wash my hair.

"Do you need a towel?" she calls out.

I look outside the shower door. The only towel in the bathroom is a hand towel by the basin. I laugh. "Yes please."

Pania shakes her head as she walks in the door and places a towel on the edge of the basin. "I should make you suffer."

"After I made you come all those times last night?"

She turns to look at me. "Was that you building up brownie points?"

I shrug. "I thought it might count."

She laughs, turning toward the door. "Just be quick. I want to get out of here."

"Yes, boss."

At first I think my words are lost as she closes the door behind her.

"I should think so," she calls out.

WE'RE on the road by 5:20 a.m., and I'm soon lulled back to sleep by the long, mostly straight motorway out of town.

It's around three hours to drive from Auckland to Whakatane, but Pania wakes me halfway through the trip when we reach a town called Matamata to stop for food.

"I was going to stop earlier, but you were so sound asleep, I thought I'd leave you to it." She smiles.

I run my fingers through my hair. "I feel much better now."

"It's still early, but there's a twenty-four hour McDonald's here and we can stop for breakfast."

My mouth waters at the thought of a Big Mac.

"Are you drooling?" We pull into the parking lot, and I press my hands together at the sight of the magical golden arches.

"Maybe."

Pania parks the car. "We'll go in and eat. It's easier than trying to do it while driving."

"Sounds good to me."

We exit the car and walk toward the entrance. I take Pania's hand in mine, and she smiles at me. "Are we doing this in public?"

"We already have. I guarantee your classmates haven't kept their stories to themselves."

She leans her head on my shoulder. "I guess."

"Is that a problem?"

We pause outside the door and she turns to me. "If it was, do you think I'd let you keep holding my hand? I've spent two years thinking about this, and I've seen how Delaney's life has changed. I'm ready."

I run my index finger along her jaw. "I'm glad because I don't want to hide."

"Me either."

We order breakfast, but I basically order lunch, twice over, as well. And the entire time we sit and eat, Pania shakes her head at how much I shovel into my mouth. It's been so long since I indulged in a Big Mac. Plus, I'm a growing boy.

People stare. I eat. Pania glows red with embarrassment. And then we climb back into the car and drive another hour and a half.

"Nearly there," she says as we pass a sign that tells me we've reached Whakatane. "I can't wait to see Mum's face when she sees you."

"Wait. Does your mom know I'm coming?" I ask.

Pania glances at me. "I told her I was bringing someone home with me. I didn't tell her who. She'll love having a guest, but she'll go overboard if she knows it's you."

I chuckle. "Why?"

"She thinks you look charming. God knows where she'd get that idea."

I narrow my eyes, but when she glances again at me, the smile on her lips gives her away.

"You think I'm charming too. I mean, you weren't complaining last night. And we've still got—" I count on my fingers—"thirty-three condoms left. Or is it thirty-two? I lost count."

Pania laughs as she pulls up a driveway. The house is one storey, and it reminds me of the first house I remember living in. Big enough for a small family. There's not much in the way of garden, but there's plenty of lawn out the back.

"More than enough for the weekend at least." She pokes out her tongue as she reaches behind her seat for her bag.

"Depends on how busy a weekend it is."

She shakes her head before opening the driver's door and climbing out. I follow suit and close my eyes, taking a deep breath of the warm air.

Locking the car with her key fob, she then leads me to the back door of the house, and kicks off her shoes on the doorstep. I do the same while she turns the door handle and pushes.

"Mum," she calls.

"She's gone to the shops." A male voice comes from inside the house.

"Her car's there."

"I'm doing some work on it. She took my car."

I follow Pania through the kitchen and into the living room. A large TV is up on one wall, a couch opposite, and two recliners sit either side.

"She'll be happy you're here. It's all she's talked about for days." The man who called out sits in one of the recliners, leaning back, his feet up.

Pania turns and smiles, taking my hand.

"Reece, this is my cousin Wiremu. Wiremu, this is Reece."

Wiremu waves. "Nice to meet you, Reece."

"You too."

"When did she go to the shops?" Pania asks.

He shrugs. "A while ago. She won't be far away."

Pania drops onto the couch, and I sit beside her.

"She'll freak out when she sees you." Wiremu grins at me. "She buys those stupid magazines with you and Josh and Delaney in them."

I grimace. "I hope she doesn't believe all the stories they print."

Wiremu shakes his head. "Pania told her not to. But who knows."

The back door opens, and we all turn our heads at the sound. There's a rustle of shopping bags.

"Do you need some help, Auntie?" Wiremu calls out.

"Yes. You could put these groceries away while I see my baby."

He grins. "On it."

An older Māori woman appears in the living room doorway. "Pani —Reece Evans?" she exclaims, holding up her hands. "Pania didn't tell me it'd be you paying a visit."

I stand and turn toward Pania. Her eyes are cast up toward the ceiling, as if she's trying really hard not to look at her mother.

"Pania's full of surprises," I say.

"Reece arrived to see me a couple of days ago, Mum. He's here for two weeks."

"Well, it's nice the two of you could visit. Wiremu's staying in the spare room right now, so …"

I press my lips together to stop myself from laughing at her obvious fishing expedition.

"We'll be staying in my room." Pania finally meets her mother's gaze, and the older woman's face lights up.

"Lovely. Make sure you show Reece how to find everything, and I'll get started on something to eat."

Pania walks over to her mother and grasps her arm. "Sit and have a coffee with us. We stopped and had breakfast at Matamata."

"I'll put the jug on," Wiremu calls out.

I stand as Pania leads her mother to the couch. She opens her arms and embraces me, kissing me on the cheek.

"It's very nice to meet you, Reece."

"It's lovely to meet you, Mrs Wilson."

She beams. "Please, call me Hana."

Pania sits in a nearby chair. "I thought you might like me bringing him here."

Hana nods. "It's good to see both of you."

We sit on the couch, and she smiles at me. "Did you enjoy the drive down?"

I chuckle. "I slept for half of it. But what I did see was beautiful.

New Zealand's been on my bucket list for a while. I just never had an excuse to come."

"And now you do."

I look over at Pania and smile. "Now I do."

HANA IS AMAZING. She fusses over me, and it reminds me of Delaney in some ways. Pania spends a lot of her time rolling her eyes and laughing at her mother fussing over me.

It's a little overwhelming.

After dinner, Pania heads along the hallway, and when she doesn't come back, I go looking for her.

I find her sitting on the end of the bed in her room.

"You okay?" I ask.

"I just wanted a minute alone."

I point back out the door. "I can go—"

She grasps my arm. "No. It's you I'm thinking about."

I close the door before sitting next to her. "What's going on? You don't have any doubts about us, do you?"

She shakes her head. "You're everything I always wanted. Not the celebrity thing, or the money you have. But you. You don't let me walk all over you, but you also know when I'm right."

"That's easy. The answer is always."

She laughs, and I nudge her arm. "You scare me, Reece. I think you're the funniest, sweetest man I've ever met, but you're still this big star and I'm me."

My chest tightens. I can't blame her. In the past, I was never reliable. I got myself together long enough to get movies finished, but in between, I'm a mess.

But I don't want that anymore. I want Pania.

"You scare the hell out of me, so that makes two of us."

She laughs. "Yeah, but you like the way I scare you. I don't like the way you scare me."

"There hasn't been anyone else." I search her eyes, but she gives nothing away.

"What do you mean?"

I suck on my bottom lip. "I haven't thought about anyone else. Not since the night I first kissed you."

Pania falters, blinking rapidly as she seems to try and maintain eye contact. "I don't understand."

I take her hand in mine and give it a gentle squeeze. "Josh and Delaney working out their issues made me rethink my own life. I've always been so scared to settle down and try just being with one person." I swallow hard. "But even though we haven't been together together, and we've been separated by half the planet, you're my person, Pania."

She's so hard to read right now, and her brows twitch as we gaze at each other.

"I'm not really sure what to say."

"Believe me, I've always let myself get lead around by my dick, but not now. Not for the past two years."

Pania clamps her lips together before dissolving into laughter. "I'm not sure whether that's a compliment or an insult."

"Trust me, it's a compliment. I didn't fly thousands of miles to get laid. Although, I'm not going to say no."

Her hazel eyes sparkle with amusement as she grasps my arm. "You're a shocker."

"I don't even know what that means, but what I do know is that I want more with you. Getting to know you these past couple of years has been a huge privilege, and now I want everything."

I scan her expression. She's such a beautiful woman, and I don't think she has any idea just how much. All I know is that she settles me unlike anyone else, and I've not had thoughts of spending the rest of my life with another person, or imagined having children with anyone.

I don't even know if that's what she wants too.

But I have this image in my head of buying her a house—similar to Josh and Delaney's, and having our own babies running around.

There's no way I'm telling her that yet. It'll just freak her out.

Hell, it freaks *me* out.

I take a deep breath. "There's something I want to tell you. Something I've never told anyone—not even Josh."

Her brows knit. "It must be big if you haven't told him. Are you sure you're ready to tell me?"

"You're the only one I can tell. And if we're going to be together, it's important you know."

She bows her head, as if thinking, and then meets my gaze. "You can tell me anything. It's between you and me."

I clamp my lips together for a moment, breathing long and deep. "I make up stories about having a family. I've been lying for years about them. It's a miracle no one's gone digging and found out, but I want you to know my truth." Dropping my gaze, I turn my head away. "I was four when my parents died. I can't remember much about them—just little bits and pieces. They left me with my grandmother for the weekend to go to a music festival and never came back."

She gasps and reaches for my hand.

"Some shitty drug dealer sold a bunch of people dodgy tablets. Most of the victims ended up in hospital and recovered, but my parents ..." I lick my lips. "I was raised by my grandmother. We moved around a lot, and I don't even know how I ended up with the accent I have." I shrug. "She died just before I moved to LA."

"I'm so sorry," Pania whispers, tears welling in her eyes.

"Josh is my family. I wanted a fresh start, so I made up the story of a loving home with parents who actually gave a shit. By the time I realised what a good friend he was to me, I didn't have the heart to tell him I lied."

Pania leans her head on my shoulder. "I'm glad you had him."

"I know people think I'm shallow, and that I can't commit, but I was so scared. I didn't want to get close to someone and lose them. I've had enough of that in my life."

She presses her nose against my cheek. "You won't lose me."

"What if I screw this up? I've never done this before."

Pania grips my hand tight. "Then we screw it up together."

"Are you sure?" I turn to look at her.

She raises her hand, running her fingers down my face and along my jaw. "You didn't ask for any of it, Reece. Not a single bit."

"I'm such a fake."

She shakes her head. "No, you did what you did to protect yourself. I can't imagine how awful it would be for the media to get hold of that."

I sigh. "I don't even care about that anymore. The only thing I'm worried about is losing you."

She leans in and brushes her lips over mine. "No chance."

"I love you." I chuckle, a little embarrassed. "Shit. I've never said that to anyone before. Not like this."

"I love you, too, you big doofus."

"You do?"

"You flew halfway around the world and got in trouble for it. Those are some pretty big brownie points."

"Say it again." I can't help but grin.

"I love you, Reece Evans. There. Does that do it?"

My heart swells. "Yes. I might want to hear it a few more times, though."

Pania laughs.

My phone buzzes, and I pluck it out of my pocket. "Fancy a road trip?"

Pania looks over my shoulder. "Where are we going?"

"Havelock North? Josh is casting a new movie, and we made some decisions not long before I left. But he's just realised I could deliver the news in person to one of our leads."

"And he's in Havelock North?"

I nod. "Apparently filming there now."

She pecks me on the cheek. "I'm in. You'll love it down there, and I get to show you one of my favourite places in the world."

Grinning, I lean my head against hers. "Sounds like a way to get to know you better and qualify this as a business trip."

Pania laughs. "Can we claim everything as an expense?"

"We can try."
"I'm doubly in, then."

28

REECE

Two days later, we're in the car again and on our way to Havelock North.

I haven't been on a car trip for years, and now I'm on my second one within days.

We pass green fields that go for miles on both sides of the road. It might be winter, but the weather is mild and there's a warm breeze floating through the car bringing with it all the scent of the countryside.

I feel more at peace than I have in a long time—at times I'm reminded of my grandmother's old house. My life is a series of long distance flights, interrupted only by work. I've spent more time at home the past two years than ever before, but that was because of Josh and I going into business.

This is different. And it's wonderful.

"How long is the drive?" I ask.

"About three and a half hours, but we can stop for breaks along the way." She smiles.

"Sounds good to me. I like the idea of seeing more of your country."

"At least you're not sleeping this time.

It doesn't take long for that to change, and I'm soon lulled off to sleep by the gentle purr of the car engine and the gentle twists in the road. My grandmother used to tease me about my ability to fall asleep anywhere, and some things never change.

About an hour later, I wrinkle my nose and shake my head to wake myself up.

The pungent smell of sulphur fills my nose. It's like rotten eggs or a really awful fart.

"Oh my God. What the fuck is that smell?"

Pania chuckles. "I took a detour to wake you up. Welcome to Rotorua."

I grimace. "Does it always smell like this?"

She pulls to the side of the road outside a small shop. "It's all the geothermal activity. There are some amazing hot pools around here."

"Now you're talking." I clap my hands together.

"I'm just going to grab some snacks for the rest of the trip. Want anything?"

I shrug. "Nose plugs?"

Pania leans over and pecks me on the lips. "You big baby. You'll be fine."

I lean back in my seat and she's back a few minutes later with a bag full of drinks, potato chips, and candy.

"Pick out what you want."

"My personal trainer is going to kill you."

She laughs. "Bring it on."

After starting the car, she pulls into the traffic. "Do you want to do some sightseeing while we're here?"

"It's not as if we're running to a timetable. Sure." I crack open a bottle of Coke and take a sip.

"I haven't been here for a while. I'll take you to one of my favourite places."

The town soon gives way to the greenery of the countryside, but it's not too far before we turn into a car park. It's not clear why we're here. There's a large building, but it gives no real clues about what it is.

"Mum and Dad used to bring me here when I was a kid. I loved it," Pania says. "If I'm bringing you this way, we might as well take a look."

"Where are we?"

She turns off the ignition and grabs her bag. "We'll take one of the shorter walks. Let me show you some of my country."

I follow her across the car park and into the building where she pays for tickets before I can stop her. It's not until we reach the other side of the entrance that I understand—I catch my breath at what's in front of me.

Steam rises from the ground in the distance, and Pania grabs hold of my hand and leads me down a walkway.

Being here makes me think of Yellowstone and how it was always one of those places I meant to visit and never got to. I've travelled the world but have usually been working, not often stopping long enough to see the sights.

This is another thing I've been missing out on.

The wooden walkway weaves its way toward a stronger sulphur smell, greenery on either side.

"We won't go too far. Just a couple of things to look at, and then we can get back on the road. I don't want to get to Napier too late, as I want to make a stop there too," Pania says.

"You're in charge. Keep leading the way."

We walk for a few minutes before she points to something to the left. It's not until we draw up to it that I realise we're looking at boiling mud.

"I always liked just looking at it. You can't touch it because it's way too hot, but it's just so freaky looking."

I slip an arm around Pania's waist and lean my head against hers.

"We went everywhere when I was a kid," she says. "Mum and Dad had trouble conceiving after I was born, so I was an only child. But we have such a big family, there were always other kids to play with. Except for when we went on holiday—it would usually just be the three of us."

The mud bubbles below us. It's hypnotic in some ways, but my head is filled with Pania's words. This is her letting me into her past, just as I let her into mine.

"Thank you," I murmur.

"What for?" She pulls away, her eyes searching mine.

"Everything."

Her nose twitches, and she grabs my hand. "There's one more thing I used to love coming to see here. Let's go."

We walk along the pathway until we get to an area with a huge white rock.

"Now, we wait," she says.

"What for?"

A burst of water comes up from the ground, and I grin, watching the geyser spray up into the air.

Pania laughs as mist settles on us.

"We're not in any hurry, right?" I ask.

She shakes her head.

"Let's stay and watch it again."

WE DON'T STOP for the rest of the trip, deciding instead to get there and go to the motel for the night before completing our mission the following day.

And at the end of a very long and twisty road, we reach a sign welcoming us to Hawke's Bay. Something's triggered in my memory from the map we looked at on my phone last night when Pania showed me where we were going.

"This is close, right?"

She nods. "We go through Napier and then head onto Hastings. Havelock North isn't much farther."

"Where did you book the motel?"

"In Havelock North. Then it's not far to go and see your friend."

I lean back in my seat. "I don't know this guy personally. His audition was amazing, but so were some of the others."

"I Googled him. He's pretty cute." She glances at me, and I take in the grin on her face.

"I'm cuter."

"Yes you are, my beautiful baby man." She does that baby voice that Delaney does when she's taking the piss out of Josh. But before I can respond, she takes a deep breath. "There's something I want to show you."

We drive along what looks like the main street of Napier. To the left is the beach with the waters of the South Pacific ocean stretching as far as the eye can see. The street is lined with pine trees, and we drive a short distance before Pania stops the car.

I close my eyes as I step out and breathe in the sea air. The sun settles on my skin and warms me.

"Reece?"

I open my eyes and meet Pania's gaze. "Just enjoying this weather. What are we doing here?"

She locks the car, walks around it, and grabs my hand. "This way."

Leading down a path to a large white fountain, we then take a right turn and end up at the base of a bronze statue, going green with age. It's a woman, her legs bent under her body, her breasts bared. She gazes out toward the water, a wistful smile on her face.

"This is Pania of the Reef," Pania says. "My dad grew up not far from here. When I was born, he named me Pania." She places her hand on the rock underneath the statue. "After her."

"What's her story?"

Pania smiles. "She was a sea maiden who fell in love with a Māori chief, living with him at night, but she had to return to the sea by morning or she'd die. He was desperate to keep her with him, and got advice from a kaumatua—a wise elder—that if she ate cooked food, she wouldn't be allowed to go back to the ocean."

I cock my head. "That doesn't seem fair."

She shakes her head. "Well, he waited until she was asleep and tried to feed her. But she woke and was horrified that he'd risk her life that way. So she returned to the sea and left him forever."

She wraps her arms around my waist, and I kiss her temple. "I can't say I blame her."

"Some say she can still be seen beyond the reef, her arms outstretched, imploring her lover to explain why he did it. Or maybe she's showing him she still loves him." Pania leans her head against mine. "I always thought it was a story about the crazy things people do for love."

"You mean like flying halfway around the world when I was supposed to be filming a TV ad."

She leans back, her mouth hanging open. "No."

"I forgot all about it. The only thing I could think about was getting to you."

Her eyes search mine, and I slowly nod.

"Reece, you didn't."

"I did. My agent called me not long after I got here and told me off. She sorted it out."

Pania rolls her eyes and laughs. "Oh my God! You're hopeless. What am I ever going to do with you?"

"Whatever you want to." I plant a soft kiss on her lips.

Waves crash against the stony beach nearby, spraying the air with salty mist. Pania takes my hand and leads me to a nearby bench where a wall shelters us from the spray, but we still get the taste of salt in the air.

"You haven't told me much about your father."

"My dad died a couple of years before Delaney went on her OE."

"OE?"

She braces herself as she leans back. "Overseas experience. It's supposedly some rite of passage for a lot of people."

"You didn't go?"

Pania shakes her head. "I got a job, but my mum still had a mortgage to pay, and all she had was me. Delaney saved her arse off, and then when she came back, her mum kicked her out, so she came to live with us."

"That's why you're so close."

She nods. "We went through everything together."

"You must miss her terribly."

Pania blinks rapidly and blows out a breath. "It's not easy. What you said about Josh being family, that's me and Delaney."

I pause, just looking at her. Her head's slightly down, and I can't see her eyes. "Come back with me."

Her head shoots up. "I can't. You know I can't."

"I'm never going home, then."

Pania leans against me, her head on my shoulder. "Suits me. I'll keep you in my tiny flat while I'm studying."

"Works for me."

She lifts her head. "You mean that, don't you?"

I lean over and kiss her softly on the lips. "You've given me more in the past few days than I ever thought possible. You love me back, and I already feel as if I'm a part of the family. I don't know if I want to leave."

"Then don't."

I let out a long sigh. "Wish I could. But like you, I have obligations."

"Think you can wait another few months for me?"

I shrug. "I'm not fussed."

She slaps my arm, and I grab hold of her, pulling her over onto my lap. Pania wraps her arms around my neck.

"Of course I'll wait. I love you."

Her lips twitch. "I love you too."

"When's your next holiday?"

"October."

I grimace. "That far away?"

She pecks my cheek. "Ten weeks."

I sigh. "It'll be back to Skype in the meantime."

"Phone sex? Video sex?"

Pania snorts. "There's no way that's happening. The video one anyway."

"Still up for phone sex?"

"We'll see." She leans forward, kissing me on the neck and nipping at my ear lobe. "We should go to the hotel."

"You're insatiable. I'm not sure I can handle this."

"Deal with it," she whispers.

"Let's go." I shove her off my lap, and she laughs as I stand and turn toward the car park. "Hurry up. I think you just made a promise to me you have to fulfil now."

"Race you." She pushes herself up, and runs past me.

I speed up to a jog and laugh to myself as she disappears into the distance.

I'll let her have this race—right along with my heart.

29

———

REECE

In the morning we head out, and I'm glad Pania knows where she's going because I have no clue.

We end up on a long road that runs parallel to a river. The water gently flows along, and trees line one side of it, the other side visible from the road. It looks like a peaceful place to swim. Next time I'm here, I want to stay longer and see everything.

We reach a grassed area where there are a ton of cars parked, and a wire fence.

"This is the spot I think," Pania says. "If Josh got it right."

"That's a big if." I laugh.

She grins and parks the car.

We walk together to the gate. I know movie sets, I've been on enough of them, and now we're closer, I can see this is definitely one.

There's a security guard on the gate, and his eyebrows rise as we approach.

"Aren't you ...?"

"Reece Evans. I'm here to see Alex Stone."

He looks down at the iPad in his hands. "Does he know you're coming?"

"No. It's a surprise."

He shakes his head. "As much as I'd like to, I can't just let you in, mate. I can talk to my boss."

I smile. "I'd really appreciate that."

We're left waiting at the gate as he ambles off into the compound, but it doesn't take long for him to reappear with another man beside him.

Pania's face lights up.

"Pania. What are you doing here, cuz?"

A tall, well built, good looking Māori guy walks up to the fence. He'd do well on screen, with his chiselled looks and two-day stubble.

Pania claps her hands like he's her long lost love. "Reece, this is my cousin, Peter. Peter, this is my boyfriend, Reece."

He plasters a big smile all over his face. "You scored Reece Evans?" He shifts his gaze to me. "I'm a big fan, man. That movie you won your Oscar for, that brought tears to my eyes. And Gabby Reynolds, what a hot—"

"Ahem." Pania clears her throat, and I bite down a laugh.

Peter's laugh is deep and loud. "Sorry. What can I do for you?"

"Reece has a message to pass onto one of the actors. Can we do that?"

He frowns. "I can ask. You'll have to wait out here, though. Who did you want to talk to?"

"Alex Stone."

His frown turns into a grin. "I know he's a big fan of yours. I'm sure it won't be a problem, but I'll go and check first."

I nod. "Understood."

"Are you okay?" Pania asks as he walks away.

"Fine. Why?"

"You just seem a little … off."

I shake my head. "Apart from the weirdness that is running into your cousin here, I'm sure I'll be fine."

She laughs. "Welcome to New Zealand."

"Did you know he was here?"

"No, I haven't seen him in forever. Last I heard he was working up north. But I guess it depends on where the work is."

I look around. The view is stunning. Lush green fields surround us, the long grass rippling in the gentle breeze. It's a great place to be filming a movie.

"Reece." Pania nudges me with her elbow.

I look back in the gate.

It's a little unnerving to see someone who could easily pass for my younger brother walking toward me. I haven't been part of the casting process—we have a casting director for that, but given that I need a sibling for the movie, even I can see he's a good choice.

Pania's cousin opens the gate to let him through.

"Reece Evans." Alex grins. "What are you doing here?"

"I've come to offer you a job."

He extends his hand, and I shake it. "Really? You came all the way here to do that?"

"I was here for other reasons, but Josh thought it'd be something special for me to deliver the news in person."

He nods. "Sounds great. Have you spoken to my agent? I haven't heard anything from him yet."

"Josh is handling all that. I'm guessing no, or maybe he's told them I'm delivering the news personally. But we're not really good at doing things the traditional way."

Alex laughs. "So I hear. I look forward to working with you guys."

"You want the role?"

His mouth falls open. "Does a bear shit in the woods? Hell yes, I want it. The chance to work with you and Josh Carter after your Oscar clean-up is mind boggling. I'd be an idiot to say no."

"Ahem."

I side-eye Pania. "Oh, Alex, this is my girlfriend, Pania. Pania, my future co-star Alex Stone."

She blushes. She *actually* has the nerve to blush as he shakes her hand. I raise my eyebrows as I meet her eyes.

"What? He's cute," she says.

Alex laughs. "I like her."

"Don't like her too much. I just got her."

All that does is make them both laugh. Time to change the subject.

"We should have dinner or something to celebrate. Have you got some time?"

He looks back over his shoulder. "I should be finished up here around four I think. It depends though. You know how things go."

"How about I give you my number, and you text me when you're ready. We're not in a hurry to leave town." Pania meets my gaze with a raised eyebrow. I grab hold of her hand and raise it to my lips. "We can stay another night."

She beams. "I like that idea."

Alex looks between us and smiles. "Sounds good. Things have gone pretty well today. I think we should be good."

"Great."

I give him my number, we shake hands again, and he turns to go back. "Talk to you later."

Pania's cousin steps through the gate, and opens his arms. She beams as he hugs her before stepping back. "Give my love to your mum."

"I will," Pania says.

As we walk away, she links her arm in mine and leans against me. "That went well."

"It did. I think you managed to wipe up all your drool."

All she does is laugh.

AFTER A DAY of Pania showing me around, my phone buzzes just after 4:30, and I swipe to answer Alex's call.

"Alex."

"Hey, Reece. I'm all yours if you want to go somewhere for dinner."

I grin. "Great. Pania's found a restaurant and made reservations. No need to dress up, it's just casual."

"Sounds good. The last thing I need today is to have to worry about dressing up. It's been a long one."

"I bet. I'll text you the details."

Pania steps into the room as I finish the call, and I catch my breath. Her dark green dress hugs her curves, and her long hair is slicked back into a top knot.

She's fiddling with her earrings while watching me. "Are you getting changed?"

I shake my head. "No, I think I'm fine like this. It's a bit early. We're not meeting until six."

"We could go for a drink first."

"We could ..." I grab her by the waist and pull her down onto my lap. "Or we could fool around for an hour and then go."

We fool around, and I can't get enough. And now I'm annoyed we made dinner arrangements. And have to leave.

It's just after six when we walk into the restaurant, and Pania buries her face in my bicep and laughs at the sight of Alex waiting at the table for us.

"I'm so sorry, dude." I extend my hand. "You know how women are at getting ready to go out."

Pania slaps my arm.

"Okay. So it was me." I laugh.

Alex shakes my hand and grins. "It's fine. I just got here myself."

"Have you ordered a drink?"

I pull out Pania's chair for her, and then take a seat.

Alex shakes his head. "Not yet. I thought I'd better wait."

"I'll order a bottle of wine if you two are happy with that. I hear it's good in these parts."

Pania scans the menu. "This one looks nice."

I wink at her. "You order what you want, sweetheart. I'm sure we'll like it."

She smiles and turns to get the waiter's attention.

"Good day?" I ask Alex."

"Long day. I was in make-up at three this morning, but we wanted to shoot the dawn, and we did so it was worth it."

"Great."

It only takes a moment for us to have a glass of red wine in front of us, and I hold mine up. "To Alex. Congratulations on joining our team."

"To Alex," Pania says.

We all take a sip before the waiter arrives to take our food order. After we've ordered, we sip our drinks and silence falls over the table for a while.

"So, Pania, do you live in New Zealand?" Alex asks.

She nods. "I study fashion design in Auckland. But I come from Whakatane."

I take a sip of my wine and reach for her hand under the table. She grips it tight before letting it go.

"Wow. So you two are long distance?"

"For now," I say. "I'm hoping once she's finished her studies, she'll move to LA with me."

Pania's eyebrows arch. I've never met anyone with such expressive eyebrows, but it means I usually can tell what she's thinking. And right now it'll be *"What the fuck? He hasn't said that to me."*

"Great. I hope it all works out for you." He pauses. "I met someone a couple of weeks ago here, but it's still early days."

"Someone on set?"

He shakes his head. "No. There's a bit of a story behind it, but I'm keeping that one to myself until I work out what direction things are going in."

I glance at Pania. "I get that. We're keeping our relationship low key right now."

Pania rolls her eyes. "Kind of. As low key as it gets while walking around publicly together holding hands."

I hold up my palms. "I can't help myself."

Alex laughs. "You two sound like an old married couple."

"Well, we have had a long-distance relationship for two years," I say.

"Kind of." Pania laughs.

"There's a story there somewhere."

Pania's smile warms my heart. "My best friend is married to his best friend. We met at their wedding a little over two years ago."

"And your best friend is Josh Carter." He points at me. "Didn't he marry a woman from New Zealand?"

"Delaney," Pania says. "She's my bestie."

Alex nods. "Gotcha. It's so nice to meet both of you. I really appreciate you delivering that news in person, Reece. My agent called me this afternoon, and he laughed when I told him I'd already spoken to you."

"You're welcome. It was actually pretty cool to be able to do that. I look forward to working with you."

He grins, and I'm reminded again at how perfect his casting is. We'll look great together on screen as brothers.

"Me too. I can't wait." He runs his tongue over his upper lip. "My mom is going to freak out. I told her I was auditioning for the role, and she was pretty excited. She's a big fan of yours."

"Mine?" I run my hand down my face. "That's awesome. Maybe you can bring her on set to meet all of us."

"She'd love that."

"And when you're back in the states, come and see us. We're a pretty close-knit team, and it'd be good for us all to get to know each other before we start filming."

I shift my gaze to Pania. Her expression is blank, and I could kick myself for inviting Alex like that, even if it's the right thing to do. She's still determined to see out the rest of her studies, and I don't have to be a mind reader to know she'll also be sad to miss out.

"By the time we start filming, Pania will be setting up her business in LA and we'll *all* be able to hang out together."

Her lips twitch, and the sparkle in her eyes is enough to show me I've made things right.

I'm not sure what our future brings, but we're on the right track.

～

AFTER DINNER, we part ways, promising to keep in touch, and Pania drives us back to the hotel. It's a quiet ride home as I reflect on my own career path.

Alex's career is still in its infancy, but there's a lot of expectation around our new film after the way the last one performed.

Once we're inside the hotel room, Pania drops her car keys into her bag. I squeeze her shoulders as she rolls her neck.

"Let me drive tomorrow. You must be over it."

She turns. "Do you really think I'm going to trust you with my baby?"

I laugh. "I'll let you drive my car when you come see me in LA."

Pania purses her lips. "You've got a deal."

I press a kiss to those lips, then nuzzle her neck. "Did you enjoy yourself this evening?"

"Alex is a really nice guy. He'll make a nice addition to our group."

I raise my head. "Our group?"

"Are you jealous?" Her eyebrows practically talk to me themselves as they rise. "Oh my God, you are."

"You said he was cute," I mumble.

She grins. "Now maybe you know how I feel when I see you on screen with other women."

"I'm acting."

Pania cups my face. "And I'm in love with you. He's cute, but you're the cutest."

"Really?"

"I never thought I'd be reassuring you of how I feel. This is something I thought would be the other way around."

I frown. "Do you have doubts about me?"

She doesn't answer me, but drops her hands and tilts her head to the side, taking a deep breath.

"I love that you're thinking of the future. It's not us, but the thought of how crazy life will get that's scary."

My heart sinks a little. She's not wrong. This is a situation where we'll have to work out how to take things in our stride together.

"I'm not saying that to hurt you, Reece. This stands a better chance of working if we're both honest with each other."

"I know."

"Now kiss me and maybe I'll forget Alex Stone even exists." Her smile lifts my mood, and I find myself smiling despite my fear I'll do something to screw this up.

"I'll do more than kiss you."

She screeches with laughter as I bend and pick her up, throwing her over my shoulder.

"I'm too heavy for this."

"No, you're perfect."

I carry her into the bedroom, and as gently as I can lower her onto her back on the bed, her eyes are so full of love, and those full lips are just begging to be kissed.

She pulls me down with her, and I'm so lost in my overwhelming emotions for her. It's not that I've never felt anything before, but I never allowed myself to *feel*. Pania makes it so easy.

This time, we make love long and slow, lying in the afterglow, curled up around each other.

"Do you know what I love about being with you?"

I meet her gaze. "My devastating good looks and charm?"

Pania's shoulders shake. "That, and we laugh together. We had that from the start."

"Remember when you asked me if hang out was a euphemism for sex?"

She places her palm flat on my chest before running a finger around one of my nipples. "Yes?"

"It kind of was."

Her brow furrows.

"I really liked you back then, even though I didn't know you that well. And I'm glad we didn't have sex because I think things wouldn't have gone well and you'd probably hate me by now."

She shrugs. "I'm not sure I could ever hate you. I might have found a photo of you and stuck it to a dart board, but I wouldn't hate you."

I roll my shoulders. "Does that explain these weird chest pains I've been having?" I sigh. "Oh, no, that's just my heart beating."

"You're such a dick." She laughs against my skin.

"And now you own my dick."

Pania pushes herself up. "I do, don't I?"

"Don't you ever forget it." I reach over and run my fingers through her hair. "I hate the thought of us being apart again. I'm not sure how I'll cope without this."

"Me too." She plants a kiss on my pec and lies back down. "I feel comfortable with you. It's not a common thing for me. Most of the time I barely tolerate people."

I chuckle. "No kidding."

"I'm just not a patient person." After a few moments of me saying nothing, she lifts her head again. "Aren't you going to respond to that?"

"What do you want me to say?"

"You're supposed to say, I know, Pania, but I love you anyway." Her imitation of my drawl is so on point, all I can do is laugh.

"You're good. Not as good as Delaney's impersonation of Josh, but not too far off."

I close my eyes and smile as Pania snuggles closer. She's not the only one who feels comfortable. Usually by now, I've cut and run, but not with her. Never with her.

I'm at peace with myself for the first time in years, and it's all thanks to Pania.

30

PANIA

Reece assures me he's driven on the left side of the road plenty of times—just not in New Zealand—so despite my concerns, I let him drive my car.

It's a little embarrassing that he's driving it after the luxury of his own car, but Reece takes to her without a care. It makes me love him even more.

After so much time on the road, it's a relief to lay eyes on Mum's house. At least now we're here, it's a while until we have to make our way back to Auckland.

Mum's standing by the door as we drive up the driveway and park. Reece steps out of the car, and I follow behind.

"Reece." She beams.

I put up my hand. "I'm right here."

Mum shoos me away with a flick of her wrist. "You I can see any time."

Reece stifles a laugh. "Hi, Mom."

"That's my boy." Mum's just about stratospheric from the looks of the smile on her face. I just shake my head, roll my eyes, kick off my shoes by the backdoor, and walk inside.

"Who crapped in your cornflakes?" Wiremu laughs. He's standing by the kitchen bench wearing nothing but a pair of shorts.

"I've become a visitor in my own mother's house."

He grins. "All she's done while you were gone is talk about Reece. And how good he is to her daughter."

"Whatever." I bite down a smile.

"It's true. I'm pretty sure she's hearing things too."

I frown. "Like what?"

"Wedding bells." He chuckles and walks off into the living room.

I shake my head again and turn left along the hallway, heading toward my bedroom. Faceplanting on the bed, I draw in a breath.

"Are you okay?" Reece asks.

"Did she let you go?"

He sits on the end of the bed. "Your mom knows I'm not here for long. She's just making the most of it."

I roll onto my back. "I know, I can't really begrudge her for it."

Reece leans over. "I'm going to have a shower. Want to join me?" He nuzzles my nose with his.

"As good as that sounds, no. We're sleeping in the same room, but Mum might get funny if we shower together."

He laughs. "Fair enough. I'll be back shortly."

Grabbing clean clothes and a towel from the pile Mum left us, he heads along the hallway.

As soon as he leaves for the shower, I pull out my laptop and message Delaney.

Me: *Skype?*

Delaney: *Good timing. Call me.*

I click the call icon and smile as her familiar face fills the screen.

"Hey." She smiles.

"Hey. We're back from our trip, and I thought I'd check in."

"Good. I've been waiting. Josh told me you two were on a business trip. Did you meet Alex Stone? He's so cute."

I laugh. "Even better in person."

"So, what's happening with Reece?" My cheeks heat up and Delaney grins. "That good, huh? Where is he?"

"He's in the shower right now. And things are really good." I bite my bottom lip. "Looks like I'm coming for a visit."

Her eyes widen. "When?"

"At the end of next term. Instead of coming here for the holidays, I'll make the trip over there. I'll be there for about a week and a half."

Delaney claps. "Love it. We can go out and do something. Josh's parents are here around then for Josh's birthday, so maybe the four of us can go out to celebrate while they look after the kids."

"How are the kids?"

She moves her computer. Melly comes into sight first, her hands over her eyes. She lifts her hands and pulls a face to a wide-eyed Addison in her rocker. "Peekaboo," she yells.

"Getting on like a house on fire. Addison found her voice, and Melly got more interested in her little sister."

"I can't wait to see them."

Delaney swings the computer back. "And I can't wait to see you. I miss you so much."

I sigh. "I know it's still a few months away, but I'll see you soon."

She grins. "I can't wait."

"Me either. I'm gonna give Melly the biggest hug. She's grown so much."

Delaney cocks her head. "Seven going on seventeen. She's more and more like her father every day."

"Is that a good thing? Or ..." I chuckle.

"Let's just say there will come a time when she'll follow in his footsteps. After her performance in the school play, I think it's inevitable."

"Really? She was that good?"

Delaney glances over her shoulder and lowers her voice. "She was amazing, but we're downplaying it a little because we don't want her to get too big a head."

Behind her, a squeal from Melly tells me Josh has arrived home.

Delaney's whole face lights up, and I adore that after all this time she still does that when she sees Josh. He leans in, and I roll my eyes as he lingers on her lips right in front of me.

"Dude."

Josh jumps, turning his head toward the screen. "Oh, hey, Pania. Didn't realise Delaney was talking to you." He laughs. "Sorry. How are you going with Reece?"

"Oh, you know. Barely coping." I look up as Reece appears in the doorway, clad only in a pair of boxer shorts. I lick my lips as I run my gaze from those shorts, up his abs and across that broad chest of his before blowing out a long breath.

"I'm guessing he's out of the shower." Delaney lets out a choked laugh.

I blink and set my gaze back on the screen.

"Yeah, I think I'd better go. Love you guys. We'll give you a call later."

"Love you too." Delaney blows me a kiss, and Josh waves.

I click disconnect and look up to see Reece standing beside the bed. "Was that Delaney and Josh?"

"It was." I close the laptop and place it on the bedside table.

He kneels on the bed. "How are they?"

"Delaney is well. Melly and Addison were playing in the background. Josh appeared right at the end, and I don't care about him anyway." I shrug.

He laughs. "Sure you do."

"He seemed fine. Asked how I was going with you. Told him you suck."

His dimples pop. "Only if you ask me nicely."

"Maybe I will. After you tell me why you're walking around this house in just your underwear."

"Your mother took my clothes to wash."

"Didn't you take clean clothes with you to change into?"

He shakes his head. "I had planned to put my boxers on and wrap the towel around me, but she took the towel too."

I snort with laughter. "It's a miracle she left you with any clothes, then."

"I love your mum. She might have to adopt me." He flops onto the bed.

Leaning over, I flatten my palm on his chest. "That would make things a little more complicated for us."

He pulls me down so my face is only inches from his. "I like complicated."

I wrinkle my nose. "Eww."

Reece laughs. "Okay. Maybe not *that* complicated." He runs his index finger down my cheek. "Maybe one day I'll have to make her my mother-in-law."

I raise my eyebrows. "Is that a proposal, Reece Evans?"

"I'm not sure either of us are ready for that yet, but I do know I'm happier than I've ever been, and I really want to do this with you."

Sliding my hand down, I palm his cock through his boxers. "I know what I'd like to do."

"Pania Wilson." His mouth falls open, as if he's offended. "It's the middle of the day."

"It's not bothered you before."

"I know, but ..."

I raise my eyebrows and lift my hand. "Don't say I didn't offer."

He crawls onto the bed, pushing me onto my back. "I've never been one to turn down an offer like that."

His blue eyes are filled with mischief.

God, how I love him.

31

REECE

On our last day in Whakatane, the morning sun peeks through a crack in the curtains, and I draw in a deep breath, unsure if I'm ready to face it.

Beside me, Pania stirs, and I stroke her back, planting a kiss in her hair.

"I don't want to leave," I whisper.

She raises her head. "What?"

"I've never been so happy. You, me—"

"Under my mother's roof."

I crook my neck to look at her. "I think I might have to take your mom back with me."

Pania laughs. "She won't fly. It's always scared her. If you want to see her, you'll have to visit."

I raise my gaze to the ceiling and huff out a breath. "If only there was some other reason I needed to come to New Zealand again."

She shrugs. "I can't think of anything."

"Me either. I'm not sure why I'm here to start with." Her palm hits my chest. "Oof. You. I came here for you."

"Don't you ever forget it."

She buries her face in my neck. "I love you, Reece. So much."

I hug her tight against me. "And you're my whole world."

"As much as I hate to say it, we need to get dressed and get out of here."

"I know."

We lie in silence, and despite knowing we need to get ready, neither of us move. We still have another day before I fly back to the US, and I don't want to think about saying goodbye.

Pania nudges my side. "We need to get moving."

"I know."

It's another fifteen minutes before either of us moves, and then we're dressed and full of food thanks to Hana.

With the car packed up, it's time to say goodbye.

"When do you fly out, Reece?" Hana asks.

"Tomorrow around midday."

"I'm sad to see you go. I hope you've enjoyed your stay."

I smile. "I have. I've been so happy here. And your daughter is such a big part of that."

She chuckles. "It's nice to see her with a smile on her face for a change. Not been a lot of that for a while."

I press my lips together for a moment while I think of what to say. It's not that often that I'm left without words.

"I love her." It's all there is to say.

She cups my face in her hands. "I can see that. She loves you too. Just promise me you'll always be good to her."

I nod. "I will."

"She'll follow you. I know that. And I'll miss her, but you can give her the life she always deserved. I'm so proud of both of you."

My heart swells, and tears prick my eyes. More than ever, I now know what family means. I thought I knew, but I'd only scraped the surface.

"You're part of the *whanau* now. You take care of yourself too."

My brow furrows, and she reaches up with her thumb, smoothing it out. "Family, Reece. You're family now."

The words leave a lump in my throat as I wave goodbye, and then we're on the road.

It's late before we finally talk about it.

I guess neither of us want to address the fact that I'm going home. If I didn't have obligations, I'd extend my stay, but at the same time I'm not sure how fair that would be on Pania as she focuses on the last few months of her course.

"I hate that you're going home tomorrow," she says.

"Me too. I'm just holding onto the fact that we'll see each other again in October. Though, that feels so far away." I smile. "When you come to stay with me, pack the dress."

Her brows knit. "Which one?"

"The one you made in class. The one the dragon lady didn't want for her display."

Pania stares at me. "Why?"

I grab hold of her hands. "Because I'm going to take you out somewhere you can wear it in LA."

Her warm smile makes my heart sing. "I like that idea."

"I can't wait to show the world I'm with you."

She does her tongue thing again, and it's distracting as usual, but it bothers me as I know it means her brain is working overtime.

I let go of her hands and run my fingers down her cheek. "What's going on in that head of yours?"

"I don't want you to roll me out to prove a point. Like 'here's my girlfriend and I've finally worked out how to have relationship'. I want you to want this because you're proud of me and—"

"What I want is to show the world we're together because I love you. And you deserve the opportunity to put a dress on display. Screw whats-her-name. Her display is nothing compared to being photographed for all the magazines."

Pania grins. "It is, isn't it?"

"You don't need her. You never needed her for your talent to shine."

She flings her arms around my neck, and I hold her tight.

I never want to let her go.

It's a quiet ride to the airport in the morning. Each minute that passes reminds me that I'll be flying away from her soon. How did I stay away for two years from something that's so good?

With my baggage checked in, we leave it as long as we can before I go through to security.

I sit on a bench and hold her hand until the last possible minute.

"You need to go," she says.

"I know."

Tears well in her eyes.

"You said you didn't want to cry. Not even happy tears."

She shakes her head. "I think I'm allowed to for this."

I dip my head and kiss her tears away. "I'll call you when I get home. I'm going to miss you like crazy."

She hugs me tight, burying her face in my chest.

"Don't you dare make my shirt wet. Your mother just washed it."

Her shoulders shake as she laughs, and when she raises her head, a smile graces her lips.

"That's better," I whisper.

"Give my love to Delaney and the kids." She sighs. "Oh, and Josh I suppose."

"I'll deliver it just like that." I grin.

She pats my chest. "I know I can depend on you."

"Always."

And with another kiss, I let her go. "See you soon."

"You bet."

I walk away and don't turn until I reach the last point where I can see her. She smiles and waves, but my heart is aching for her already.

Waiting is going to be hell.

32

REECE

"Have you got ants in your pants?" Josh laughs as I pace the living room.

"What?" I stare at him.

"That's what you said to me the day I waited for Delaney and Amelia to arrive."

I drop to the couch. "I'm sorry I teased you. The waiting is driving me crazy."

"That's why I'm driving."

I frown. "You are *not* coming with me."

Josh's smile is so smug, I'm sure my blood pressure takes off. "Do you really think you can keep Delaney from her best friend?"

I drag my hand down my face. "How are we all going to fit in the car?"

"Delaney's taking her car, and we'll drive back together, but you can't deprive her of meeting Pania at the airport."

Standing, I turn toward him. "She's my girlfriend. It's not good for the kids to be there. Do you really want them seeing our reunion?"

"Reece Evans." Delaney stands in the doorway, her hands on her hips. "Do you really think after all this time that I'm not meeting my bestie at the airport?"

I whimper. "But—"

"Don't you dare use the children as an excuse. They'll be just fine. Addison's only three months old."

"I wouldn't cross her if I was you."

Grumbling, I look at my phone. "It's time to go anyway."

"Yes, which is why my children are in the car, and I came back up here to find out what you're doing."

We follow her back out. Josh is right. There's no point in trying to stop Delaney even though I just want to whisk Pania away and do every little dirty thing I've thought about these past months. It's only work that's kept me away from her, and I look forward to spending the next few weeks together.

There is some part of me that's glad Josh is driving as I jiggle my right leg, wanting to go faster but unable to speed things up.

"You're worse than an animal in heat."

"Now you know what it was like watching you."

He chuckles. "I'm impressed you two have stuck this out. It's not easy being apart from the person you love."

"I just want her with me now, you know? Whether we travel the world or stay in LA, I just want us to be together."

We pull up to a red light and he looks at me. "I'm sorry if I haven't been as supportive as I should have been in the past. You've really got your shit together, and it's a beautiful thing."

I hold up my hand. "Don't you dare make me cry."

"You clown." He reaches over and ruffles my hair.

The light turns green and I draw in a deep breath.

Not long to go.

JOSH GRIPS my shoulders as we wait before giving me a gentle shake. The plane's landed, and once Pania's cleared security, she'll appear at the door I've had my eyes on for the past fifteen minutes.

A lump in my throat forms when she appears. I've missed her, but really had no idea just how much until she's right there. My heart soars.

Her eyes are tired, but they're full of all the love I've come to know as she lays eyes on me.

I start walking, meeting her and her luggage trolley half way. She lets go of it.

"Hey, you."

Sliding my arms around her waist, I pull her to me. She gazes into my eyes.

"I thought you were never going to get here." I pout.

"You are such a big baby, but I love you very much." She slips her arms around my neck.

I laugh. Some things never change between us.

"Might not ever let you go now."

"Well, you won't have to for a little while."

I kiss her, ignoring the fact we're in a crowded airport and that anyone could take a photo of us. I don't care. All I want is Pania.

"Ahem." From behind us comes the sound of someone clearing their throat loudly.

I break away from Pania and turn.

Josh, to Delaney's delight, is making a gagging noise and pretending to put his finger down his throat.

"Dude."

"You used to do the same to him." Pania wags her finger. "Payback's a bitch."

Delaney passes Addison to Josh and steps forward, her arms open. Her eyes fill with tears, and my stomach falls at the words we exchanged back at the house.

I turn back to look at Pania. She smiles at me, but it's clear she's fighting too from the way she's blinking.

Taking a step back, I draw in a deep breath as Delaney and Pania embrace.

"I've missed you so much," Delaney says. "I'm so glad you're here."

Pania hugs her tight. "I've missed you too. Can't wait to meet your baby."

"She's right over here."

Pania gasps at the sight of Addison. "Hello, beautiful girl. You're so much like your big sister."

Addison blinks, those long eyelashes framing her big blue eyes always get me.

Pania reaches for Addison and Josh passes her over. She snuggles into Pania's chest as Pania rocks her gently.

"You might not get your baby back now," she says to Josh.

He laughs, and it's a welcome distraction because my chest might just burst at the sight of Pania holding a baby—especially the daughter of two of my best friends.

And that's how we leave the airport. Pania cradles Addison while talking to Delaney, Josh is hand in hand with Amelia. I'm left pushing the luggage trolley.

It doesn't upset me. It's amusing considering the way we left the airport when Delaney moved here. Josh pushed the luggage while I walked out with one arm around Delaney's shoulders, the other hand holding Amelia's.

I guess payback really is a bitch.

33

———————

PANIA

I love being here.

Reece is out of bed before I wake.

I yawn as I look at the phone. It's after ten, and even then it's hard to keep my eyes open. I could stay and doze, but I'd rather get up given I'm not here forever.

Pulling on some trackpants and a T-shirt, I make my way to the kitchen.

"Good morning, sleepyhead." Delaney's way too chirpy. "Want some coffee?"

"Sure." I run my fingers through my hair. "Have you seen Reece?"

"Josh dragged him into the office. Now that you two have let Alex know he's got the part in the next movie, they've got the whole thing cast. They're working on the next step of production."

I slide onto a breakfast stool. "Real work. I'm guessing Reece won't like that."

The coffee machine whirrs and the scent of ground coffee fills the air. I take a deep breath and close my eyes.

"He'll get over it. I told him to leave you to sleep, he kept bouncing around wanting to wake you up. But I know that flight is a killer."

It's like stepping back in time as she froths the milk. Day in, day out we'd make coffee in the diner.

My eyelids are so heavy, and my brain switches off.

"Here you go. Want something to eat? I made bacon and eggs for the boys, but you can have whatever you want. I even have Marmite for toast."

I open my eyes to see Delaney place a steaming mug of coffee in front of me.

"I can make something."

She grips my shoulder. "No, you sit back and relax. Melly's at school and Addison is asleep for a change. It'll be quiet for a little while."

I smile. "Sounds great. If you're making something, some Marmite toast would be nice."

"Coming right up." She sounds way too bright for this hour of the morning. Even if it's not early.

She dances around in her swanky kitchen, and it makes me smile. Delaney's dream was always to cook, and I followed her into it wanting to stay close to the woman who's like a sister to me.

Now we're both following our dreams.

"Are you okay?" she asks.

I meet her blue-eyed gaze. "Can I ask you something?"

"You know you can ask me anything."

"When did you know Josh was it?"

Her lips twitch. "The first or the second time?"

I shrug. "Either."

"Is this about Reece?" She's giving me a smug look now, the same one I usually give her. It's insufferable.

"Just answer the question."

Delaney laughs. "Honestly, I don't know. We just were. From the moment we met, we clicked and just never stopped." Her expression straightens. "Except for the interruption in our relationship. He's my one."

I take a sip of my drink, taking my time to respond. "I don't want to worry Reece, but I'm still a little scared of this whole thing. I love him, and I know he loves me, but now I'm here it's all a little over-whelming."

Delaney reaches across the bench and places her hand on mine. "You know, when I moved here, I felt the same. Josh and I were solid, but I was so miserable the first few weeks trying to work out where I fit into this crazy world."

"What did you do?"

She leans back in her seat. "Floundered a bit before Josh and I sat down and had an honest conversation about it. For me, it was coming here and getting used to having staff and feeling like I wasn't neces-sary in my own home. That was before dealing with the bright lights and the social side of it." Delaney runs her finger around the top of her mug. "We tackled it together. Just talk to Reece. And I'm here whenever you need me."

I reach up and run my fingers through my hair.

"You know I'm team Pania for life."

"I know."

She smiles. "I'm just really glad Reece brought you back to me."

AFTER BREAKFAST, I place my dishes in the dishwasher and turn to Delaney. "There's something I want to show you."

She smiles. "What is it?"

"I've made a couple of project dresses over the time I've been studying, and Reece told me to bring one just in case I want to go out and show the world we're together."

Delaney clasps her hands together. "That's beautiful. He's putting your needs first."

"I want to, but the thought still scares me a little."

Her sad smile makes me frown.

"What?"

Delaney sucks on her bottom lip. "It won't be easy. I'd do anything to protect you from what's said about me online. But I'm here for you, and so is Josh. And Reece loves you so much. He's been unbearable since he came back from his trip."

I chuckle. "That bad?"

She looks everywhere but at me. "It's been like having a moody teenager. Maybe it's good practice for when the girls are older."

Grasping her arms, I keep laughing until she meets my gaze and laughs too. "I'm glad he had you. I can't imagine you made the past few weeks easy for him."

She turns her palms up, gripping my arms. "You know it. Anything to distract him from moping."

"I know I can always rely on you."

"So, show me this dress."

I lead her to our bedroom and open the wardrobe, pulling out my dark blue, sparkly gown.

Delaney gasps as I lay it on the bed.

"I made more, but this one meant the most to me."

She brushes the blue crepe fabric with her finger tips.

"Oh, we have to go somewhere for you to wear that. Whether Reece and Josh come with us or not."

"Really?"

She's got a mischievous twinkle in her eye. "Oh, you bet. If you decide not to go public with Reece, you can go public with me."

I laugh. "I'm not sure about that."

She grabs my hands. "Oh, let's do something fun. Let our hair down. It's been forever. I haven't had a night out since before Addison was born, and I'd love to just hang out with you. Do you remember Melly's friend Maria?"

"Lorenzo's granddaughter?"

Delaney nods. "Her mum babysat Melly before. I'm sure Laura would take care of the kids while we had a night out. I'll call her today and see what we can arrange." She lets go of me and picks up the coat hanger. "I can't believe your tutor didn't put this on display. It's beautiful."

I shrug. "What can I say—she hates me." I bite my lip. "Should have seen her when Reece turned up though." I clasp my hands together and press them against my cheek. "Oh, Mr Evans. How wonderful to see you."

Delaney laughs when I flutter my eyelashes.

"And then he was somehow polite and rude to her all at the same time. I wish I could master that."

She places her hand on my arm. "I've always loved the way you are. You don't need to be like Reece or anyone else. You're uniquely you. And you've always had my back." Addison's wail comes over the baby monitor, and Delaney squeezes my arm. "Sounds like I'm being summoned. I'll just change her and bring her to the living room and you can play after she's fed."

"I'll make some more coffee."

Delaney grins. "See, you always know what I need."

I spend a lazy day drinking and eating with Delaney, and spending time playing with Addison until it's time to pick up Melly from school.

It's a little after four when Josh and Reece come home, and Delaney pounces on Josh the second he walks in the door.

"We need a place to go. I've got a babysitter all sorted whenever we need to go."

Josh glances at Reece. "Where are we going?"

Delaney grasps her husband's arm. "Well, I'll tell you what we're wearing and you can find somewhere. You know this city so much better than me, and your name will get us in anywhere."

"You're my wife. It's your name too."

She smiles. "Yes, but you making the call will make all the difference."

"You just want to dress up and not worry about the details."

She pats him on the chest. "That's right."

Josh kisses her temple. "Leave it with me."

After dinner, I take care of Melly's bedtime while Delaney takes care of Addison. Even from the along the hallway, I can hear Josh making calls, and it makes me smile as he does what he can to make his wife happy.

Delaney's already back in the living room when I get there, and she waves at me to sit next to her on the couch. She pulls me down beside her. "Josh has something to tell us."

I look at Josh, sitting in a chair opposite. "What's going on?"

"I called Gabby. She's involved in a charity for under privileged children, and I remembered seeing something about a gala night." He takes a deep breath. "So for a donation, I got a table. It's a red-carpet event."

Delaney's eyes widen. "Oh, you are *so* getting laid tonight."

"It might not be the best table because we're late to the party, but it's tomorrow night and formal dress."

"Do we need to go and buy new shoes for this?" Reece asks.

Josh glares at him. "Smart ass."

I look between them. "So Gabby will be there too?"

He nods. "Yes, and Delaney's favourite shopping partner, Antonio."

Delaney grabs my arm. "Oh my God! We need to go shopping with him because I tell you, he knows where to find *all* the bargains."

I swallow hard at the thought of walking a red carpet, and meet Reece's gaze. He winks at me, bowing his head slightly, and it shouldn't but it helps me recover my confidence a little.

I might even have some fun.

34

PANIA

Butterflies occupy my stomach the whole day. Not because this is, I guess, my first official event as Reece's girlfriend. But because for the first time, I'll be exposed to the life Delaney has now.

I know how nervous she was at first, and still is, at attending events with Josh. But over time she's grown in confidence, reporters talk to her because of her YouTube channel, and she's just so damn gorgeous, it's hard to get a bad shot of her.

It's nearly time to get ready, and Delaney walks into the living room where I sit with Reece.

"I've been thinking a lot about your dress, and I have the perfect accessory for tonight," she says.

I frown. "I don't need—"

She hands me a velvet box, and I open it. Inside is her diamond teardrop necklace—the one Josh gave her as a wedding gift.

I shove the box back at her. "I can't wear this."

Delaney squeezes my knee. "Of course you can. It's just one night, and it goes beautifully with the dress you're wearing. I'll lend you the matching earrings too. You just can't have my engagement ring."

I laugh. "Delaney."

She leans over to hug me. "Sisters share. When they're not squabbling. I want you to shine tonight."

"What about you?"

Delaney moves back and looks at me. "I've got other jewellery. And I've got the last dress you sent me that I haven't worn yet that I'll match with something."

"Go and get changed," Reece says. "I'll be right behind you."

I throw my arms around Delaney's neck. "Thank you."

"I love you and I'm so glad you're here," she whispers.

"Me too."

By the time I'm finished in the bathroom with my hair and make-up, Reece is in his tux and sitting on the end of the bed.

"You look beautiful."

He reaches out, and I walk toward him. Sliding his arms around my waist, he rests his head on my stomach.

I close my eyes and just enjoy the quiet moment with him.

"Pania," he murmurs.

Looking down, all I see are his blue eyes so full of pride.

"Can you tell I'm nervous?"

"You don't have to be. We're all right here with you."

I blink back tears and then swipe at the corners of my eyes with my index fingers. "Have I made a mess? I don't want to look like a panda."

"Pandas are cute."

"I still don't want to look like one." I laugh.

"Would you like to me to say something completely sexually inappropriate to make you laugh instead?" He grins.

"No. Just help me with my dress."

I slip it on over my head and it cascades down my body. I shiver when Reece's warm breath tickles the skin on my exposed back as he zips it up. His touch sets me alight.

"Are you cold?" he whispers as his lips brush the nape of my neck.

"No, quite the opposite."

For a moment, I just stare at myself in the mirror. I tried it on as I was making it, but it's not the same as wearing it out for a big event like this. The bodice hugs my curves, the sweetheart neckline making my boobs look much better than they do in most of my other clothes. The tulle is layered on the full skirt.

It makes me think of dresses worn by Disney Princesses.

The jewellery box clicks behind me and Reece's hands are warm on my shoulders as he connects the clasp of Delaney's necklace.

She was right. The diamond sparkles like the skirt does.

"I remember telling Delaney on her wedding day that she could put these in because I didn't want to tear a lobe. So, I'm giving these to you to put in yourself." He laughs and offers me a much smaller box.

"Thank you."

I switch out my earrings in front of the mirror and turn to see Reece, his arms open wide.

"That dragon lady has no idea what she's missing out on. She needs you so much more than you need her."

I place a hand on his chest. "You're the best. Anyone ever tell you that?"

"The only one who ever mattered was you."

He offers me his arm, and I take it.

In the living room, Delaney wears a dress I made her a year or so ago. It's lavender chiffon with a high waist, gathered at the top with crossover shoulder straps. I made it so she could wear it during her pregnancy if she had to.

She squeals when I walk into the room. Her eyes fill with tears, and she claps.

"Pania." Melly gasps. "You look like a starry sky."

I bend, opening my arms and she runs over to hug me. "That's exactly the look I'm going for."

"I'm staying to babysit Addison." She puffs out her chest. "I'm being responsible."

I chuckle. "You are, my sweet girl. I'm so proud of you."

She kisses my cheek, and then I straighten up and take Reece's offered arm again.

"Shall we go?"

I grin. "Yes."

Leaving Delaney and Josh behind to say goodbye to their children, Reece leads me downstairs and into a waiting limo. We're doing this whole thing in style.

He grips my hand tight as we sit and wait for the other two.

"I know you're nervous, but I'm right here."

"I'm sure I'll be fine."

Delaney arrives next, followed by Josh. They sit opposite us, snuggled together, and I wriggle a little closer to Reece. He slips his arm around my waist, and then we're on the road.

Everything's lit up, and all I see are shiny colours in the night sky as we're driven toward the event.

The limo slows, then comes to a stop.

Delaney smiles at me as the limo door opens. "We'll go first. Watch out for the camera's flashing, they'll be blinding."

I squeeze Reece's hand harder, but his hand on the base of my spine gives me a little rub, and I take a deep breath to relax.

Once Josh and Delaney are out, Reece steps out, turns, and offers me his hand. His confident smile gives me confidence, and I take it to steady myself as I step out of the car.

Despite being warned about it, I blink as flashes go off all around us.

Reece leans in.

"Smile, beautiful."

I turn to look at him, and he gazes at me with so much affection, I know I'm ready to face whatever challenges we'll have.

We'll do it all together.

Once we're inside, there's far less photography, and a lot of mingling. We're shown to the table, and I'm relieved to take a seat after our walk into the building.

"How do you do this?" I ask Delaney.

She grunts. "It's exhausting. But now we're here, we get to eat and dance before we go home again." Her hand brushes my arm. "You'll look so beautiful in all the magazines. That dress really is to die for, and it suits you."

"Thank you."

I keep my eyes on the door, watching each new arrival. Some designs I could name the designers on sight, others I'm not so sure of.

"You know this is going to drive your tutor crazy," she says.

Despite all my bravado, the thought of that makes my stomach flip. But I'm simply living my life. I might be part of a world I never seriously thought I'd live in, but now it's real, and no matter what happens with my studies or anything else, I'm Reece's girlfriend.

And my life has been enriched by having his love and his trust.

"What's that look for?" Reece says as he takes his seat next to me.

His brows knit when I make eye contact and say nothing.

"Do you want to go home?" he asks. "Any time, just say the—"

"I'm happy right here with you." I lean against him.

His warm arm wraps around my shoulders. "Good." He kisses my temple. "I promise we don't have to do this kind of thing too often. I'm much more of a homebody now. Maybe even more when I have my own actual home with you."

I cup his cheek, pulling him closer to kiss him softly on the lips. "That all sounds wonderful to me."

With it being a charity event, drinks and food are served to our tables, and then there are speeches before the dancing starts. It's all a bit of a blur as I spend more time looking at how people are dressed than anything else.

"Dance with me?" Reece takes my hand.

I let him pull me to my feet and follow him to the dance floor where he takes me in his arms.

"Having a good time?" he asks.

We move slowly to the music, and I close my eyes and lean into him. His familiar scent grounds me. "Yes."

"I know you were nervous."

"I've had fun. It's just been a nice dinner with you and our friends. And now I get to dance with you."

He presses his lips to my hair. "I'll always take care of you, Pania. We'll have more nights like this whenever you want."

"I like that idea."

We finish our dance in silence, and are on our way back to the table when a familiar looking redhead walks our way.

"Reece." The affectionate way she says his name makes me grit my teeth.

"Jessie," Reece replies. I blink and shift my gaze to my boyfriend.

"It's so good to see you. I didn't know you'd be here tonight." She doesn't even look at me, which just pisses me off even more.

"Oh, last minute thing with Josh and Delaney. I think you two have met before. Jessie, this is Pania, my girlfriend."

"Girlfriend? You?" She snorts and waves her hand. "Sorry. It's just crazy coming from you."

"I can see you still haven't learned any manners." The words are out before I can stop them, and Jessie stops laughing, her lips tightening into a straight line. "Delaney's here if you ever want to apologise to her."

Jessie's face drains of colour. "It was nice seeing you. I should move on."

She scuttles away, leaving Reece staring at me in disbelief.

"I don't know why you're friends with that woman. She's awful."

He screws up his nose. "She has hidden qualities."

"Does she hide them in her vagina, or ..." I hold up my palms in a questioning gesture.

"Pania." Reece buries his face in his hands.

"It's just a question."

He chuckles. "I shouldn't laugh, but you are incorrigible."

I lean my head against his shoulder. "I know. That's why you love me."

"I do."

35

PANIA

By mid-morning the following day, I've still barely moved.

We didn't drink a lot last night, but we ate and danced and even though we got home at a respectable hour, sleep was slow to come.

I got as far as the couch this morning and there I've stayed.

"Do you want to go for a drive?" Reece asks. "I've got something to show you."

I look up from the magazine I'm reading and tilt my head. "Are you sure you want to show me and not your other girlfriend?"

He sits on the couch beside me. "You're my only girlfriend. I saw this house that I want to look at. Thought you might want to come with me?" He nudges my arm.

"I'd love to. Now?"

Reece hooks his arm around my shoulders. "No time like the present."

"Lead on."

I follow him down the stairs and out the front door to his car. He opens the door for me and waves me in.

"Didn't you say I could drive your car?"

He hesitates before waving into the passenger side again. "Yes, but not this time. It's a surprise where we're going."

"But I don't know anything about LA. Just give me directions and—"

"Next time."

Settling into the comfort of his leather car seat, I let out a little moan. I'm going to miss this thing so much when I go home and go back to driving my shitty old Honda.

He starts the car, and the gates open for us to exit.

We drive about two metres down the road, turn right, and pull up a paved driveway that leads up to a beautiful house. The veranda around the outside of the cream stucco two-storey house has large arches that would look beautiful with climbing plants around them.

"We're here," he says.

"What?" I look at him and back at the house.

"This is it."

I laugh. "We could have walked across the road, you egg."

Reece grins. "But where's the fun in that?"

Next to the driveway, there's a large gravel parking circle, and a BMW with a real estate logo on the side sits nearby. A beautiful blonde lady gets out of the car and walks toward us.

Reece climbs out of the driver's seat, and I undo my belt and open the door.

"Mr Evans." She smiles a dazzling smile that I catch a glimpse of when I step outside.

Here we go.

"Please, call me Reece. This is my girlfriend, Pania." Reece holds his hand out to me as I walk around to join him.

"So happy to meet you both." She holds out her arm. "Shall we?"

Inside are polished wooden floors, until you hit the stairs which are laid with thick dark carpet that reaches up the hallway and into the bedrooms.

I'm in love with everything I see.

The spacious rooms fill me with ideas of how to furnish them.

Returning downstairs, I gasp as we walk into the kitchen. Grey marble benches with shiny chrome appliances—more than enough to excite Delaney, and even I'm impressed.

We walk back outside hand in hand, but my head is spinning at the thought of what I could do with this house. We'll make it a home.

"What do you think?" Reece asks.

I take a moment to answer, because I'm overwhelmed that he's looking at buying something like this. I grew up in a small, three-bedroom house in Whakatane, sharing a room with Delaney when she moved in with us.

Never for a moment did I consider I'd end up living in something like this. And while it won't be for a while yet, one day, this will be my home.

"Pania?" His voice falters as if he's done something wrong. "If you don't like it, we can find something else. I just thought the house was perfect, and it's so close to Josh and Delaney. If I'm away filming, you can just walk across the road to see her."

I blink rapidly, unable to hold my emotions in. "I love it."

His smile makes me love him even more. It reaches from his lips to his eyes, and he takes my hands in his and squeezes them. "Really?"

"I love the house, and I love how thoughtful you are about the location." I drop my voice. "And if Bethany looks at you like that again, I'll cut out her eyes."

Reece laughs in my ear. "I love you."

"I love you too. And I love this house. I'll never forgive you if you don't buy it." I turn in his arms. "That's if you love it too?"

"I want a house that we can call a home one day. One that we can settle down and grow old in. This place suits me just fine." It's times like this I especially love that drawl of his. It makes his words even more swoon-worthy.

"As long as you're happy with it, then yes."

The look of love in his eyes is enough to make my heart pitter-patter. "I'll make an offer. I like the idea of being so close to our friends too. Especially if we have our own kids later on."

I don't say anything more—I can't. Instead, I cup his face in my hands and press a long kiss to his lips.

The click of Bethany's heels makes me turn around.

"Sorry to ask this. I couldn't help but overhear some of your conversation earlier. It might sound insane, but are you Pania Wilson? The lady who designed Delaney Carter's wedding dress?"

My stomach falls to the floor. "Yes?" I know my voice is shaky, but in all the times we've ever been anywhere, it's been Reece that people have fawned over. No one ever really sees me.

She smiles. "Oh my. It was to die for. I'm getting married in a few months, and I was wondering if you're available."

Reece steps in while I'm metaphorically picking my jaw up from the floor. "I'm sure Pania would consider it. She's going back home to New Zealand shortly, but if you send me through the details, we can take a look at what you need."

"That sounds good."

"I've caught you by surprise, haven't I? I tried to find out if you had a store or a design studio but came up with nothing. You're living in New Zealand?" she asks.

I nod. "I live there. I'm just here to spend time with Reece and Delaney."

"Well, I loved the gown you made her for the Oscars. She looked simply gorgeous. I can't imagine that kind of thing comes cheap."

My mouth is so dry.

"It doesn't, but I'm sure it's fair considering the work Pania puts into her designs." Once again, Reece comes to my rescue. He might just have earned himself a blowjob tonight.

Bethany's eyes widen. "Oh, I'm sure. I'll get that email together and send it to you."

"Sounds great." He beams.

"It was so nice meeting you both."

"You too." I smile. My head is spinning over what just happened. It's so random, and so wonderful.

Bethany gets into her car, turns, and heads down the driveway and out onto the road. Reece and I just stand there, leaning against his car.

"Did that just happen?" I ask.

"You're famous." Reece nudges my arm.

"Stop it." I laugh.

"I'm proud of you." He grins. "I think we're about to buy a house."

"I can't wait to tell Delaney."

He walks to the car and opens the passenger door. "Let me drive you there right now."

I laugh. "You really are an egg."

It doesn't stop me from climbing back into the car, and we drive the ridiculously short distance back to Josh and Delaney's house.

I head inside and up to the living room where Josh is on the couch with Melly.

"Where's Delaney?" I ask.

"In the bedroom. Addison's having a nap, so Delaney went for some quiet time. I think she's just watching TV if you want to look in on her," Josh says.

"Thanks."

I walk along the hallway to their bedroom, knock on the door, and then push it open.

Delaney's lying on the bed, watching TV with a packet of potato chips beside her.

"A woman after my own heart."

She laughs. "Come and share these. There are plenty."

I climb up onto the bed beside her and lie on Josh's pillow.

"Where did you two go?"

I pluck a chip out of the bag. "We went to look at a house. Reece is going to make an offer on it."

She turns to look at me, her mouth open. "No."

"Yes. It's right across the road."

Delaney laughs. "No way."

I nod. "He just wanted me to take a look before he decided. And it's perfect. He said he wanted to get somewhere close so it'd be easy for me to visit you if he goes away."

"Aww. That's so sweet."

"And then the real estate agent heard our conversation and asked if I was Pania Wilson who designed your wedding dress."

Delaney's mouth falls open again. "I think I just did a little wee with excitement."

"She wants me to design her wedding dress. Thank God Reece was there because I was a bit of a mess."

"Are you going to do it?"

I take a deep breath. "I guess it depends on what she wants and when the wedding is. I don't have a clue about how much to charge or anything yet. That was something that was always down the road."

She puffs up her hair with the palm of her hand. "I'm sure your manager will be able to work on that."

I laugh. "You're the best manager a girl could have."

Delaney grabs my arm. "I'm so proud of you. And I'm so glad my body could be of service to you."

"Ahem."

We both look up to see Josh standing in the doorway. He holds up his hands. "I'm not even going to ask what that was about."

Delaney and I look at each other and dissolve into laughter. By the time we've finished laughing, Reece has joined Josh in the doorway, an equally confused look on his face.

"We're going to get takeout for dinner. Any preference?" Josh asks.

Delaney shakes her head. "Whatever you want to get is good with me."

"Me too," I say.

"I thought we might get some Chinese."

"Are you taking Melly?" Delaney asks.

Josh's lips tighten. "Actually, it was her idea."

Delaney laughs. "I should have known. That girl has you twisted around her little finger."

He shrugs. "So does her mother, but I don't hear you complaining about that."

She picks up one of her pillows and throws it toward the door. It misses by a mile, but the door's already closed and they've gone.

36

PANIA

I'm not sure I've ever felt so empty at the thought of going home. Our time together has gone by way too fast, and for the first time in my life, I want to be somewhere other than back in New Zealand, surrounded by what's familiar.

I have all that family back home—but I also have family here. And now I know how Reece felt leaving my mum's place.

"Ready?"

I look up and meet Delaney's gaze. They're all taking me to the airport this time, and my heart's so heavy at saying goodbye.

I'm not sure what my expression even is, but it's enough for her to frown and pull me into her arms.

"I've loved having you here," she whispers. "Come back soon."

I nod, hot tears spilling onto her shoulder as she hugs me tight. This isn't me. I never cry over anything.

"I'm going to miss all of you," I managed to get out.

"We'll miss you too. And we'll take good care of Reece. Promise."

I sniff. "Good, because he's useless at taking care of himself."

She lets out a laugh, and before I know it, I'm holding hands with her and laughing too.

"What on Earth is going on in here?" Reece stands in the doorway with his arms folded.

"We're talking about you," Delaney shares a smile with me before turning.

He shrugs. "Huh. Figures."

"What?" she asks.

"Always talking about me behind my back. I know how hot I am, ladies."

I'm the one who snorts first this time, but Delaney's right behind me as we burst into laughter.

Reece crosses the room, and I turn toward him. His eyes crinkle at the corners as he takes in the sight of me. "I'm glad I made you laugh, but have your eyes been leaking?"

I swallow. "Just a little."

"It's not like you. Are you going to miss me that much?" I press my lips together, and he frowns. "That's not good. Are you trying not to say no?"

I throw my arms around his waist and bury my face in his chest. "I'm not going to miss you at all."

"Good. That's what I thought." He kisses the top of my head.

"I think I'll leave you both to it."

There's a soft snick of the door as Delaney leaves, and then I'm left, still with my face buried in Reece, not wanting to leave the comfort of his arms.

"You don't have to go," he whispers. "I'll keep you in the manner to which you're accustomed."

All that does is make me laugh. "So, we're going to look for a tiny apartment with a living room that doubles as a bedroom."

"I would live in a tent in Josh's back yard if I had you with me."

"Stop being so nice."

He kisses my ear. "I'll be waiting. You know that. And any time you need me ..."

"I know. I love you."

"I love you too. And you're still the only woman I've ever said that to."

I raise my gaze to meet his. "Are you sure?"

He chuckles. "Positive. No one's ever given me all that you have. And I'll never take that for granted."

It's hard to find words when your heart's in your throat. There are only three months standing between Reece and I making this permanent, but it feels like a lifetime.

But once that time's over, we can make our life together.

And that makes it worth it.

It's a quiet drive to the airport. And it's weird to be in a hired limo because Reece wanted us all to travel in style in one vehicle, complete with Addison's car seat and Melly's booster. But I get to sit next to Reece and snuggle up with him all the way there.

After checking in and dropping off my luggage, we stand before the security entrance and the last place we can all be together.

Delaney hugs me tight. "Call me when you get home. I need to know you're safe."

"Okay, Mum."

She laughs in my ear. "I should think so. Love you."

"Love you too."

She lets me go, and I bend a little so Melly can slide her arms around my neck. She's too big for me to lift these days, but a hug will do. "And I love you too, little miss. Take good care of your mother and sister for me."

"I will. I'll miss you."

I kiss her on the cheek. "I'll miss you too. To the moon and back."

Finally, I stand and face Josh. "Is Amelia supposed to take care of me too?" he asks.

I grin. "I'm pretty sure you can take care of yourself."

He leans over and pecks my cheek. "Let us know if you ever need anything. We'll all miss you."

"Never thought I'd hear that from your lips, Josh Carter."

He chuckles. "You're pretty fun to be around when you're not glaring at me." He looks at Reece. "We'll wait outside for you."

I turn to Reece as he nods. "Thanks."

"Bye, Pania." Melly waves to me as they walk away, and I bite my bottom lip so hard, the taste of copper floods my mouth.

Reece pulls me into his arms, and I let out a long breath against his chest.

"I'll miss you like crazy," I say.

"Not as much as I'll miss you."

I take a deep breath of his freshly laundered shirt. "It's not a competition."

Looking up into his face, I catch my breath at just how handsome he is. And he's mine. All mine.

"We'll talk every day."

I sigh. "I'm not going to hold you to that. I know you'll be working, and I know Josh told Delaney that and couldn't always do it."

He straightens up. "Well, I'm not Josh."

"I know that." I laugh. "But I'm just saying I don't expect unrealistic promises. Just keep loving me, and I'll love you, and we'll work it all out in the end."

He tilts his head, and his lips curl into a smile. "I know we will."

"I should go."

Reece kisses me, long and deep and lingering on my lips afterward. I know how hard this is for him. It's tearing me apart inside. But I have to be strong. I owe it to myself.

"Go before I drag you back out of here."

I laugh and turn away.

"Pania. Wait."

Reece grabs hold of my hand, pulling me back to him and looking at me with those beautiful crystal blue eyes.

I smile.

"Do you think I should grow a beard? I mean the stubble is sexy if I say so myself, and I think ..."

I roll my eyes and kiss him on the nose. "I think you should do whatever you want. It's your face, and I won't be here for when it's really scratchy if you decide to."

"But will you like it?"

I clamp my lips together for a moment, trying not to laugh. So many times I've seen Melly use this delaying tactic to stay up later. Now my twenty-seven year old boyfriend is doing the same thing.

"I'll love whatever you do, Reece. Just be you."

He runs his thumb along my knuckles. "Are you sure?"

"You'll do for me. Beard or no beard." I press a kiss to his cheek. "I have to go so I don't miss my plane."

"Maybe I want you to."

Sighing, I tug my hand from his. "Don't make this harder than it is."

He gives me a short, sharp nod. "I know how important this is to you. And I know how hard you've fought for it." His lips quirk. "Give 'em hell."

"You know me."

"Call me when you get home. I'll worry."

I swallow hard, sliding my arms around him and giving him a quick hug before I pull away. "I promise."

With tears in my eyes, I walk away from him. It's the hardest thing I've ever had to do in my life, and I could curse myself for being so stubborn. But for some stupid reason, I want Judith's approval.

Life's weird. The whole don't-meet-your-idols has gone both ways for me. I found love with one, and am frustrated as all hell by the other.

That's something I need to sort out.

37

———

PANIA

Coming home sucks. Dragging myself out of bed to go to class is really hard.

Three more months. That's all. And then I can be with Reece all the time. It doesn't hurt that he comes with the added benefits of Delaney and family.

Judith's eyes are on me as I enter the class. I'm jetlagged, and all I want to do is sleep. What I don't need is her on my back.

As soon as the class is full, she pounces.

"Ms Wilson, did you have a nice holiday?"

I nod. "It was wonderful. Tiring, but wonderful."

"I'm surprised to see you back here after your photo was in so many magazines."

Boom. There it is.

"Such a lovely photo of you. And no mention that you made the gown in this class?"

That's it. I think I've reached the end of my limit here.

As much as I wanted this woman's approval, I should have also listened to that whole don't-meet-your hero thing.

The past few weeks have really shown me just how much backing I have to go out on my own. And it doesn't matter if I fall on my face, I have friends and a loving boyfriend who will back me to the moon and back.

None of this is worth it. This whole conversation wouldn't be an issue if Judith had made a different choice—I'd never have had the dress with me to wear in the first place.

"No. I think I've said before that I can't control what the media say. They asked who made the dress, and I told them. It's not my job to buy you publicity."

Her mouth falls open. "I beg your pardon."

"You know, I came to this class eager to learn, and I've learned so much. I'll always appreciate that. But I've done nothing to get the snark from you other than just be friends with Delaney. And I've come to realise having a famous boyfriend is going to make things even worse."

Sam nudges my arm. "So you and Reece Evans really are ...?"

I turn to her. "Yes. And thank you for being my one friend in this class. You have so much talent, Sam, maybe one day *we* can work together."

She beams, but Judith scowls and shuts her down.

"You know I always thought fashion was such a joyous thing. The designs, the fabrics, the art in making these wonderful unique creations. And I love it. But I haven't enjoyed this class, and I'm really wondering why I'm still here."

Judith takes in a deep breath. But I've heard more than enough out of her for one lifetime.

"So I'm just going to pack my shit and go. You can shove it up your arse."

I grab my bag and poke the few items that belong to me inside. There are a few gasps around the room, and someone over the other side actually starts clapping.

Giving Sam a quick hug, I walk out and don't look back.

Life's way too short for this shit.

I can't stop fidgeting. After leaving class, I came straight home where I paced the living room, trying not to second guess what I'd done. But there's only one conclusion I can come to.

The time for putting up with crap in my life is over when there's so much more waiting for me.

I don't want a long-distance relationship—I want to share a home with Reece and be near my best friend. And I don't need to finish the course to have a career doing what I love.

Pulling out my phone, I dial Delaney.

"Yo," she answers.

"I need some help."

"Anything. Tell me what you need." I could cry at the concern in her tone. She knows it's not like me to reach out like this.

"Do you remember when the signs were there for you to join Josh?"

Delaney laughs. "You mean when I nearly set fire to the diner kitchen? Uh huh."

I bite my bottom lip to stop laughing. "Yeah. Then. I think I just had a moment."

She gasps. "What did you do?"

I draw in a deep breath and slowly let it out. "I just told my tutor to stick it."

There's silence for a moment, but then Delaney gurgles.

She snorts.

She lets out a choked laugh.

And from the other side of the world, my best friend dissolves into laughter that she seems to have given up fighting.

"What's so funny?" I huff.

"I'm only surprised it's taken this long."

"What do you mean? I thought you told me I should follow my dream."

Delaney sighs. "You did. You are." She's silent for a moment. "Reece told me you were having a hard time. It's my fault."

"It's not your fault."

"Your tutor clearly has a thing about you designing things for me. And she can shove it right where—"

I laugh. "That's fair."

"Anyway, you were there for me for years. From studying cooking when it wasn't really your first love, to going into business with me, and being by my side the whole way through Melly being born ..."

I clear my throat. "Wait. Is this chatty Delaney, or are we rehashing the past for a reason?"

She chuckles. "I'm just proving that I can go on a trip through memory lane just like you can when you're trying to make a point."

Waving my free hand in the air in frustration, I purse my lips. She's right. It's just taken until now to realise how annoying it must be when I do it.

"Okay."

"My point is that I'm here for you just as you were there for me. I'm making money of my own from my food videos now, and maybe we can go into business together again."

My heart leaps. Delaney's wealthy now, but her heart is still solidly in place. It's not the first time she's made an offer, but maybe ...

"I don't know if I can accept anything like that."

"You also have Reece behind you. And Josh knows how much I miss you. If you're not going to finish the year, come here."

I swallow hard. A lump the size of a golf ball appears to have formed in my throat. It's not the first time Delaney's suggested such a thing, but it's the most tempting given all I have waiting for me in the US.

"Delaney, I ..."

"Take a chance, Pania. We'll be here for you no matter what. And I hate interviews, but I'll gladly do whatever I can to get your name out there."

"You ... You would do that for me?"

She laughs softly. "Do you even have to ask? I'll do anything for my sister."

I lick my lips just to give them some moisture. "I'd have to talk to Mum about it."

"Of course you would. You know you can go home any time to see her too. It's not like we'd keep you trapped here."

I laugh. "Reece might."

"Reece loves your mother too. I think he'd be on that plane with you." She pauses. "It's your decision, but I think it's time. Let's make this an adventure together."

My eyes fill with tears. I always thought it would be hard to beat the relationship I have with Delaney. She's right. We are like siblings, and through our whole lives we've mostly done everything together.

These past two years without her being a constant in my life have been the toughest. Add Reece to the mix, and it's even harder to ignore.

"We should surprise Reece. He did it to you."

I laugh. "He'll freak out."

"That's the whole point. He's been moping around since you left." Delaney lets out a contented sigh. "I'd love to see that reunion."

"Pervert."

"Always. Let's do this. Tell me what you need, and let's make this happen."

"You're the best. I hope you know that."

Delaney laughs. "You can tell me that when you get here. We've got some time to work through the paperwork and get you on that plane. I'm *so* excited."

38

PANIA

I'm not sure I've ever been so nervous. It's such a bizarre feeling, but I think it's only right that I feel this way considering I've just turned my whole life upside down to travel across the world to try something new.

The more I think about it, though, the more I think I understand how Reece must have felt when he threw caution to the wind and came to me. He didn't know if I'd reject him—at least I know he'll want me there.

I smooth down my dress. It's one I made myself a couple of years ago at home—a simple black dress—but it works for the event we're going to. Delaney's wearing something similar.

Delaney grips my hand. "You go in, and we'll be right behind you. The press will want to talk to Josh and I've got to try and slide in who dressed me."

I grin. "I'm so glad I've got you here with me."

"You'll be fine. Just get in there and scare the shit out of Reece."

My stomach churns. Nothing makes me nervous. No one has this effect on me but him. The thought of being in his arms tonight makes every nerve in my body come alive.

She gives me a gentle shove. "Go."

I walk into the glittering room. It's some industry event with dinner and dancing that Josh booked a table for. He's taken care of all the details, so Reece hasn't been involved with who's representing their company. All he's been told is to show up.

As I scan the room, my nerves start to disappear. I don't really understand it, but knowing Reece is here somewhere soothes them.

I come to a halt when I lay eyes on him.

He's so handsome, with his stubble and his shining blue eyes. All dressed up in a tuxedo that just makes me want to jump his bones even more.

What else I see makes my blood boil.

I never thought I was the jealous type. I experienced it when I saw the photos of Reece with Gabby. I've seen Reece in movies, and I understand that they're acting. Hell, I've watched Josh strip off and screw women on screen but know the only woman he'll ever want in real life is Delaney.

But right now, there's a gorgeous blonde who looks like she just walked out of a Vogue magazine, laughing and joking intimately with *my* man, with her hand on his arm like she owns him.

I narrow my eyes and stalk toward them.

"Hi."

Blondie keeps talking, but Reece's eyes meet mine, and widen.

"Pania?" His voice isn't much more than a whisper, but his mouth curves into a wide smile.

"What's going on?"

He looks down at his arm, shakes off the blonde's hand, and takes a step back.

She very obviously doesn't take the hint, not stopping for a breath as she just keeps talking.

With barely a glance at me, she shoves her empty champagne glass in my direction.

I shove it back. "Wait. Do you think I work here?"

Finally, she turns her head and meets my gaze. "You don't?"

I open my mouth to speak but gasp instead as Reece grabs hold of my wrist and pulls me to him.

"This is my girlfriend, Pania."

Tension tightens blondie's face so much, she won't need a facelift any time soon. "Oh."

Reece gives me such an affectionate look, my stomach flips. "My beautiful, amazing, very clever fashion-designer girlfriend, Pania."

I bite my bottom lip, blush, and then fix my gaze back on hers. I've never backed down from anything before, and I'm not about to do it now. I cock an eyebrow and don't blink.

She takes a step back, and Reece slides his arm around my waist, hugging me to him. I remember Delaney being anxious about not fitting in—neither of us fit the Hollywood stereotype—but as Josh loves her, Reece loves me. I know he'll always have my back.

The blonde licks her lips as if she's trying to work out what to say. "Oh. Nice to meet you."

"Sigourney and I made a movie together a couple of years ago. You probably saw it. *The Long Walk*?" Reece says.

Oh I remember. It was a romantic movie about a woman with only a few months left to live who falls in love. She dies at the end.

"I'm not sure. I usually remember your films, but I can't seem to place that one." I flash a bright smile at Sigourney. "Maybe it wasn't very good."

He chuckles in my ear and pinches my bum. "All my movies are good."

I wiggle my hips against him, and turn to murmur back at him. "Oh, *you're* usually good."

"Behave." He places a kiss on my temple. "At least until we're out of here."

Sigourney looks a little uncomfortable and steps back even farther until she finds someone else to start talking to.

"So, what's the deal with her?" I ask, crossing my arms and tapping my foot. "Why does she think she gets to touch you like that?"

Reece purses his lips before raising his hand to his mouth and letting out a laugh. "Well, hello to you too."

"Don't you try and sweet talk me."

He places his hands on my wrists, pulling my arms apart. "She wouldn't stop talking. I just zoned-out after a while. What are you doing here?"

"I came to surprise you." I pout.

He tugs on my arms, bringing me closer before sliding his arms around my waist. "You did that. I'm so happy you're here."

And without a care in the world as to who sees us, he kisses me long and deep, lingering on my lips as he pulls away.

"That's a better welcome." I nuzzle my nose against his. "Now, what did that woman want? What's her name? Susan?"

Reece raises an eyebrow. "*Sigourney* is hoping to meet Delaney tonight. She thinks knowing me and making friends with her will help her get a part in our next film."

I roll my eyes. "Couldn't she just audition like everyone else?"

"Sure, but making friends is always advantageous in this town." He chews his bottom lip. "She'd be better off just approaching Josh instead of trying to get to him through his wife."

"Uh huh." I nod.

"Speaking of whom. They're here."

I turn, and grin as my bestie walks into the room with her husband behind her. Heads turn where Josh goes. His career's in the stratosphere with the Oscar win, and he's the man everyone wants to know. But his eyes are firmly on Delaney. They always are.

She's the one person he's always out to impress.

Out of the corner of my eye, Sigourney straightens up and puts on a dazzling smile.

My gaze locks with Delaney.

She squeals, and all but races across the room, gathering me into her arms.

"I couldn't see. How was the reunion?"

Reece clears his throat. "You set me up?"

"It was a surprise." She looks between me and Reece. "Everything's okay, right?"

"Apart from a blonde near-misunderstanding, we're fine."

Delaney's eyebrows creep up. She looks around the room. "Josh was right behind me."

"He's caught up over there." Reece points.

She leans in closer. "Why is that woman looking at me funny?" Delaney murmurs.

"Reece said she wants to be your new bestie to get into Josh's new film."

She turns her head, her mouth falling open. "That's not how it works. I have nothing to do with his business."

I smirk. "We both know he'd do whatever you said, he's so pussy-whipped. But I also know you wouldn't try to influence him. Unless he was considering casting your old mate, Jessie."

Delaney's top lip curls. "Josh knows better than that."

Nodding, I hook my arm through hers. "He really does. That's how I know he's the right guy for you."

The smug expression that spreads across her face makes me laugh. She's so confident in their love, and it even makes me a little giddy thinking about how deep that goes. It's what I want with Reece.

Wait.

That's what I have with Reece.

I wasn't worried about him when I saw Sigourney talking to him. It was the way she hung off him that made me see red.

Turning my head, I meet Reece's gaze. He tilts his head a little, his brows knitting as if to ask me what I'm thinking. Maybe we haven't spent the last couple of years in the same country, but time and distance gave us the opportunity to get to know each other as friends. It's acted as such a good foundation for our relationship.

"Love you," I mouth.

He smiles that dazzling smile of his and shoots me a wink that makes me sigh.

"I'm so glad you two are together," Delaney says. "Now I have you here, and my best friends are in love with each other. Things couldn't have worked out better."

I lean my head against hers. "I'm not sure what I'm doing here yet, but I guess we'll work it out."

"Sometimes, I think I should be jealous of Delaney," Reece says.

Delaney leans over, summoning up her baby-talk voice. "Aww, poor wittle Reecey. Is he feeling left out?"

"I don't know what you did, but you're in trouble when she brings out that voice." Josh chuckles as he approaches, placing his hands on his wife's waist and scooping her against him.

"Breathing gets me in trouble." Reece takes my hand and smiles. I'm not sure what the future holds, but I do know I want it to be with him.

"Let's go to our table." Josh plants a kiss on Delaney's neck.

AFTER WE'VE EATEN, there are a few speeches by the organisers, and then the music starts and so does the dancing. Josh pulls Delaney to the dance floor, and I snuggle against Reece in my seat.

"Did you want to get out of here?" he asks.

I place my palm on my throat. "Why, Mr Evans. Are you propositioning me?"

"I'm not even sure we'll last the drive back to my place." His whole face lights up in a smile, and my heart lurches. God, how I adore this man. "I still can't believe you're here. Aren't you supposed to be studying?"

I bite my bottom lip. This is the one part of this whole thing I was dreading. I made such a big decision without telling the one person I should have.

His brow furrows. "Pania, what aren't you telling me?"

"I quit."

"What? I thought—"

"After I got home, it was just awful. There were photos of us in magazines, and I was tired, and Judith was just such a bitch, and—"

"You quit?"

"I told her to shove her course up her arse."

Reece claps his hand across his mouth. "You didn't."

I shrug. "I did."

He snorts, and it makes me laugh as I think back to Delaney's reaction.

"Want to know what I think?" he asks.

"Do I have a choice?"

He leans in and brushes his lips to my skin, just under my ear. "I'm just surprised you didn't do it sooner."

"That's exactly what Delaney said."

He pulls away, that soppy look all over his face again. "Because we both know you so well."

I cock my head, reaching for his hand. "Well, technically, you know me just a little better."

"How do you figure that?"

"I've never had sex with Delaney." At that, he laughs so loudly, heads turn and I clamp my lips together, shaking my head. "I think that might be our cue to leave."

He kisses my temple. "Works for me. The sooner I get you home, the sooner I can get you naked."

"You and your one track mind. I'll just say goodbye to Delaney."

"We'll wave to them on the way out." He stands and extends his hand. "Let's go home."

"Home?"

I take his hand and let him pull me to my feet.

"Well, Josh's place. I've sold my apartment and I'm waiting on the house we bought to settle. Yesterday, I spent my last night in my apartment."

I screw up my nose. "Damn it."

Reece shrugs. "We could break in, but there's no bed. But there's a big comfy one at Josh's place."

Grinning, I squeeze his hand. "That sounds wonderful to me."

"When did you get here?"

I bite my bottom lip. "Yesterday."

His eyes narrow. "Why didn't you tell me?"

"This was Delaney's idea, and I wanted to surprise you."

He wraps his arms around me. "And we could have had one more night together."

I place a kiss on his jaw. "What's one night when we have forever?"

"Oooh you're good."

"Take me home and let me show you just how good."

BY THE TIME we get into Reece's bedroom, we're a tangle of limbs and partially removed clothes.

He lifts my dress over my head while I'm in a daze from his kisses.

All my cares about anything else have flown out the window, as all I want is *him*.

He squeezes my breasts together through my bra. "Oh, my darlings, I'm so glad you came home."

I laugh. "You're an idiot."

"I've missed you." He plants a kiss on each breast before he unhooks my bra and drops it to the ground.

"And the rest of me?"

I start unbuttoning Reece's shirt. I'm not even sure where he discarded his jacket and tie. Maybe the hallway.

He runs his fingers down my spine. "I missed all of you. I'm glad you're back because I think my balls were turning blue."

Tugging the hem of his shirt out of his pants, I push it open, exposing his chest. I leave the rest to him while I reach for his belt buckle.

"I guess we'll have to do something about that, then."

"*Taku whaiāipo,*" he whispers. His pronunciation is terrible, but the meaning isn't lost on me as I stop what I'm doing.

"My sweetheart." I place my palm on his chest. "Where did you learn that?"

"Google? I hope it's right."

I plant a kiss on his throat. "I love that you did that."

"I just want to make you happy." He grips my arms and leans back. "How do you say 'strip me off and ride my cock'?"

Wriggling loose from his grip, I cover my face with my hands. "Just say it in English."

He leans forward. "Hurry up. Isn't that what you said to me that first night?"

I laugh and nod.

He drops his pants to the ground and leads me to the bed.

I lie down on the crisp sheets and close my eyes as Reece climbs into bed beside me.

"Pania," he whispers.

I open my eyes to see him leaning over me.

"I might have missed you a bit too."

Reece kisses my throat. "Just a bit?"

"Okay, a lot. Are you happy?"

He raises his head again. "Happier than I ever thought possible."

And then his hands and mouth are everywhere, and I close my eyes again, loving every moment of his touch. I've craved it during the time we've been apart, and although I know I'm not getting sleep any time soon, it'd be so easy to drift off as he worships my body.

"Don't you dare go to sleep." He chuckles.

"It'd be so easy to do. I'm tired, and you're relaxing me."

Reece slides his hand down between my legs. "Let's see if this wakes you up."

I lean against him as he strokes my thighs one by one, inching closer, and touching me everywhere but the one place I want him to touch.

"Don't tease me."

His fingers spread me out until finally he runs his index finger over my clit. "I just want this to last."

"Why? I'm not going anywhere."

His eyes meet mine. "It's going to take a while to get used to that."

I smile. "Believe it."

Taking a deep breath, I relax into the bed as his fingers do their work.

I grip his arm, feeling the muscles in his bicep move in time with his strokes.

"I love it when you do that," he murmurs.

"Do what?"

"Feel me touching you."

"How did you …?"

He looks deep into my eyes. "Because I do the same thing to you. You just haven't noticed."

My eyelids flutter, and I fight the urge to close them. "You do?"

His lips twitch. "I notice everything, Pania."

My heart melts at his words. Where once I was unsure of what the future held, Reece makes me grow more confident by the minute.

He slips a finger inside me, and I'm lost in sensation as he draws it back out and over my clit.

"You're all mine now," he whispers. "Never giving this up."

Tears prick my eyes. "You'll never have to."

Heat traverses my body, and I give in to the urge to close my eyes. Reece's lips graze my right nipple, and it's all I can do to hold this sensation.

"Reece," I cry out.

"Give it to me," he whispers.

I shudder, and he wastes no time moving between my legs.

"Oh no, you don't."

He laughs as I push at him, rolling him onto his back and then straddling his hips, taking his length into me. He moans, brushing my hair from where it's fallen over my chest.

"God, you feel so good."

"So do you," I whisper.

"Fuck me, my beautiful girl."

His hips rise as I rock mine, every stroke in sync. Reece cups my breasts with his hands, his fingers making gentle movements over my skin.

I love him more than I can bear.

He moves his fingers to my back, dancing them down my spine and pulling me down for a kiss.

"I want to spend my life doing this with you. Only ever you," he whispers.

I push up on his chest, his lips placing gentle kisses on each nipple before he suckles on them.

He lets me go, leaning back and looking into my eyes with so much love. His body tenses underneath mine, and I throw my head back, crying out his name as he thrusts harder.

"Pania. Oh God! Pania."

Reece lets out a loud groan and slows as we both come down to earth.

He's panting underneath me, but I'm still floating from being back together with him. For good. There are still logistics to work out, but nothing is going to keep us apart now.

I lean over and kiss him, and he rubs his nose against mine.

"I don't even have the words to tell you how I feel right now," he whispers.

Tears well in my eyes. "I know. I feel the same way"

I lift myself off him before rolling onto my back. "If you were trying to wear me out, you did it."

"I feel as if I just flew across the world." He laughs.

I kiss his chest. "I'm just going to the bathroom. Be back in a minute. And then we're going to sleep."

"You don't have to tell me twice."

As I walk to the en suite, he wolf whistles.

"Stop it." I laugh.

He's still lying on his back when I return and climb into bed with him. I rest my head on his chest and listen to his heart beating. It's constant, reassuring, and everything I could ever need. His hand caresses my spine, and I let out a contented sigh, being right where I need to be.

"You okay?" he asks.

"Yes and no."

Reece reaches for my chin and pulls my head up, studying my expression. "What's wrong?"

I pull back. "I know I've made the right decision coming here, but ..." I frown. "I feel like I failed. Studying under Judith was all I wanted."

Reece shakes his head. "You didn't fail. Sometimes our heroes just turn out to be pretty shitty after all. I'm just really happy you're here now."

"Me too."

"Stay with me," he whispers.

I nod. "That's the plan if you'll have me."

His grin's so wide it's a miracle it doesn't split his face in half. "Oh, I'll have you."

"I love you."

Reece kisses me so deeply, I'm pretty sure he sucks my tonsils out. "I love you too. Once the house sale is completed, the move in date won't be long afterward. We'll have our own home together."

My heart swells. "That's wonderful."

"I think you'd be a lot happier near *whanau*."

I laugh. "You remembered."

He shrugs. "A few words, but I'd love to learn more."

"Give it time, I'll teach you."

Reece nuzzles my neck, and I let out a soft moan. He stops.

"Keep going."

"Did you tell your mom you were coming?"

I lean my head against his. "I went to see her before I made my final decision."

"Is she okay?"

"I love that you're worried about her." I pull back and reach to stroke his cheek. "She's fine. She loves the shit out of you, and she'll kill you if you fuck this up, but she's fine."

He laughs. "I won't fuck it up. I love you too much, and I adore your mom."

"That's one of the reasons I love you so much."

His eyes twinkle with mischief. "I'll give you everything you could ever want, Pania."

I lick my lips. "Lucky that all I want is you, then."

"Oh, you'll get so much more."

39

REECE

The thud of music reaches me from my bedroom near the end of the hallway.

I reach out, but Pania's already out of bed, and I'm alone. Climbing out of bed, I pull on jeans and a T-shirt and head out the door.

As I step out into the hallway, Josh opens his bedroom door and smiles. "Morning."

"What's with the music?"

He laughs. "Come and see."

The strains of "Mr. Blue Sky" by the Electric Light Orchestra come from the living room.

Delaney's got her back to me as she swings her hips, her arms swaying in the air. Amelia wiggles around to the beat. Pania is smiling, and laughing, and dancing up a storm too.

They're lost in their dance, and as Delaney turns, she's got this look of absolute bliss, her eyes closed.

"Reece," Amelia screeches, running at me and launching herself into my arms.

I pop a kiss on the top of her head. "Hey, princess. What's going on?"

"We're dancing." She twirls before grabbing Josh's hand. "Come on, Daddy."

He looks back at me, but I shake my head and hold my palm up.

And then he joins them before grabbing Delaney's hips and moving with her.

For a moment, I just watch them. This is what family looks like.

"Come on." Pania approaches me and takes my hand in hers. Her eyes shine with happiness, and I lean over and kiss her softly.

I follow her lead, and before I know it we're all dancing around the living room, laughing. I pull Pania into my arms and twirl her around.

As the song ends, I flop onto the couch, Pania dropping onto my lap.

"I still have no idea why we do this." Josh laughs.

I cock my head while fixing my gaze on him. "Well, Joshua, if you paid attention to Delaney's hobbies, you'd know it's a thing in Grey's Anatomy."

"Except they dance things out. We just dance when we're happy," Delaney says.

Josh glowers at me. "How did you know that?"

"I've had a lot of spare time while I haven't been man-whoring the past two years."

Delaney hisses at me. "Reece."

I turn to see Amelia staring at me wide-eyed.

Shit.

Pania laughs. "You're on your own. I'm not helping you out with this one."

For a moment, I'm lost for words. "Why don't we have breakfast?" I shrug.

"Let's do that," Josh says.

I'VE HAD breakfast in this house a million times before. This time, it's different.

Delaney and Pania talk up a storm as they catch up. Josh cuts up Melly's pancakes, and she's so much like him in her dramatic telling of something that happened in school. I love every single person at this table. They're my family.

The thought brings a lump to my throat.

Delaney nudges my elbow. "You okay?"

I slice up my bacon and nod. "I'm fine."

She lowers her voice. "I know you better than that, Reece Evans."

I put down my knife and fork and take a deep breath.

"Uh, there's something I need to tell you and Josh. It's about my family."

Pania meets my gaze. She gets to her feet and walks around the table to stand behind me, placing her hands on my shoulders. It's reassuring and bolsters my courage to tell them.

"Your family?" Josh asks.

"My parents. The ones you're always talking about meeting."

Pania squeezes my shoulders.

Josh scrunches his nose, like he does when he's thinking hard about something. I'm sure he's remembering the times I've referenced them. I tried not to overdo it, but sometimes ...

I take a deep breath. "My parents died when I was a kid. I was raised by my grandmother." Delaney gasps, and I shift my gaze to her. "The way they died, I was ashamed. So, I made up a story."

She blinks a bunch of times like she's fighting back tears.

"Oh, Reece. I'm so sorry."

"You're not angry with me?"

I can't stop looking at Delaney welling up because of me.

She shakes her head. "Why would we be? My dad left when I was little, and my mother threw me out because I was pregnant. Not all of us had wonderful parents like Josh and Pania."

I pause for a moment, taking a deep breath.

"My grandmother was amazing, but we moved around so much. And then I met you ..." I meet Josh's gaze. "You became the brother I never had. But I'd concocted this story, so I stuck with it." I blow out a breath. "Maybe because I wanted it to be true. And your mom and dad are the best."

Delaney reaches out and places her hand on mine. "We *all* love you, Reece. You did what you thought was the right thing for you. I think it says a lot now that you can open up to us."

Josh blows out a long, loud breath. "Agreed. You *are* family."

"I know I've probably outstayed my welcome a bunch of times in the past couple of years." I smile. "But Delaney was just the icing on the cake. Pardon the cooking pun."

Delaney laughs. "You've never outstayed any welcome. You have your own room here."

I chuckle. "That's true. Anyway, you guys mean so much more to me than I can ever tell you. And you gave me Pania, and that makes me feel really blessed."

Pania wraps her arms around my neck and kisses my cheek.

"I know I'm hard on you sometimes, but you've never let me down when I needed you," Josh says. "Come here."

He stands, and Pania lets me go so I stand too. We grasp hands and pull each other into a bro hug.

"I feel like the luckiest man alive," I say when we pull apart. "I have all of you, and Pania with her *whanau*."

"Ooooh look at you." Delaney smiles at me.

"I know, I know. I'll be bi-lingual any minute now."

Pania laughs. "It might take a little longer than that."

I cock my head. "You all changed my life, and I'm so grateful."

"Glad to hear it. Now sit your arse down and eat your breakfast before it gets cold." She kisses me on the cheek before returning to her seat.

"Yes, ma'am." I grin.

"Mummy," Amelia says.

"Yes, sweet pea?" Delaney turns to her daughter.

"Pania said arse."

Pania claps her hand over her mouth and guffaws.

"Naughty Pania," I say. "Don't worry, Amelia. I'll punish her later."

"Will you wash her mouth out with soap? That's what Mummy says to me."

I look at Delaney. She's also got her hand clamped across her mouth, and her face is reddening at what seems to be a huge effort not to laugh.

"I'm not sure. I'll find some way to make her suffer." I shoot Amelia a wink, and she returns to eating, seemingly satisfied with my answer.

Pania's got an eyebrow arched and directed at me when I meet her gaze again. I shovel more food into my mouth and wink at her too.

She just shakes her head and goes back to eating.

Punishment can wait until later.

CHAPTER 40

PANIA

This is the life. California, in April, relaxing with my best friend in her backyard. The warm sun is relaxing as we lie back on loungers under a large umbrella, a table with drinks and potato chips, and Addison on a blanket on the grass between us.

"It's so weird to think three years ago, we were working so hard in the diner with no clue that this would be our life," Delaney says.

I smile. I'm not officially in business yet, but the building Reece and Josh bought for their production company offices had space available, and I moved in. I've been busy making designs and looking at fabric swatches. Good things take time.

Dropping my sunglasses down my nose, I raise my head to look toward Reece as he pushes wickets into the ground.

"Where on earth did you get a cricket set from?"

Delaney chuckles. "The first time we went back home. I promised to teach Josh the rules in our wedding vows, but we never actually got to that." She pops another chip in her mouth.

"So, if those three are playing, who's doing the teaching?"

"Melly can teach them."

I facepalm. "The rules will change every time to benefit her."

"Of course." Delaney waggles her eyebrows. "That's my girl."

I reach out and grab a chip. "It won't take them long to realise they're being duped."

"It'll just be fun until that happens."

"Amelia Carter," Reece calls out. "I don't think it works that way."

Delaney and I glance at each other.

"What's going on?" Delaney asks through her choked laughter.

"Your daughter is working on a scam that means she never has to retrieve the ball."

Delaney nods. "Uh huh."

"Apparently, the only person who has to run after the ball is the person with the letter R in their name."

I run everyone's names through my head before laughing. "I'm pretty sure that's just you."

Reece glares at me. "That's right."

"That's a legitimate rule. They don't play it for international matches, but ..." Delaney tries so hard to keep a straight face, but loses it, dissolving into laughter again.

"Delaney." Josh moans.

"Fine. There's no such rule. Melly, you'll have to take your turn fetching the ball."

"But, Mummy." Melly pouts.

"You've got younger legs than both of them. And I think you're much fitter." She turns her head and winks at me.

"What do you mean?" Reece asks. "I'm in better shape than Josh."

"That's debatable." Josh chuckles. "I saw you take that extra helping of dessert last night."

"What are you doing?" I whisper at Delaney.

She laughs. "Give them five minutes and they'll be stripping their shirts off to out-muscle each other. I'm just here for the show."

I stare at her. "Oh, you are wicked. You don't mind me perving on Josh?"

"Of course not. What else are best friends for if not to look at hot guys?" She sips her drink. "I'm just glad that you're here with me to perv on our boys. It's so good to have you here."

"I couldn't be anywhere else."

Delaney holds out her glass. "Here's to friendship and a lifetime of perving those two."

I reach over and clink mine against hers. "Hear, hear."

Sure enough, it takes next to no time before the two of them are kind of playing cricket, not a shirt in sight. And Melly sits on the grass, ignoring their pleas to chase after the ball.

"Wanna go for a swim? The pool's heated," Delaney asks.

"Sounds good to me."

We abandon our chairs, and Delaney scoops up Addison to carry her to the pool. After going through the gate, I dive straight in, the water cooling me down, while Delaney goes the long way and down the steps.

Addison squeals when her feet touch the water. She's nine months old, and it won't be long before she's walking, but for now she loves being on her mother's hip.

"Let me take her." I hold out my arms, and Delaney passes her over.

"Hey, baby girl."

Addison blows bubbles at me, giggling as she kicks her legs in the water.

"You are such a cheeky wee thing. Lucky you're so cute."

Her blue eyes grow big as I dunk her bottom in the water.

"It's not that cold."

"Bub bub bub," she says, and I laugh at her response.

"Oh, *taku māreikura*, you are so precious."

Delaney cocks her head. "That's beautiful. What does that mean?"

I plant a kiss on Addison's forehead. "My angel."

Addison giggles as I dunk her again.

Warm hands slide around my waist.

"I love watching you with her," Reece murmurs behind my ear.

"I thought you were playing cricket."

He chuckles, his hot breath on the back of my neck. "We gave up. Amelia just sat in the way."

I swing Addison onto my hip and turn toward him. "At least you had fun for a while."

Reece reaches for the baby. "Come to Uncle Reece, little one. Let's go for a swim."

Addison reaches for him, and she's soon giggling again as he swings her through the water and out again.

It's enough to bring a lump to my throat.

"He's a keeper." Delaney touches my arm.

I look back at her. "I know he is."

Melly leaps into the pool, her bright orange water wings keeping her afloat. She's a strong swimmer, but she loves the damn things. I remember her going through so many pairs of them when she was little because she was also good at ripping them.

"Look at me, Reece." She pushes herself off the bottom of the pool toward him and just floats there.

"You're a smart girl too. You and your sister," he says.

She screws up her face. "She doesn't do that much."

"She does heaps more than she did when she was born." I reach out and stroke her hair.

Melly shrugs. "I guess. She can't play cricket, though."

Before I can point out she didn't play either, she dives under the water and swims the short distance to her father, who's just walking down the pool steps.

"Daddy, look at meeeeee."

He shakes his head. "You don't need those wings. Show me how you swim without them. Addison will need some soon."

"Okay," Melly yells.

The water wings go flying as she pulls them off and dives under the water. Even though I know how good a swimmer she is, I hold my breath until she emerges at the other end of the pool.

"You're so clever." Josh laughs as she takes a deep breath and swims back into his arms.

She beams.

After she's swum for a while, Melly shows signs of slowing down, and little Addison is yawning.

"I think we need to get out of the sun," Delaney says.

"Good idea," I reply.

Everyone's lathered in sun screen, but I think we've all reached that point. Besides, the day has moved on and it'll be evening soon enough.

"Come on, Amelia. It's time to go in and get ready for dinner," Josh says.

"Did you two want to stay to eat?" Delaney asks.

Reece shakes his head. "Not tonight. I've got an early start tomorrow."

I will my eyebrows to stay in place. It's not easy when I know he's not even working tomorrow.

"No worries. I'll probably see you sometime anyway." She smiles at me.

"Sure thing."

Josh leads Melly inside with Delaney and Addison right behind them.

I close my eyes to the silence as we're left in the pool. The water swishes around, and I open my eyes to see Reece standing in front of me.

"We're alone."

I cup his face. "We are."

He reaches down and grasps my butt. I wrap my legs around his waist and shoot him a sly smile, feeling him hard against me.

"Really?"

"Really," he says.

"You never stop."

"Not with you." His contented smile reaches his eyes. If I ever had any doubts about Reece's ability for commitment, they're long gone.

He reaches for the strap of my swimsuit, and I swat his hand away.

"We are *not* fucking in their pool." I laugh.

"You're no fun."

"Would you want Josh and Delaney fucking in *our* pool?"

Reece raises his index finger to his chin. "I see your point."

I shrug. "We could just go home and fuck in our pool. Problem solved."

His grin illuminates my heart. "Now *that* sounds like a good idea."

"I'm full of good ideas."

Reece pulls me closer and plants a kiss under my ear. "Let's go home, then Ms Wilson."

"Sounds heavenly to me."

I pull away from him, and he waves his hands, pointing toward his groin. "What do I do about this?"

"That looks like a you problem, not a me problem." I grin.

"Pania." His desperate tone does nothing as I wade toward the steps and walk out of the pool.

"No one can see you. Come on."

I slide on my jandals and wrap a towel around myself. "Ready."

"Thank God we don't live far from here." Reece follows me out of the pool, grabs a towel, and does the same, wrapping it around his body. He walks a little awkwardly as we make our way to the back door of the house, and I laugh to myself at the sight.

"I can hear you," he says.

"Sorry. Once we get home, I'll sort you out."

"I'd be grateful." I clamp my lips together to stop any more laughter.

I stick my head in the back door. No idea if they'll hear me, but they'll know we've gone home. "Delaney, we're going home now. See you later."

There's no response, and I turn to Reese. "Come on then, let's get you home."

He waddles toward the side of the house, and I can't help it as laughter bursts out of me.

"I can still hear you, Pania."

"I know. I'm sorry." Tears roll down my cheeks from laughing so hard, but I can't help it. "I'm not really sorry," I whisper.

We walk across the road to our house. I love the house almost as much as I love Reece.

Almost.

Apart from it being so close to Delaney, it's my little piece of luxury I never thought I'd have.

And best of all, Reece and I chose it together.

I lead him around the side of the house and through the gate to the pool. Throwing the towel off, I dive straight in, gasping a little as the water hits me.

Reece walks down the steps. "If I jump in like that, I might break something."

I chuckle. "Wouldn't want to do that."

He makes his way down the steps into the pool and into my arms. "I love you," he murmurs in my ear.

I close my eyes as he nuzzles my neck. "I love you too."

"No regrets?"

I pull back. "Not a single one. What about you?"

He shakes his head. "Only one."

I cock an eyebrow.

"I wasted two years when we could have just been together."

And then he kisses me, and I know I'll just have to take his problem and make it mine.

Because I love him.

ALSO BY WENDY SMITH

Coming Home

Doctor's Orders

Baker's Dozen

Hunter's Mark

Teacher's Pet

A Very Campbell Christmas

Fall and Rise Duet

Falling

Rising

Fall and Rise - The Complete Duet

The Aeon Series

Game On

Build a Nerd

Bar None

Hollywood Kiwis Series

Common Ground

Even Ground

Under Ground

Rocky Ground

Solid Ground

Stand alones

For the Love of Chloe

Only Ever You

The Friends Duet

Loving Rowan

Three Days

The Forever Series

Something Real

The Right One

Unexpected

Chances Series

Another Chance

Taking Chances

Lifetime Series

In a Lifetime

In an Instant

In a Heartbeat

In the End

At the Start

ABOUT THE AUTHOR

Wendy Smith lives with her two children and two cats in Auckland, New Zealand, and she's not sure who's responsible for her grey hair. She's a multi-platform bestselling author, whose book In the End, written as Ariadne Wayne, was named one of Apple's best books of 2017. All her stories come with a quirky sense of humour, and she cries over everything.

Find me online
www.wendysmith.co.nz
wendy@wendysmith.co.nz

www.ingramcontent.com/pod-product-compliance
Lightning Source LLC
Chambersburg PA
CBHW061340310726
48974CB00001B/126